Hunt for the Blower Bentley

By Kevin Gosselin

Paperback ISBN 978-1-78092-018-4
PDF ISBN 978-1-78092-019-1
ePub ISBN 978-1-78092-020-7

Published in the UK by MX Publishing
335 Princess Park Manor, Royal Drive,
London, N11 3GX
www.mxpublishing.com

Cover design by www.staunch.com

For my race team, Nickie and Graham & Dr. J.P. Elliot, who did the simple thing of saving my wife's life.

PROLOGUE
Portsmouth, England May 1939

Stephan was glad that Fowkes, the cousin of engineer D. H. Sessions, had a gambling problem. A huge, debt-inducing gambling problem. A gambling problem that caused him to take silly, errant risks. Fowkes' gambling problem had even caused him to steal items from his rich relative to pay his bills. And Stephan was often the man to buy those items because D.H. had exquisite taste in all things.

Noticing the time was nine o'clock, Stephan finished his Young's pint with a final gulp, put on his hat and walked out of the Sailor's Return pub to go meet Fowkes. It was just a few blocks down Prospect Street to their meeting place, an alcove that had once been used to stable horses. Instead of a pair of nags, there was close to 200 horsepower, in the form of a Bentley with a blower hung off the front stabled there tonight.

Stephan walked straight up to the right-hand side of the car and peered through the glass at the driver. Fowkes' face was cut across by one of the three wiper blades that had parked vertically. It was easy to see he was scared and desperate like a street dweller with empty pockets and emptier stomach.

Getting out of the car, Fowkes shut the door but kept his hand on it as if he needed a bit of a support. As if he couldn't stand on his own.

"This is it then." Stephan stated like fact but structured like a question.

"It is."

"I thought it had a fabric body?"

"I don't know. Maybe it did when it first left the factory, maybe it didn't. Who cares?"

"I care. A leather body would have been a bit lighter. But regardless, how long ago did you take it?"

"A week."

Stephan felt the blood fill has face. He was told it would be freshly purloined. Not stale.

The cousin must have noticed the change in his expression and explained before Stephan could erupt. "D.H. has been busy. Called in to help run Bailey's factory near Leith."

"What sort of factory?"

"Don't know. A part of a part of a submarine."

Interesting, thought Stephan, a nice bit of information to file away for later.

"How much you owe?" Stephan asked the cousin; if he were as bad a negotiator as he was a gambler this would be a strong first opening move.

"I don't owe much." Fowkes said with a straight face and strained voice. "Not what this car is worth, that's for sure."

"That car is only worth what someone will pay for it. A car is never worth a thought."

"Right." The cousin forced a laugh. Stephan knew he wanted to play like he was a chum. A pal.

"I didn't mean to be funny. I'm not here to chat like a couple of birds. I am here to buy a car and not tell anyone where I bought it. This will benefit me. And it will benefit you. And the mutually beneficial number I am thinking about is 1,000 pounds."

The cousin rolled his eyes up a bit as if he were figuring sums. Stephan wouldn't have been surprised if he stuck out his tongue. It took a minute, but the cousin answered. "You see. You and I know what this car is worth. D.H. paid dearer than 3,000 pounds for it. And, he just had a bit of work done to it down at Gilbert's here in town. I just collected it last month from there. And because of all that, I'm gonna need 1,500."

"Is it because of the work done or the debt owed?"

"The work done, mate. The work done."

"It is in fine fettle, but not a lot of people are splashing out on cars now, are they?"

"A few are. I just saw a new reg on a Rolls not two weeks ago."

"And were they willing to talk about it?" The cousin didn't answer. "Fewer, I would say. Now, I am charitable. 1,200 pounds." Stephan then held out his hand.

Fowkes spat in his.

"What are we, out at the dogs? Here's the money." Stephan thrust the elusive, large and dirty wad of bills at the cousin and got into the car.

After a minute of familiarization with the bristling-with-gauges dash, Stephan set the retarder, put the hand throttle on and started up the Blower. Stephan then slid the small pistol out of his pants pocket, wrapped it in his scarf and held it an inch from the head of the cousin who was standing next to the door counting his money. Pulling the trigger, Stephan watched the cousin get pushed back into the brick wall and slump down to the ground.

With the Bentley idling, Stephan stepped out of the car, snatched back his 1,200 pounds and quickly jumped back into the driver's seat. Cranking hard on the cord-wrapped wheel, Stephan snicked the grey Bentley's gear lever into first, then pulled out onto Commerce Street, prepared for the blast up to Newcastle. It had taken more than a month to acquire this tool. Now he needed to use this most recent acquisition.

1
Goodwood Revival 2008

The cars around Faston exploded with sound. And with a flip of a switch, so did his Lotus-Climax 18. Revs dipped and rose. Fuel choked the air. Faston engaged the clutch and then snicked the gear lever into first. And he then waited. Head straight ahead, but eyes off to the side watching the starter.

The flag dropped and rubber pelted his face shield. Faston reacted without thinking when the race began. He got the skinny-tired Lotus to hook up and was able to pass the Lotus of Elliot coming out of Madgwick to move up a spot into 14th out of 30 cars.

Bang! All old racecars made impressive, unique and frightening sounds when pushed hard. Especially when heard from behind the wheel. And this Lotus was not any different. Faston tried to push past the fear that something might break and concentrate on the race at hand. Bang! Again and again the Lotus creaked and groaned. The wheel shimmied in his hand. But so long as the car pulled hard, tracked straight and had brake pedal feel, Faston pushed on. He had to have faith in the mechanics of Kelly Van Ness, the man whose car this was.

The race swirled around him. Being mid-pack in a Formula One race, even a retro race, was three hundred and sixty degrees of noise and action. A complete assault on the senses. Faston loved it and feared it. And loved it more for the fear.

The nimble cars around him pecked at the slightest opening, trying to move up a spot. Elliot and Warren, his other grid mates in a Cooper-Climax, both proved good competitors, and the three of them raced within the race. Faston, aware of the action around him, worked his line and drove smoothly. The Lotus erred towards stable over steer, and he was able to balance the grip and power through the longer turns.

At Fordwater, the undulating surface tested Faston's nerves. Bumps there had the Lotus climbing to the top of its suspension travel. Then slamming back down. Bang! Tall tires squirmy with lateral forces. But he stuck to it, staying flat out, letting the car drift to the outside, tires near the edge of tarmac, to prepare for St. Mary's.

The Lavant straight was where Faston was able to relax a bit. To prep for the rest of the lap. Especially for the chicane. A couple of deep breaths here gave his brain enough oxygen to overcome his strained breathing on the rest of the lap. Faston thought he would have preferred the circuit without the chicane, as it was before 1952. But there it was, a big kink with a big crash if you missed it. Hay bales more menacing for bringing attention to what they wouldn't save you from.

Faston settled into his pace. Bang! Creak. Breath. He let the race come to him until the end was approaching. Wanting to make a pass, Faston tried to exploit the handling of the Lotus on the long, high-speed turns. The Lotus twitched through the tight corners. Drifting wonderfully on the longer turns. A bit too much drift on lap 11 as a Maserati 250F tried to pass Faston on the outside of Fordwater just as his Lotus got rocked by an undulation and slid to the top. The cars bumped. Faston's left rear tire touching the Maserati between its two right-side wheels. Slewing abruptly back against the g-forces, the Lotus cranked into what a motorcycle rider would call a tankslapper. It was moments like this in racing where some guys would back off. Faston had the opposite reaction. He tried harder than ever to keep the Maserati at bay. And he would have to keep it behind him for two more laps.

Faston knew of two ways to keep a driver behind you. One was to drive a conservative defensive line. The other was to just outdrive the other racer. To use their presence behind you as motivation to keep your foot on the gas a little longer. To drift that much closer to the edge of the track to maintain speed. And it was this latter strategy that Faston employed.

Giving a symbolic tug on his harness, it couldn't get any tighter, Faston aimed to turn his fastest lap and keep the 250F in 13th place. Focusing on the inside front wheel and ensuring it clipped the apex, Faston was able to string together a smooth line and fast laps. The Maserati driver went from filling his mirrors to being six car lengths behind. When the chequered flag came, Faston was not sorry to see it.

Crossing the finish line in 12th place, Faston was ecstatic pulling into the pits. Or as ecstatic as one could be with a helmet, harness and arm straps holding him in place. His stewardship of the Lotus over, and the car returned to Van Ness in one piece, Faston could now enjoy the rest of the weekend.

After unclipping his harness, HANS device and helmet, Faston lifted himself out of the Lotus with his arms, both quivering from a draining of adrenalin. As a result of a lack of altitude on his escape, he caught a toe as he exited the cockpit. It took a couple of steps and a helping arm from one of Van Ness's mechanics to steady him. Looking up to see who might have glimpsed his inelegant dismount, Faston saw that Van Ness, Caprice and someone who seemed to be a good friend of Van Ness had all witnessed it. And all three were laughing.

Van Ness was first. "Glad you saved your crash for the pit, Faston."

"Me too. Just a touch and go. Like I had with the Maser in Lavant."

"Right. That too. Let's see the result of that." Van Ness and his friend walked around the Lotus and looked at the right rear tire while Faston took the opportunity to catch up with his wife.

While Van Ness looked the part in his two-piece brown suit and trilby, his friend looked a mess in a misfit tweed blazer, distraught bow tie and puckering wool pants. Caprice, on the other hand, looked stunning. She was wearing a light-wool, grey dress that had a loose fold down one shoulder. It was fastened with a high-waist and broad black belt with silver buckle. Her shoes were perfect black and grey pumps with a T-strap slid over seamed stockings. On her shoulders lay a heavy cream-colored shawl jacket that exaggerated her sway as she walked along. The sensible black hat, aerodynamic is how Faston would describe it, was the crowning touch, allowing Caprice to shy away and then turn back with a friendly or fiendish glance.

"Nice race, luv." Caprice said kissing Faston on his sweaty cheek.

"Thanks. Moved up a couple of spots and didn't bankrupt us. I'd say it was a well-done day. Who's the guy with Van Ness? And did I say how sharp you look?"

"You didn't say. But thanks. Him? Hmm. A guy who wants to meet Faston Hanks. He heard us in the grandstand during the Richmond Trophy and was adamant that he be introduced to you."

"I thought Van Ness and the tweedy fellow were old friends."

"No. They just met. But he is one of those gentlemen who seem to form a quick bond."

"What's his name?"

"It's Aron - one 'o' one 'n' - Stores."

Just then Van Ness tapped Faston on the shoulder. "Nothing done that my boys can't take care of. Cosmetic only. Might leave the marks, adds some patina to the Lotus. What do the people in NASCAR call it, a Bristol tattoo? I'll change the Dunlop, though. And, eh, Faston. This is Aron Stores."

"Heard much about you and your gifts." Aron offered on a robust Scottish accent.

"What gifts are those?"

"Finding cars that go missing for long periods of time and are worth lots of money."

Faston just smiled in return with Caprice arm in arm with him.

Aron continued, "And I have an offer for you to help me complete my quest to find a certain Bentley that has proven rather shy the past several decades."

"I love Bentleys. The early cars are dynamic. Which one are you interested in?"

"Well, when do you plan to head back to the States?"

Caprice squeezed his arm to the point of stopping blood flow, knowing that Aron was hinting at starting the search now, and in turn disrupting Faston and Caprice's planned post-Goodwood vacation to Liege.

"Not for a week." Faston could not feel his fingers due to Caprice's grip.

"Good. I'd love for you two to join me at Toftcombs. Once there, I will tell you all about the Bentley."

"And where is Toftcombs?" Caprice asked.

"Right outside Edinburgh, if I recall right." Charles piped in. "Known for its minstrel gallery and for being the home of Prime Minister Gladstone's family. Shall we head out tomorrow? Should be there in time for dinner."

"See you all tomorrow. Drinks are at seven sharp."

"I need a drink now," Faston said to Caprice and Charles, each taking a different meaning out of it.

2
Newcastle, June 1939

Getting back to his appointment in the North was draining. The brilliant chaps who ran the war and civil defense decided that it would be best if all street signage were taken down. Signage that the government never really bothered to put up in the first place, leaving the task to the AAA. This delabeling of the roadways was so that any German forces who happened to set foot on this island would have a devil of a time making their way. The odd side effect of this was any law-abiding citizen who travelled outside their own village had better bring a good map and a willingness to chat it up with locals so that the right road could be found. A brilliant side effect as there is no one more snooping or mistrusting than an uneducated British isolationist in village-by-the-backwater.

Right now, the Bentley was in a nearby garage that he rented from a local who couldn't make a go of the business as it transitioned from repairing carriages to repairing cars. But that was not as a result of under-investing in tools. The shop had everything Stephan needed.

On the drive up, Stephan noted that the Bentley's wheel pressed close to his chest. He wanted to shorten it back to a more standard position, say by two inches or so, but after closer inspection it was too involved a job for him to tackle. To get a few inches he would need to contact a machinist to get some parts knocked up and he was not about to do that.

Next, Stephan was wanting blackout screens and other modifications fitted for the headlamps. Thankfully, he was working with the more powerful Zeiss units. The originals, as had been Stephan's experience, shed as little light on the road as a first-year deacon shed on the mysteries of the church. Stephan had in his mind a lighting arrangement that he could activate from the cockpit. He didn't like the look of the standard hooded arrangement alone. He wanted something that could completely black out the lenses and pivot them in different directions. So he cut circles out of wood to match the large projector headlamps. He then inserted a pin at the top of each lens so that the wooden circle could be pivoted off to the side of the lens. The next part took some fiddling. He found some threaded rod in the shop and screwed together an ungainly but effective pair of activators for the lenses. He didn't want to cut into the beautiful dash, so the handles of these were located beneath the dash. With his chin on the center of the dash, Stephan could just reach the controls with both hands, such that he could completely turn on or off the lights without powering them down, as well as pivot them through 90 degrees of vertical arc.

A further inspection of the big 4 ½-litre revealed that a larger than standard silencer had been fitted at some point. Not one to really want to attract attention, even more so in his current situation, Stephan left it as is. There was plenty of wind and induction noise to satisfy his motoring fantasies anyway. In fact, one of the hardest parts on the drive north was staying off the floorboard with the accelerator just to hear the blower work its aural wonder. The blower had been one of those cast without the Villiers name, as Stephan recalled the court case of the inventor trying to get some money out of the bankrupt Bentley firm some eight years or so back.

Stepping back and looking at the light grey color, Stephan was able to take in the shape of the car. The upright windshield was a bit pedestrian to his eye - it announced the car as more doctor than soldier - but he could do nothing about that. As the coachbuilder had not installed a full-length running board to connect the taut front and rear fenders, Stephan and other drivers and passengers were left with the step-plate that looked to him like an upside-down aircraft wing. Overall, the impression was of the gentlemen fighter thought Stephan. Someone who had spent some time at University but never forgot that you earn respect with your fists as well as your brains.

Inside, it was more of the same. The soft finishes of leather and the cloth hood were both in a nearly matching light grey to the exterior. Changing those would be difficult, but changing the paint color would be, at least a rough paint job, not that hard of a job. And that is why earlier in the day he'd arranged for the car to be sprayed a midnight blue. Tonight he would spend sanding and cleaning the car for tomorrow's paint. The wheels he wanted painted red.

To complete the transformation from stolen car to Stephan's car, he decided to remove the front bumper. He'd have removed the rear spare tire but was sure he'd need it. It was four in the afternoon, and Stephan promised the painter he'd have the car to him by morning. Stripping off his suspenders and opening himself a bottle of local Newcy Brown, Stephan got to work preparing a device that would fulfill his needs like no other. The work went easily yet deep into the night. With an end goal as large as Stephan's, the intermediate tasks on the way seemed not to be work at all.

3
Goodwood Revival, 2008

"Pass the tea, and please, please tell me why we are going to Scotland?" Caprice asked while pushing around her English breakfast. Faston knew she never liked the mushrooms that rolled around the plate and brushed against the more savory bacon and sausage portions of the breakfast.

"The Goodwood Park puts out a nice spread, hmm?" Charles said with a mouth full of food, some black pudding sauce even appearing and sticking at the corner of his mouth. "These beans are delicious. And others may pass on the fatty ham, but I for one, am a sucker for it."

"It is a nice way to break fast, Charles. For sure. This tea is smoky perfect."

"Faston, are you a bit upset that you had that moment there in the 18? I mean, you aren't the smoothest driver and have been getting all sorts of coaching back at Lime Rock."

Faston immediately flashed back to the touch of his Lotus 18 and the Maserati. "I think the coaching was exactly what kept me on course. I didn't look at him. I looked ahead, kept a light grip on the wheel and focused…"

"Why is no one answering me?" Caprice dropped the spoon on the nice china of The Richmond Arms restaurant.

"Faston doesn't want to lie to you, Caprice. Simple as that." Charles answered.

Staring at a sculpture on a hall table of a head cut in two and positioned inches apart, Faston thought about his own split feelings regarding a trip to Toftcombs house in Scotland. Aron Stores was, how to put it, engaging. That twinkle in his eye. Faston had seen it before in enthusiasts who had the sickness. The oil mixed with water in the blood. The turning to jelly of the logic and decision when it came to cars. And Aron had certainly seen a similar look in his eyes as he told of a Bentley that he wanted to find. But a twinkle in the eye was not something Caprice liked to make decisions on.

"It's true. I don't want to lie to you. What happened the last time I lied to you? Nothing good."

"True, we had a rough weekend; you were minutes away from missing the Fall Festival as you were out tracking down that Porsche prototype."

"Right, so I don't lie anymore. I just want to go. The man is putting us up at his house. We can easily stay for another seven to ten days."

"My, I am ill-equipped for another ten days of gallivanting about England." Charles offered in.

"Charles, you are always ill-equipped to be gallivanting. Even in your own home." Faston laughed as he patted Charles on the back to let Charles know he was still glad to have him about, no matter his fashion sense. "And Caprice. You love old country houses. And this new one is not usually open to the public. You'll love it. I hear they have a ten-acre garden and are near some other sensational show gardens."

"Stop pandering. I just want to know that this will be a worthwhile trip and not just a headache for all involved."

"Oh. It will be a headache. But a good one." Faston smiled.

"I don't want to lie as Charles said."

"The man doesn't want to lie." Charles parroted.

"I don't want to lie. But a Bentley. I have been into them more and more. As a group, the owners are fanatical about every little detail and history of the cars. Almost psychotically so on the pre-War stuff. Some phenomenal people will be watching, greeting, and searching with us at least. All, while you garden."

"All while I garden? I think I will get roped into this search somehow. At least I'll have to hear about it over drinks and dinner. Drinks and breakfast. Drinks and walking. Drinks and shooting."

"Don't be ridiculous, Caprice." Charles smirked. "Faston never drinks when he shoots. Now, let's get going. Plus, I hear Faston has arranged for some sensational transport."

"Of course I have. It's right out front. All loaded with our luggage." Faston said and got up to lead the trio outside.

Sensational their transport was, Faston thought while looking over, lusting and drooling around the Jaguar MK2 3.8 manual the chaps at JD Classics had loaned to him. With a promise of an article in return. Opalescent blue over blue hides, 9471 CR was a spectacular example. With the recent JD Sport upgrades to suspension and air-conditioning, this particular MK2 was the perfect small-island-crossing material. It was even supercharged and possessed the optional overdrive unit.

"Are those competition wire wheels, and do I see some shock reservoirs under there?" Charles asked as he was on his knees near the Jaguar, looking underneath at the immaculate undercarriage.

"Yes. And yes." Faston answered as he placed the luggage in the boot.

"And why are you so into sports cars?" Caprice asked, sliding into the right-hand seat.

"Because they are better. And, Caprice, the passenger gets in on the other side."

Pushing her large sunglasses down off her head, Caprice turned to the front of the car and held out her hand palm up. "I know. Now give me the keys. I'm driving. You can get in the back and fiddle with the tray tables like a two-year-old."

"But it is a JD Sport…"

"Chop. Chop. We have to get to Toftcombs for drinks."

Faston looked over at Charles who only had a one-word comment. "Shotgun!"

4

Newcastle, July 1939

"You've met Stephan before, haven't you?" the aide to the secretary of the ARP, Thornley, asked of the head of Section 1 ARP, John Mounts. "Don't believe I have," Mounts nodded. "Stephan..."

"Sidlow it is. Nice to meet you.' Stephan made sure to look Mounts right in the eye and gave him a firm, quick, one-pump shake.

"Yes," Thornley went on. "The Air Raid Protection is getting a bit stressed and stretched. Damn organization sprung up from a sprat in no time. Got a kick in the pants compliments of the Communist Party here, about the only good thing they've done, but here we are. Twelve regions, all running around a bit like their own fiefdoms."

"And we all remember how it was when each Lord had too much power and his own fiefdom," Mounts quipped.

"I'm a bit young to remember that," Stephan deadpanned.

"We all are," Thornley brokered the tension. "Stephan here is in charge, really a roving measure of consistency and capacity, of the half-dozen eastern edge ARP civil defense regions."

Mounts looked Stephan down. "Is that so? Where did you serve before this appointment?"

Stephan could tell the man was testing him, prodding to find out more about a new boss. "I could ask you the same question? But I trust you earned your appointment, so extend me the same. Because I have earned it."

"Enough with the quiz." Thornley stuttered. "It's enough that Sir John Anderson wants the man in the post. So the man gets the post."

Mounts stood a bit taller, Stephan noticed. "No worries. Just trying to get to be a bit closer to a man that could potentially send me more money or assets. A bit of looking into the future."

"I didn't take it any other way." Stephan said. "Now, if you'd excuse me and Thornley for a while, I myself would like to get to know my duties a bit better."

"Nice to meet you. And to see you on your rounds of the regions, if you ever make it out of the joys of London."

"There are some ills to go with the joys of London. Good day."

Mounts stepped out of the office that was carved out of the courthouse and left Stephan and Thornley alone. Stephan, who wore a two-piece wool field-cut uniform with the ARP oval badge, set his cap down on the desk that stood between the two men. Stephan took out a small loose sheaf of paper from his jacket along with a similarly small pencil, and prepared to jot down a note or two. He liked writing down things, then throwing out the scraps. The act of writing down the words worked wonders in aiding his memory.

"Don't worry about Mounts. He and the other chiefs of the ARP regions are good blokes. They are all used to having serious responsibilities on their shoulders and can be relied upon."

"I would assume nothing less. So, when Sir John rang me and asked that I take on half the country, I said yes. But, as you know, you don't ask him detail questions. So that's why I'm here. To start at the top of the country and to figure what I need to do on the way down south to keep it all safe and secure."

"That is very much up to you. First, since you'll be travelling a lot, I've gotten you a driver, an Austin and a pass to get you on any train. Now, what are you laughing at?"

"I prefer to drive. So I made sure to get a car that can properly handle the mileage. It's parked outside." Stephan motioned over Thornley's shoulder and out the tall arched windows.

After getting up and peering out the window, Thornley asked, "Which one? The Singer or the MG."

"The Bentley. It's parked a bit further down. Got a couple of kids gawking at it like it's the latest fighter of ours."

"Taking the King for all his free petrol, are you? But, lovely car, a bit old for my taste, I think. To be honest, it looks almost new. I do think that Singer quite rakish, for a little thing."

"It's been well maintained, you could say."

"What color is that anyway? Black or blue?"

"It's whatever you think it is. That's why I like it. It looks like two different colors to different people. Suits my two different moods."

"And what are those?" Thornley pondered, still looking out the window.

"Feeling efficient. And feeling effective."

Thornley stifled a laugh at the back of his throat. "Now, lets get to figuring out what I need from you."

Stephan took out his initialed pad and pencil and made notes. Notes about when Thornley wanted updates. Notes about what the updates should entail. And notes about what his travel schedule was expected to be and so on for an hour. Stephan was careful to clarify any details he was unsure of. He didn't want to make mistakes that would bring undue attention his way as he would be doing enough to attract the wrong sort of attention soon enough.

5

Near Biggar, Scottish Borders, 2008

Caprice did an admirable job of making great pace without resorting to the manic moves in and out of traffic that Faston knew he would have made on the drive north to Toftcombs. As they drew down the drive, Faston took in the horses, some miniature, grazing in the field. The heavy rains of summer's last days had saturated the greens to a point that had Faston thinking that if he touched the grass or a tree, it would bleed off on him, staining his hands with pure, liquid nature. This location in the rolling boarders area reminded Faston of his and Caprice's inn back in Connecticut. And that made him very happy.

The facade of Toftcombs, though, was of a completely different style; Faston thought it might be baronial, to his usual very modern architectural preference. Toftcombs was built in the soft red brick of the region, with a crenellated portico over the front entrance and its overall smallish scale, smallish being relative when speaking of a home with eight bedrooms and nine bathrooms. Its asymmetric style, with one turret off to the left corner, also added to the mystery and approachability of the property. Faston always felt that perfectly symmetrical large, old properties were too governmental. They spoke too much of power and not enough of vibrant home life.

With drinks at seven coming up in just an hour, Faston was hoping to have a walk around the property to stretch his legs after 400-odd miles and seven hours in the back of the MK2. Even though the MK2 has small shelves built into its seatbacks, its leg rear legroom is not as generous as one would think. For room in a Jaguar saloon, one had to go for the inflated looking Mark X.

"Charles, help Caprice with the bags, will you? I've got to walk around and get some feeling back,"

"Yes, sir; anything else, sir?" Charles mocked Faston.

Faston watched as Charles took his typically horrible and inappropriate luggage along with Faston's and Caprice's linen Tumi bags out of the trunk of the MK2. Satisfied that Charles wouldn't make Caprice do all the heavy lifting, Faston began walking around to the right of the main house. What he saw behind the house that arriving guests could not see from the approach was the huge L-shaped set of renovated stables.

Seeing the large stone walls and six gleaming oak doors cloaking the contents of an equal number of bays, Faston quickened his pace toward the building. The six bays were not alone. On the shorter leg of the L-shape was a two-storey all-wood building with one larger oak bay door, this one open, revealing a spotless garage. Empty, but spotless. A staircase ran across the back of the bay leading up and to the right toward what Faston guessed was an office or owner's retreat. If he were Aron, Faston thought, that is where he would put his computer, sofas, TV and booze.

Without hesitating, asking or caring, Faston walked into the open garage bay and looked around. The construction was all post-and-beam pegged together with old-world craftsmanship. Faston liked it. One of the things that united this style of building with the modernist style was a pride in how it was constructed. No need to hide anything that was done with such a fine level of finish. At closer inspection, Faston noted that this part of the building looked newer than the longer part of the L. It was just a subtle difference in tone. The richness of hundreds of years of oxidation on wood is hard to duplicate. No matter how much you pay. And no doubt Aron had paid handsomely for this building.

Turning to look for a way into the bays that were closed from the outside, Faston glanced over shelves brimming with original workshop manuals for Bentleys, MGs, Bristols and many other car manufacturers. Spotting an ancient door, Faston walked over and tried it. A slow turn of the fine handle rotated down ninety degrees. There was no window in the door, so Faston was bursting inside to see what was on the other side. Pulling on the door, Faston was prepared and flexed to give a monumental tug, but all that was needed was the slightest one-finger pull, and the door opened.

Lights flickered to life overhead. There must be a motion sensor, Faston noted to himself. Glancing down from the lights, he took in a stunning collection of about a dozen cars. Ranging from limousines to sports racers, the collection immediately broadcast both breadth and quality. If the man's wines and food are half as good as his taste in cars, Faston let his imagination run, I'll be having a phenomenal time here.

The car closest to him was one of Gordon Buehrig's gorgeous Cord 810s. In a correct ivory with wide whitewall tires, she – this car was defiantly a she - looked like a ghost of a debutante, lithe, pretty and with angles enough remaining to balance the curves. She even seemed to be blinking as the pop-up headlamps were folded down. Peering in through the side windows, Faston could take in the engine-turned dash. And a rather spartan and nautical interior in blue cloth with grayish piping.

The Cord 810 is a beautiful car, Faston was thinking, but the Lancia Aurelia B24 is a sex symbol of a car. An at-her-prime Anita Ekberg. With their fully independent suspension and powerful V6, Faston loved these Lancias for what they were. A more respectful but equally powerful contemporary to Ferraris and Porsches. The one Aron had, in black with black interior, looked just sinister enough. Stored with the top down it showed that the owner had the good sense to use his car only when the weather allowed for the full experience. Driving this car with top up would be like a vegetarian going to a steakhouse for dinner.

A couple of Jaguars and an early Morgan Plus4 separated Faston from the last street car stored in the stables, the stunning Aston Martin DB 2/4 in two-tone paint. Grey over blue. It was a wonderful Aston. The one for enthusiasts. All the world knows about the Bondish DB5 so this example goes under the radar. A wonderful British grand tourer.

Next, there was a 1963 Howmet Turbine, white and blue. Almost GT40 in appearance save for the large roof-mounted scoop that fed air to a repurposed helicopter engine. Thinking about how fun and shocking this car must have been in the early sixties, Faston laughed out loud. Running kerosene jet fuel, this is one car that Faston rather liked looking at more than driving, let alone racing, in.

Next came a Tuthill-prepped early 911 rally car. Complete with rock chips and quiver of hood-mounted spotlights. As Faston began climbing in to get a better look at the prep work of the chassis, Tuthill was the best in the business and he'd love to learn a trick or two, he heard the door open and Aron's distinctive voice.

"I fear you'll have to wait until tomorrow to take it out for a spin. The neighbors, even being far off, very much dislike me blasting around in uncorked racecars in the evenings. Much better we go out in the morning."

"That's generous, but I'd rather take a taste of V8." Faston said pointing to one of the most unique racing cars he'd seen in a while.

"The '81 Oscar India. I had that prepped some years back for racing. I was sick of Yanks; you Yanks, having all the fun in your V8 Mustangs at the races. I figure the Aston V8 is as close as we have to a Mustang from the UK, so I went for it. Take a look. And we'll take her out tomorrow instead of the P-car."

And go for it he did. While Aron undid the hood latches on the dark-blue-with-white graphics racer. Under the hood was the distinctive Aston V8 running Webers. The exhaust was a custom stainless bundle of tubes, larger than original diameter; the shocks were adjustable, as were the sway bars that seemed as thick as Faston's wrist. The tires were Hoosier slicks. Inside, there was neither leather nor wood. No Wilton wool carpets or overmat, just cages, instruments and a full-race OMP halo seat, dark blue with matching white stripes. Fantastic.

"So, how does it stack up against Mustangs?"

"It's a bit heavier, but the grunt from the Pagnell lump puts me out front."

"I must say, all your cars a unique. So, what can be so special that you need me to help you find it? Looks like you do no mean job of finding-or building-whatever you're after."

"If I could have told you in a garage, I would have blown the gaff at Goodwood. But I can't. And every mystery tastes better with a drink."

"I couldn't agree more."

"Now, lets go inside and have ours. Caprice and Charles have gotten a head start on us already."

"About Charles..." Faston went on.

"No need to explain. He's not the first guest to have mistaken the bath soaps for a breath mint."

Faston let Aron place his arm around him to drag him out of this stable of oil and dreams and into the drawing room of Toftcombs where Faston hoped to hear more about his next potential adventure.

6
Scotland, July 1939

While he was in the North, Stephan thought he would
take care of a potential little problem. Not that it was a
problem at all. Or that it would be in the future. He just
did not let things grow into problems. Problems brought
people down. And Stephan never, ever, liked being
brought down.

That is why he spent a couple of days making
his way up the coast to a factory in Leith. Finding the
factory itself was a hassle without the road signs around,
but Stephan managed to locate it. And to locate D.H.
Sessions. Always be safe, Stephan believed. That is why
he followed D.H. for a couple of days. Learning his
routine. Learning who his friends were. Learning when
he should approach him.

Session's routine was just that, routine. He rode
a bicycle about four miles inland to the factory from his
guest rooms within a rather large, stately home. His
friends were not friends. They were coworkers. In three
nights, he never saw D.H. go out to eat, or even for a
pint, with any of the other factory workers. There were
no apparent social situations at which Stephan could
meet D.H., so Stephan would have to figure out some
other way to get into contact. Close contact.

Stephan figured the best time would be to
arrange some sort of meeting along the road that D.H.
followed to and from the factory. Driving the Bentley up
and down the road while D.H. was in his office, Stephan
spent some time finding a good location. The road was
mostly well-bordered by the type of lower-middle-class
homes typical of a hard-working town like Leith. But in
the last half-mile of the road to D.H.'s quarters, it
opened up a little. The homes became harder to spot,
then nonexistent. The side roads became more like side

paths, unpaved and twisting strips that disappeared off into the countryside. It was onto one of these turnoffs that Stephan turned the Bentley and drove until it and he could not be seen from the roadside.

Stephan walked down to the main road and back toward town. It was going on seven at night; the sun was still shining strongly as it wouldn't be night until close to nine-thirty. Although Stephan would have preferred it to be dark out when he approached D.H., he had to meet the man now.

So Stephan headed back to town, walking at a slow pace as he did not want to cover too much ground, and looked out for the bicycling D.H. Over three days, D.H. had gotten round to this spot in the road within the same 15-minute period. Only one car, a tiny Austin, had passed in the time that Stephan ambled along. He was glad he had only this one passerby to think about. To put in the back of his mind. To remember.

Once he was a few hundred yards closer to town, Stephan turned and headed back to the road where he had turned off. Looking back over his shoulder often for the approaching cyclist, he was within 25 feet of the turnoff when he saw D.H. gliding his way. It was a very mild slope downhill, and D.H. was not pedaling; he was just coasting along. Looking as stern as always, as if he were figuring a difficult sum.

"Hey, hey there," Stephan spoke out loud and waved down D.H.

As Stephan knew he would, D.H. pulled over. "How's it. What can I do?"

"Just got my car stuck up the turnoff here and need a hand changing a wheel. I usually could do it myself, but it is at an awkward spot in the road, and the jacking situation seems shaky. Do you have a few moments to help? Or, if not, could you send help for me?"

Stephan watched as D.H. checked his watch, and gritted his teeth, but in the end he agreed to help.

"Superb. Now, lets get there and back and the job done so you and I can both get home."

"Fine."

Stephan and D.H. walked for a minute or two without saying a word more to each other. D.H. pushing his bicycle with one hand so that he could keep the same pace with Stephan. But after another minute, just as the pair were out of view from the road, D.H. asked, "What were you doing driving on this road anyway?"

"Trying to find a mate's house. Damned lack of road signs combined with an outdated map made it rather hard for me to get there. I was trying to turn around and get back to the main road there and got stuck with my flat."

"Hmm," Was all that D.H. could mumble.

Stephan felt that D.H. thought him a rube, or at least an incompetent. That he had to help this sorry fellow. As the road made a few more of its tight twists, the Bentley would be visible in a moment. Stephan bent down to tie his shoe, to give him a moment to think and space to act.

"You alright?" D.H. sneered downward.

"Yeah, I'll catch up, just don't want to trip and dirty my suit."

"No, you wouldn't want that."

Stephan let D.H. get a dozen or so steps ahead and began walking behind him. He knew that the sight of his Bentley would be a shock, and it was.

"That looks just like my Bentley, the very one I left in the care of…"

Stephan knew who he had left the car in the care of. A gambler. He didn't need to hear it again. That's why he swung hard with the lead hammer from the Bentley's toolkit, aiming at the base of D.H.'s skull.

Stephan didn't miss, and the hammer didn't even make a sound. Stephan bent over to make sure D.H. wasn't breathing. He wasn't.

Stephan then looked around, found a large stone on the side of the patch, and arranged it next to D.H., as if he had fallen off his bike and hit it.

"Unfortunate that. Out for a ride, doing your part. And supper will go cold."

Stephan got into the faultless Bentley, began its complicated starting procedure and prepared for a fast blast to his office to complete his report to Thornley then on to his next civil defense region check in.

7
Toftcombs, 2008

"Like Nick in the Thin Man, Faston could be summoned
from a mile away by the sound of a drink being mixed in
a silver shaker." Caprice noted, as Faston walked in just
as Aron's man was beginning to pour a martini into her
just-emptied glass. "Thank goodness the man has a proper, 1920s-
sized martini glass, otherwise if you're on number two,
you being dizzy on the couch would not be too far
along." Faston winked at Caprice as he strode over to the
drinks table and gladly took an icy drink in his hand.
Looking at the gin on the edge of freezing, its viscous
texture mixing with the zest of lemon that was added
was a joy in itself. The first sip of a martini was always
better than the rest of the sips combined, so Faston took
a big, long pull. It coated his throat and stomach with a
cool warmth that meant the good part of the day was
starting. "This is spectacular, Aron."

"Spectacular." Charles agreed from a sofa that
he already seemed to be a part of.

"And," Faston continued after the interruption,
"it has a hint of yellow. Is this actually an aquavit and
not a gin?" Whatever it was, Faston thought, the man
does have excellent taste in food and drink.

"Not a bad guess." Aron noted. "It's Old Raj.
Distilled here in Scotland. And a touch of saffron is what
sets it off from the rest of the gins. A bit nutty."

Faston raised his eyebrows over the diminutive,
and now empty, glass. "I'm not sure about the nutty
taste. I'll have to try another."

While Faston waited for his second drink to be
mixed, he watched Aron arrange a couple of chairs
opposite the sofa that Charles was sitting on. Next, Aron

went over to the built-in bookshelves and pulled down a binder, placed it on his lap and waited.

"Faston, come take a seat and let me tell you why you're all here."

Faston, as ordered, took his seat across from the sofa where Caprice and Charles were perched sipping their second martinis. Faston gulped at his second. Aron had not even taken the oily surface off his drink.

"You know," Faston admitted, "I don't need a special reason to be here. The collection of cars you have. The taste in sundowners and the grounds around your home. This is like a vacation from our vacation."

Caprice raised her glass in a silent toast.

Charles pawed at the lemon twist in the bottom of his glass in ignorance.

Aron just laughed. "Thank you, Faston. You're too kind. But I do have something very special in mind for you to find."

"Lay it on me, brother."

"Pardon?"

"I, we, can't wait to hear." Faston finished his second martini and nodded to the servant who began mixing a new one from scratch.

"When I say Bentley, Faston, Bentley," Aron repeated. "What car is it that comes to mind? What car is it that defines the brand for you? And if you say one of the modern-day disasters, I know I have the wrong man here for the job."

"No need to worry there. I don't hate or love the new Bentleys. I really wasn't aware that they made anything after 1989."

"Good to hear. So, what car does it for you?"

"Uh, humm, let me see. And I bet my answer is no different than most, although the first Continental comes close, I would have to go with a Blower."

"Of course you would!" Aron blurted. "And that is why I want you to be my weapon in finding one of the missing Blowers."

"One of the missing?" Charles asked. "Isn't there only one of the original 50 still unaccounted for?"

Aron looked stunned for a moment and then pleased. Faston could tell then and there he and Charles would get the job, as they bled old car history. They were marque-agnostic. Be it Bentley, Ferrari or Porsche, Charles and he lusted after and had researched them all.

"Well played, Charles, you are right. But only one of the original 50 has a trail that went cold. And there are some spectacular stories regarding these old cars."

"Tell us a few of the stories, if you don't mind." Faston all but demanded, as he grabbed his third martini, took that familiar long first sip and sat back to listen. "I don't know all the Blower histories so would love a refresher."

"Oh my, a good story to start. How about that of MS3940. One of the many four-seater Van den Plas-bodied cars. Was exported to India. And, after a while the engine, with supercharger, was fitted to a speedboat. Can you imagine? That cobbled together speed boat got sunk, though, and the engine is still believed to be lying at the bottom of Bombay harbor."

"Then there was the young American, Billy Fiske, who had to have a Blower. The child won the bobsled Olympic gold when he was 16. And that was when they raced face-first. Face-first on those rickety wooden sleds. Even a Blower must have felt sedate after that. Well, he was a rich boy and wanted to be like Birkin, so he ordered up a Blower and went racing. Sold it after a few years though. But then the kid joined the RAF and was the first American pilot killed in the war. Quite a story."

Caprice, Charles and Faston had all stopped drinking and started listening to the remarkable stories of these legendary Bentleys. Faston got the feeling that Aron wanted to get to his car, but seeing how rapt his three guests were, he continued telling the history of different chassis numbers.

"Finally there was MS3939. Another four-seat VDP-bodied car. This one went to an H. Olswag in South America, but he was killed while driving it. Then, the biggest travesty of all, the car was rebodied with a Model A Ford body. Must have shocked a few folks though when that Model A puffed up and blasted past."

"And that brings us to SM 3912. The one Blower with an unknown fate."

"And the one you want us to find?" Faston presciently confirmed.

"Yes," Aron agreed in a voice just above a whisper, "SM 3912. Originally delivered to Lord Brougham & Vaux in August of 1930. The only one to wear a Phillips body. It was indeed one of only six not to be shod with the iconic VDP four-seater body. It was a stunning machine." Here, Aron opened his folder and pulled out a remote control.

Faston, Charles and Caprice all exchanged looks of shock and humor at the combination of old world and new technology. Fingering the remote, Aron hit a button that caused a picture, a rather nice Maud Earl non-sporting-group dog painting nestled within the bookshelves, to disappear, revealing a flat-screen television. Images of a large 1930s car appeared in black and white.

With more manipulation of the buttons, Aron zoomed around the image giving Faston and Charles a solid feeling for the car. "As you can see, SM 3912 is a large and imposing coupe."

"You know," Charles interrupted. "I think there is a rule of the automotive universe that a car's importance is directly related to how many replicas have been made of it."

Aron, Caprice and Faston all waited for Charles to continue. But he didn't. He, disgustingly to Faston, spun his little finger in his ear, and sat back in the couch with his second martini.

Shrugging his shoulders, Aron continued. "As I was saying, SM 3912 is beautiful. There are just two pictures around of it, one with the top up and one with the top down. Starting with the bonnet, SM 3912 has some very identifiable features. There are the two sets of 13 louvers on the bonnet."

"How many hold-downs?" Charles asked.

"Three on either side." Aron answered, continuing, "Then there are the swaggish front fenders. Tapering to a tight point with no running boards, they are rather unique of a Phillips-bodied Bentley. And especially the rear fenders; they seem to be symmetrical front to back, as if they could be mounted on either side. Of course, being hand-beaten, there is no doubt they could not be fitted to either side, but they do look that way."

"The step boards are also rather peculiar. First, that there are no step boards at all and not fender-to-fender running boards. With a flat top and a curved, aero-shaped underside, they hint at the great speed the Blower was capable of. It is my opinion that they look like gas tanks; they aren't, but that is what they look like to me."

Aron took a breath, and then pressed on. The way he pushed through the visual facts of describing SM 3912 was proof to Faston of a man obsessed for years. He didn't need notes for sure. He probably even had dreams, or nightmares, about this car. "The body itself has a shape that is part sporting, part demure. Like the personality of Lord Brougham & Vaux himself. The partial boat-tail hints at the sporting pedigree. The upright windshield and triple-wiper arrangement hint at the more proper two-seat tourer aspects. The hood also looks weather-tight and not like an afterthought."

"So," Caprice began to escape the boredom of hearing all the little coachwork and craftsmanship details of the car. "Who owned this big, expensive car? Just our Lord?"

"Quite the opposite. Lord Brougham & Vaux owned the car for only a very short period. Only managed to pile on about 4,500 miles. He sold it on to a Mr. E. T. Scarisbrick of Ormskirk, Lancashire."

Charles muffled a laugh.

"What's so funny?" Faston needed to know.

"He said E.T. owned the car. Think he drove home in a Blower?"

"Anyway. Go on, Aron." Faston asked of his host, his blank stare revealing he had no knowledge of the Spielberg movie.

"As you said, E.T. owned it."

Charles again laughed in his hand, but this time Aron pressed on.

"Yes, E.T. Scarisbrick. Everard Talbot. Served as a second lieutenant in the Great War. He was one of the owners who began to pile on the miles in the few years that he owned the Blower. But he, too, sold it along. This time the car went to London, into the possession of Mr. M. Stone, who owned the car briefly and had a rather middish-sized accident with it."

Faston grimaced silently, but Aron must have picked up on his pain at hearing of such a beautiful car getting in a crash. Aron tried to comfort him, "Just the odd bit and piece was fixed up on it. A new rear axle was the big item. And then it goes on to the next

charismatic and unlucky, I should say, owner, Mr. D.H.
Sessions from Portsmouth. He is the last owner that most
enthusiasts know about."

"Most?" Faston perked up.

"Yes, all the above information is easily
available from the W.O Bentley Foundation. They have
a chap there by the name of Alan Bodfish. He can dig up
all sorts of useful, esoteric and enlightening information
on most Bentleys. Knows the Blowers like a postman
knows his route, could recite it all from rote. Knows
which dogs bite and which don't, so to speak."

"So, I assume you're saying that you have more
information about SM 3912 than Mr. Bodfish?" Charles
asked.

"I hope so." Caprice added from her slumped
and evidently bored position on the sofa.

"I do. I do." Aron stammered with excitement.
"Don't tell Alan though. He'd be quite jealous. You see,
most people believe the last record of SM 3912 is that of
parts being sent to Gilbert & Co for repairs in 1939. But
that is not the case. I have a few interesting breadcrumbs
for my Hansel and Gretel to follow."

"I'm Gretel then."

"Fine," Faston agreed, "You do know Gretel
was the little girl?"

"I didn't," said a defeated and now silent
Charles.

"Although not registered via the traditional
manner, SM 3912 does have a paper trail for a few years.
And it was in the ARP that I found the records."

"ARP?" Caprice asked, as a non-car term had
her interest revived.

"Yes, the Air Raid Prevention Corps was a
rather large, involved and important group of home-
based citizens who ran the shelters, organized spotters

for German bombers, basically did anything that would help prevent harm from an air raid."

"What did you find that matches up the ARP and the Blower?" Faston asked, his empty martini glass sitting on the table as he was too engaged to even think about another drink.

"Petrol receipts." Aron answered.

"Petrol receipts?" Faston, Charles and Caprice all repeated in unison.

"Yes, petrol receipts for SM 3912 for a bit over four years, from 1939 to 1943." Aron clicked a few pictures across the flat screen to show scans of the actual fuel receipts. Their yellowed edges and tight handwriting formed perfect examples of mid-century schooling and supplies. "Yes, and although there is no marque associated with the number SM 3912, the fuel consumption is so enormous that I can't imagine another car of the era that could drink petrol in such a robust fashion."

"Maybe an Auto Union Grand Prix car," Charles suggested.

"If they didn't burn a more toxic mix of fuel, you'd probably be right. But the numbers and fuel consumption show that it averaged about 8 miles per gallon so they seem to point to the last of the Blower Bentleys."

"Do you have anything else?" Faston asked. "This is good, but it doesn't give me a bunch of hope. The name of the owner…"

Aron interrupted Faston. "Unfortunately not. My research team is not really a research team. They are a couple of people who know the types of cars I like, and when they find stuff, usually the cars themselves, they forward the information on."

"And that is why you called me?"

"Right. I believe you and Charles have the wherewithal to pick up the paper trail somewhere and at least find out what happened to SM 3912. That would be a victory in and of itself. I'll cover all your expenses. Now come on, on to dinner."

Aron placed his tweed-clad arm around Faston and guided him toward the dining room.

Sitting down at the table, Charles tucked his napkin into his collar and looked at Faston. "We humanities people stick together and research together. I have a friend whose specialty is primary source research for World War II. Don't know how much he knows about the home front and all the battles and organizations like the ARP that popped up and then disappeared after the Jerries were beaten, but I can give him a call."

"See, the soup isn't even finished being ladled, and we are already making headway." Aron smiled. Faston however, wasn't that interested in food. His hunger for anything except information about SM 3912 had vanished. But when he saw a decanter of super second-growth Rauzan-Segla '87 set upon the sideboard, his thirst, at least, returned.

8

Padova, Italy, October 2008

"Coys is very proud to begin our Auto Moto d'Epoca sale of important classic and sporting automobiles with something that is, rather special. Or could be rather special." The auctioneer at the podium spoke with an Italian-accented English that echoed throughout the room. His dark grey double-breasted suit, accented with a purple tie, gave him the air of royalty. Behind him screens displayed the price of bids in Yen, Euros, Dollars, Pounds and other denominations. A still larger screen, directly centered behind the serious leader of today's million-dollar sale, projected images of the cars.

Patrick was glad that the lot he had come to Padova to bid on was the first to go under the hammer. He hated auctions. He hated the people who attended auctions of high-end cars as a social outing. And he especially hated auction house employees who treated him as below their station and not worthy of their attention and invitations to champagne brunches sponsored by Veuve Clicquot.

Seated in the middle of the room on chairs that had a pattern of people playing in a park rendered in shades of yellow and blue, Patrick could not sit still. His lot was coming up. And he was determined to go home with it, the actual value of the piece being no guide for how much he would pay. It was a part he needed to have to put his plan one step farther down the road.

"Patrick, what do you think someone will be able to escape with this heap for?" The auction attendee whom Patrick had been chatting with asked.

"I've no idea, really." Patrick responded sharply. "I'm thinking eighty thou. Are you bidding on this lot?"

"Not me. I'm here for the recently restored Espada. But $80,000 for anything of that ilk seems square."

"Euros. So more like $100,000. With commission." Patrick winced thinking about the large premiums that auction houses made off both buyer and seller. Like real estate agents. Double dippers.

The gavel rapped on the dark, solid podium, and the image of lot number one flashed onto the large screen. It was not a perfectly restored Pierce Arrow or Cooper. Nor a Porsche or Brabham with original race patina. Lot number one was a bare chassis in a dreadful state of repair.

"As I said, ladies and gentlemen, lot number one could be something special. With say, just a little bit of polish." This understatement got a soft ripple of laughter out of everyone in the audience except Patrick and Tim. "We are on the continent, so the bids will be announced in Euros."

Patrick sat up in his chair and watched as the images of lot number one flashed in slide-show fashion behind the auctioneer, who began, "The proverbial barn find. Disinterred from a shed in Portugal, this Bentley four-and-a-half litre chassis has proven to be of unknown serial number and provenance. It is as you see it. There is no motor. It has some bits and pieces that seem to have hung on long past the coachwork, including a larger than standard fuel tank. It also has seen some crash repair done in period. But does that all matter? Your Bentley Boy dreams begin at 160,000 Euros."

Patrick noticed there were no takers, and he was not going to be the first to bid, he wanted to pay as little as possible for the Bentley chassis as they would be making a significant investment in it.

"140,000 Euros." The auctioneer intoned with no takers. "120,000. Alright, lets jump down to 50,000 Euros."

At 50,000 Euros a couple of phone attendants' arms rose up, but no one in the crowd, except Patrick, put a paddle in the air. Patrick was glad the action was not too hot on these rusty bits, as it bode well for a good deal.

The auctioneer, Patrick was thrilled to hear, ratcheted up the price in increments of 2,000 Euros. And the back and forth between himself and the phone bidders thinned out to just himself and another bidder at 68,000 Euros.

"70,000 Euros, to the bidder on the phone. It is with you at 70,000 Euros. Going once, going twice…"

Patrick held up his paddle and with his other hand; he showed a wide open palm and all five fingers. He knew he would have it.

"Thank you sir. 75,000 Euros. 75,000 Euros." The auctioneer looked over to the phone attendant who shook his head back at the auctioneer.

"Sold!" The gavel came down, and the boards lit up with the final sales price in all the currencies of the collector car world. "To the man in the…blue velour track suit."

Patrick felt a pride and joy he usually only felt when he won a race. And in a sense, he thought, he had won a race. Or part of a race. One that would have the largest purse he'd ever competed for.

9
Edinburgh, October 15th 1939

With his nighttime duty done, Stephan went back to his
rooms at a thin and meager guesthouse to try and grab
some sleep. It wouldn't be easy. To sleep. To unwind.
To shed the day and the deeds of that day. Stephan,
though, had a duty to see out and a superior to report to,
even when things were not pretty. Not ideal. He laid
back in his bed. The windows open on this warm night.
Stephan was able to hear the Bentley cooling down.
Pinking and clinking below his second-floor perch. He
could even smell it. The oil, the gas, the success.

His duties the past several months had been
monotonous. Once down in the south of the country, he
had innumerable small duties to attend to. From filing
and approving local ARP wardens to overseeing more
dramatic precautions, he was kept busy with busy work.
Stuff like ensuring that all the hydrants were painted
with a mustard gas reactive agent. This way, if the
Germans decided to use the insufferable poison, anyone
passing by a hydrant would know that a chemical
weapon had been unleashed upon them. That would
cause some panic, Stephan thought.

On making his way north, while continually
getting lost, Stephan had filed report after report to
Thornley and been in contact with region leader after
region leader. It was, some said, a false amount of
preparation and evacuation for civilians. Most had gone
home. Most had come to believe that the war would not
be affecting them. Affecting their job. Affecting
everything.

The pressure of the looming German invasion
was beginning to weigh on Stephan. He knew it was
coming. Britain knew it was coming. But how do you
prepare for such a thing? He was exhausted from his

work and from keeping his motivation high. Stephan had felt the need for himself, from his reports and the citizens too, that he needed to be a solid force. Be the person who defined the war-time morale even before the war came home. It was draining. It was acting. It was not who Stephan was.

Stephan felt proud of what the Bentley had done this evening. Listening to it cool off, he felt like the proud owner of a prize racehorse or dog. The man who had a living thing that helped its owner. Stephan did indeed feel that the Bentley was a living thing. It certainly drank enough petrol to be quite a trencherman. A glutton.

Stephan needed tonight to go seamlessly, to go as he planned. He had been unable to eat dinner, he was too busy thinking about the task ahead, but he did go ahead and complete the job. He succeeded. He would be on the winning side. But the task was not easy or obvious.

He had to find a spot high on a hill, overlooking the Forth of Firth and he had to get to this spot unseen. He had to remember the proper order in which the signals had to be given. One flash too long or too short and the directions he was trying to communicate would be off by a tenth of a mile. Or more. He had only one chance. And he took advantage of that chance. He did his duty and turned his back. He didn't behave like some murderer or other criminal and linger about the site. Seeing how people reacted to his work. Did people call what he did work? Because he would call it something else entirely.

Stephan was restless and did not fall asleep until at least 6AM. He slept fitfully for hours. Only jarred into consciousness, like the others sleeping or not within earshot, by an explosion. The first bomb missed its mark. The sound was hollow. The second, and the third, did not. Air raids of the home country had begun. Now Stephan could do his job. Donning his uniform in a hurry, Stephan rushed out to help and to see how his ARP was performing.

When Stephan arrived, smoke still hung in the air, curling around the iron of the Forth Bridge. People of every kind were walking toward the water. Stephan's first priority was to observe the movements of the ARP personnel. They were doing a crisp job. Being efficient. Organizing witnesses and writing recaps of the day's events.

Stephan was looking at what was the result of the Luftwaffe's first attack on Britain. Stephan was shocked it could occur so swiftly. As he stood above the Forth, a slight man wearing the base ARP uniform and pin approached him.

"That's the *Southampton* with the slight lilt. She took a good hit. So did the *Mohawk*, took a hit, but seems to have held up better then the '*Hampton*.'"

"How'd it happen?" Stephan asked flatly.

"Nine of 'em, I think. Nine Junkers JU-88s, had the audacity to bomb the Forth. Don't know what they were after. But we got at least two of them, the boys from 602 and 603 Squadron swatted them like flies."

Stephan cringed at hearing of the two downed Junkers. This was war, he thought. This was what he had worked so hard to become a big part of.

"What's your role, man?" Stephan asked of the fortyish man who informed him of the battle tally.

"A spotter. Saw them coming in myself. Was part of the chain that got the warning to the Spitfires. The ARP is running well, sir."

Stephan thought the man had no idea who he was. "So, how did they come in?" Stephan asked, desiring as many facts as possible.

"All unorganized. Scattered. Don't know if it was the weather or the fight that got them scattered, but they scattered. Not quite the war machine we've been warned of, eh?"

"I wouldn't call it victory for Britain, yet." Stephan warned the man and turned to find the ARP representative in command. He needed more details before his reports were finished and could be forwarded to headquarters.

10

Home Front Archives, London, October 2009

"You've got to remember, the entire British populace felt they were in the fight with the soldiers. Diary writing took off with the start of the war. People really knew how important a moment in time they were living in. How could they not, with War Bond posters plastered around every building corner? Every front page for months talking about the unstoppable." Here, Charles' friend Koustas took off his horn-rimmed glasses, paused and switched thoughts. "The people were in no way sure of the outcome. Only in hindsight do we know the outcomes of wars. That the Germans could not win. Or that the Confederates could never beat the industrialized north. Or that Vietnam would not be a cakewalk. But at the explosive time of the start of World War II, nothing was sure. Hence, the number of women in their forties finally getting married."

"Guys would take whatever they could." Charles nodded.

"You take whatever you can, whenever you can. War or not." Faston said while outlining both a slim and a thick female form.

"Even the sheep would look good if you were about to head off into the metal teeth of the German war machine." Koustas indelicately put the feelings of the British people.

Faston felt that he needed to get to the point with Koustas, or they'd be here all day, drinking Madeira, telling jokes and dispensing theories and thoughts without getting any research done on SM3912. "Alex, these records are pretty vast. How much has been categorized? And how can we search it?"

"Not much. And not well."

Faston groaned out loud.

Koustas patted Faston on the shoulder. "Don't worry, we can narrow it down to a few areas that might lead to your car. First, the receipts are from the central office of the ARP, so that narrows it down a bit. And the amount of fuel that is used, or could be extrapolated that was used, is not inconsiderable."

"And that means?" Charles asked the leading question.

"Oh, sorry. That means that its owner was a rather important person.

"I don't know any unimportant people who owned Bentleys at that time. The cost was too much," Faston noted. Then thinking how he should have thought of this before. Anyone who owned a Bentley, especially a Blower Bentley, had to have a high profile. At least in some area, he had to be known.

"You're right." Koustas concurred, "and he was probably associated with some high-level position regarding the home front. MP. Director. Secretary."

"Sounds promising and overwhelming." Faston said while scanning the stacks and mounds and boxes and terminals. "How do you suggest we dig in?"

"I've been thinking about that since Charles called two days ago." Koustas said, rubbing his chin. Then he snapped his fingers. "And I figured three of us, three different paths to perambulate down. Since I know the least about the car and its history, I figure I stick to searching the numbers associated with it in the databases that have already been catalogued. I wouldn't be able to work out any connections that aren't number perfect. You two should be able to do that, so that is why I have some special treats for you. Charles."

"Yes, Mr. Koustas," Charles responded like one of his less than eager students.

"Charles, you will dig in to the personnel records of the ARP. See if you can spot a name associated with Bentleys. They're organized by city, so you can sort it out that way."

"Sounds tedious."

"It is, Charles. And Faston, you get the odd lots. The three-dimensional. The possessions of ARP members stocked here. They are not organized. A few researchers have gone through some of the stuff looking for things associated with their specific course of research, none of which have been automotive in content. So you should be making fresh discoveries."

"Cracking," Faston responded with a soft voice, showing his disdain and dislike for the hard work of finding something missing for decades. Pushing up the sleeves on his cashmere Suitil sweater, Faston popped open the first box that Koustas had pointed out to him and looked inside.

Minutes later, Charles raced back from his spot out of eyesight. "I've got it."

"No, you don't." Faston replied. He'd fallen for Charles 'got it' joke too many times already.

"I don't got it," Charles said, wrinkled his lips, and then went back to research, grumbling something about needing a teacher's assistant.

Hours later, Faston stood up on legs that had become asleep and numb and made a demand. "Let's get something to eat."

"The Gastro Pub name is as ridiculous and abused as much as a slow horse," Koustas noted as the three researchers sat down at a large, communal table in the middle of the clean-lined pub. "But this place earned the name. Great food. Real ales. Real owners."

"Did I not tell you that Koustas was also the local food reviewer for the paper?" Charles asked Faston.

Beaming, Faston replied, "No, you didn't."

"I know. I didn't want to tell you because I thought it would make you too happy. And it has."

"Check out the blackboard." Koustas led the group. "Pick out the food, and I'll pick out the beer. Then we can talk about anything remotely promising that we found in our hunts. See if we need to change course or stay on our headings."

Noticing that a loose, energetic and bold hand had written the menu on the blackboard, Faston hoped that the same spirit was in the food. And as he read down the offerings, his hopes rose and his appetite grew. The menu was a celebration of the pig. From cracklings with paprika to belly over field greens to stuffed trotters and on toward rillettes, sausage and cured meats.

"Locked and loaded. I know what I'm getting," Faston declared.

"Me, too."

"I always get the same thing," Koustas said as the bartender emerged from the behind the bar to take their order.

Faston went first and ordered the sage-crusted pork sandwich, served with a marrow daub. Koustas ordered next and got the Gorgonzola stuffed and burnt-bread crumb crusted chop. Charles went for the fish and chips.

Faston took in a deep breath, to calm himself from saying something to Charles for his poor choice. But he didn't, instead he went back to discussing the search so far. "What have you found that has been the most interesting so far?" Faston asked, but he left no pause as he filled in Charles and Koustas on his most interesting find. "For me, it was a bunch of receipts for aluminum pots and pans and other odd bits. Not that there was money noted, just that it was noted how much aluminum a person donated."

"Oh, yeah," Koustas remarked knowingly. "Had lots of aluminum drives during the war to get metal to build bombers. Took the pots and pans, melted and refined the metal, and off it went into the sky to make hay."

"From frying sausages to flying sorties." Charles noted with some flair.

"Exactly," Koustas continued. "Exactly that, made the cast-iron bits the elements of choice in British kitchens for the next 20-odd years. The war rippled into every part of our lives for a very long period of time."

The server came to the table and set down three pints, each holding a meager head over a copper-colored liquid.

Koustas grabbed one glass and raised it toward the center of the table. "Cameron's Castle Eden Ale. Hand-pulled."

Faston toasted with Koustas and Charles and took a long pull of the ale. Its sweet malty flavor soon gave way to a citrusy, hoppy flavor that Faston thought would make the beer an excellent session ale.

"This is one to session, eh?" Koustas asked, looking at both Faston and Charles.

"I agree," Charles said, as he set down his glass that was half-emptied in one large pull. "Delightful."

"This is great stuff," Faston concurred. "I've been brushing up on beer. In the summer I can only have so many sundowners and sauvignon blancs. Give the liver a bit of a break with a beer. From inky-black Scotch Ales, to citrusy Blue Moon, to a Dogfish 120 IPA that I think had so much hops in it that it seared my tongue."

"Faston has pawned off some awfully good stuff and awfully awful stuff on me the past few wrenching sessions," Charles said as he licked his lips, Faston guessing he was remembering the Dogfish 120.

"It's a world-of-its-own beer."

"For sure. Lots of variety. But compared to wine, where it is a variety of subtlety, beer seems to be a variety of in-your-face flavors. Either way, good all around. So, I noted the aluminum recycling as interesting, no relation to our Blower, but interesting. You two?" Faston said, passing his hand over the table.

"Mine wasn't so much of a trail, and I know I spent too much time looking at it, but it was unique. An infant's gas mask. You put the whole child in it. Must have looked like an alien. Odd, very odd. Imagine some war profiteer made a killing producing the gas masks and they were never used! Never even tested."

"That would be useless, Charles, I agree," Koustas noted as he finished his beer and ordered another round for the table.

"I did my fair slog through war registrations. Insurance receipts and so on." Then lifting his left hand up, "I even have the paper cuts to show it."

"That leaves me," Koustas stated. "And I, too, found not so much as lots of nothing. I did find a few files and boxes that were from the ARP, though."

"Better than I did," Charles noted.

"Me too, I was dying to see those initials."

"We'll dig into them when we head back."

"I'd say I can't wait," Faston noted, "but that would be a lie." He finished as the bartender brought over the trio's lunch order. For a moment, Faston could put the Blower aside and tend to his own appetites as there was no hard deadline to meet in finding the Bentley.

11
ARP Headquarters, January 1940

This room, Stephan thought, was exactly what most of the British populace was fighting for. It was stolid. It was wood. It was old. And most importantly, it was proper and impressive. It was the type of room in which people made sensible decisions regarding things that were often not sensible at all. This room was a cavern of responsibility. When you stepped into it, you felt the weight of the 'right thing'. You felt the weight of the British Empire. And to most, the British Empire was what everyone was fighting and dying for these days.

Stephan had come to the ARP headquarters as part of his duties. It was the first time that the heads of the ARP were getting together. They would discuss the war. A war that, up until now, had impacted the people of Britain far less than Stephan or anyone else thought it would have. Sure, there were attacks and planes and some bombs, but overall most felt that the Germans were aiming spitballs at the people of Britain. Not the poison gases and giant bombs people feared. But that was all to change.

"The U-boats are giving us a bit of a hassle, eh?" The man seated next to Stephan asked.

"Well, I think they are giving people who fish and travel hell." Stephan responded, barely looking in the man's direction. Stephan was annoyed, tired and just wanted to get this meeting over and back to work.

"Of course. Of course. Lucky us just get to dodge bombs in the comfort of London," the man responded then got up and went to the sideboard to have a glass of sherry.

Leaning into the high-backed leather chair, Stephan felt a grasp on his shoulder that almost sent him through the coffered ceiling.

"It's you, eh," Thornley asked, with a smile that Stephan noticed as he craned his neck around to catch a glimpse of his direct superior. Pulling out and taking the seat next to Stephan, Thornley continued, "Been doing a bang-up job with the ARP. We are fully staffed. Nearing 1.2 million in uniform. Quite a hassle getting that many armbands and bells out. Though I do think the populace finds it a bit reassuring, and maddening, the constant reminders to block out the windows and barks to 'Put that light out'. Keeping the morale rather high and the reports up to date. There has only been one misstep."

Stephan, outwardly, remained a placid lake of emotion. Inside, he could feel his stomach tighten as if he was in a fight and about to take a punch to the gut. "And what was that?"

"Something to do with a car."

Stephan's stomach tightened further. The punch was going to be a hard one. Looking around the room, Stephan grew concerned. "And what car-based misstep did I take, sir?"

"Using old Morrises as roadblocks!" Thornley laughed, and that attracted all the room along with the announcement of using a lightweight car as a roadblock meant to annoy potential invading tanks.

"I did have the town fill the old things with dirt, twigs and rocks," Stephan responded as his entire body uncoiled. And the room burst into a good laugh that broke some of the tension.

Stephan was seated and not laughing. The rest of the room was now sharing stories of their own about the ingenuity and flexibility of the locals as they made an effort to defend their piece of England.

Then the room stopped its lively buzz with the awkwardness of a recalcitrant horse approaching a jump it did not like. Sir John Anderson had entered the room and looked around, Stephan receiving a nod from the old man with new responsibilities.

"We have a rather full agenda, Thornley, let's get started," Sir John explained as he sat down in the chair at the center of the table, near the windows, that all in the room had known to leave available.

"There is now, today, hitting this island a weight of bombs never before launched at a country." Thornley stood by a large map of the room, explaining what Stephan and everyone in the room knew to be true. They lived it. They saw the planes. They charted their progress. They saw the coming of bodies and broken homes. "It is a shock to the populace who thought that this day would not come. The initial German assault was lighter and more sparse than we all imagined."

"But today it is the ARP who plays a very vital role in the protection of this country. Before I talk about where the bombings have been and what we have learned, I want to talk about the incendiaries." Here, Thornley moved over to two other images on easels. The first showed a small unexploded incendiary device; the other showed it more in detail. "The incendiary is not only designed to burn structures, but also to overcome our well-executed blackouts by creating a glowing target for the nighttime raids. We find close work with fire brigades, and training to show how one person can easily snuff out a fire, have resulted in excellent post-attack mediation of the incendiaries."

"All of us in here," Thornley evenly noted, "have felt the impact of the attacks. But none more than Stephan Sidlow, our Eastern board representative. He has seen the most attacks while traipsing across this island."

"And in high style, I'd say. A Birkin." One of the lower-ranked ARP reps jabbed.

"Enough," Thornley brought down the man.

"It's alright," Stephan said, while smiling to the room. "High-speed, surely. But not high-style. It is a bit of a truck to drive. Should I go on, Thornley?"

"Yes, do. I was about to turn it over to you."

"I was asked here to talk to you all about my experiences and to offer tips I could share with this group. I think I have implemented a few tools and picked up a few exigencies that might allow you all to strengthen your part of the Air Raid Prevention Corps."

For the next hour, Stephan lectured, debated and educated his peers with new information about attack speeds, bombing tendencies, and best practices relating to warning residents and keeping calm those in shelters. He told them what they needed to know and what he wanted them to know. It was a natural role for Stephan to play: the leader, the man looking out for his men. But it was still a role.

12

Home Front Archives, London, October 2009

Late into the second day of archive rummaging alongside Koustas and Charles, Faston finally unboxed several dusty, yellowed pieces of paper that might give him something more than an allergic reaction. Maybe. Faston wanted to share this with his co-searchers and take a break. "Guys, come over here, have a sit, and listen."

Koustas and Charles came creeping and creaking out of the stacks. Koustas with his shirt unbuttoned down to his navel and Charles with his pants rolled up to the point he looked like a deranged Katherine Hepburn painting the low tide off Stratford, Connecticut. "Jesus, gentlemen. I know it's hot, but really. Some dignity. You know those old postings of 'Keep Calm and Carry On' that we keep seeing?"

"Yes." Was the answer in stereo.

"How about Keep Clothed and Carry On, huh? Man. You both look like you suffer from derangement."

With neither man making any effort to appease Faston, he thought it best to look at the documents and, of course, carry on. "What do you two think of these records here? They seem to be from an internal investigation."

Koustas took a bold dive into the materials. Grabbing the folder stamped "Investigation Closed. 1944 December." He folded the outer carrier back onto itself and looked at the contents. Faston could see his mouth water and then dry. He, too, had been titillated by the few lines still readable today.

"This is a God damn shame," Koustas pronounced, showing the documents to Faston and Charles. Faston averted his eyes. He knew what was inside.

"All that blacked-out text looks like a bunch of pen skid marks. Something blow up and obscure the thing?" Charles asked.

"No," Koustas answered, "Like the Nixon tapes, blank sections, someone wanted to hide something in here."

"It is enticing and then devastating," Faston said. "Like having a pretty woman chat you up in the bar then ask…"

Charles interrupted, "…if you like to party and how much for how long? This man knows that disappointment! Let me tell you."

"Don't tell us, Charles, stop." Faston shut him down while Koustas was studying the documents in the ARP-branded Investigation Closed folder. "You seem as keyed in as a bulldog preying on a table scrap. What are you thinking?"

"As you no doubt noticed, Faston, the first few lines are not blacked out. That is why you are so interested in this section, is it not?" Koustas noted.

"And why is that? What does it say?" Charles asked.

"Read it to him," Faston obliged.

"Alright," Koustas said, then coughed and breathed in like a classic orator. "Here we go. And I quote, 'What was once thought to be multiple internal targets seems to be narrowing to one. Travel schedules overlap with a regularity and pattern not easily swallowed. There is mounting evidence that BLACKED OUT has been BLACKED OUT and on numerous occasions has arrived BLACKED OUT. Despite the train schedule not allowing such distance to be covered. For instance, from BLACKED OUT to BLACKED OUT there is BLACKED OUT and BLACKED OUT. BLACKED OUT…"

"What?" Charles asked.

"I will not read 'blacked out' over and over again for three more pages. I won't." Koustas replied.

"Any idea who wrote it?" Faston asked. "You did catch the bit about surprising distances covered in surprisingly short amounts of time? What could do that back then besides a high-powered car? Nothing."

"Not the slightest idea who wrote it, Faston, but I do agree it is a unique measure of time travel noted at a time when most people had to deal with a limited array of travel choices," Koustas acknowledged. "Regardless, it does not seem to be an official investigation, despite the stamp."

"Why not? Seems official to me," Faston said, as his stomach turned with a drop that can only be felt with a grave and approaching disappointment.

"No title. No letterhead." Koustas clipped. "The war departments and every other government department back then, and even now, are very big on letterheads and mastheads and titles and attribution. So and so says this, and you best know that so and so said it, right? There is no official marking of any kind on this letter, and that is troublesome and at the same time like wafting bits of history. It is like waving your hand over time and pulling in the bits of history and facts and hearsay to your mind to distill and interpret."

"Koustas, I'll waft a simmering sauce, but historical facts are quite another thing." Faston laughed. "This thing leaves me unsure of what to add to the sauce pot. I am getting no taste beyond the initial shock. But you seem to have a growing appetite for it."

"I sure do. And that is because I think I have a way of decoding a bit of what has been blacked out."

"You're kidding." Charles guffawed.

"Is this CSI?" Faston asked, lowering expectations.

"Not kidding at all and not out of place on CSI, either. Follow me." Koustas, sweaty and unbuttoned of shirt, disappeared into the stacks for a few minutes, only to return clutching a bulky, heavy typewriter.

"What the devil is that? Looks as bulky and ugly as an XJS."

"This is an Underwood typewriter, the most common style used by British forces in WWII. Funny enough, one ship sank in early 1940 carrying over 20,000 of them. Must have caused a hold up in the communication. But back to this Underwood."

Koustas set up the dusty, black and battered machine on a desk and went off to the supply closet. Faston was getting annoyed with Koustas. His descriptions were always so dramatic. And this was no exception, as he soon returned with ribbon and paper. After a few minutes' fettling and banging on the keys, Koustas sat upright in a typist's perfected position and turned to Faston and Charles.

"In 2004 an Irish graduate student was able to crack the 'felt-pen' editing of some classified U.S. documents. None too happy, them. But I think I can apply his theory to these documents as long as we establish the font, size and lettering then add them to a computer document."

"Remarkable," Charles obliged.

"Pathetic," Faston responded. "Our government, I mean."

"I agree with both," Koustas went on. "The process is real. It's no good for long samples of text that have been blotted out, but smaller sections, those of one and two words, can often be deciphered. The student was able to fill in the blanks regarding suppliers to Iran and Iraq about helicopter secrets. Odd stuff. Wonderful that it combines the new and old."

"So it takes some thinking? And time?" Charles asked. "I've got to take a break. Faston, fill me on this when I get back from a trip to the pool."

"Ugh," Faston moaned. "And do leave the boxes of research materials here. The toilet is no place to look at historical documents. Now, back to deciphering."

"Right. What we need to do is measure the font size and spacing, input that data into the computer and it will give us a list of words that fit the space, give or take a few pixels."

Faston then watched as Koustas took out a ruler and measured several areas of the documents, writing down numbers in a neat hand with a beautiful Dunhill mechanical pencil. He then took out a booklet to try to match the font.

"Oh my, quite a number of possible fonts," Faston blanched as he saw that the booklet contained thousands of different typefaces.

"Oh, yes. Since the beginning of typesetting there have been those who have sought to beautify the words by the shape that the letters themselves take. Sort of steel-based illumination. But I am sure that the font of these Underwood machines is Underwood Special Roman Gothic. I just want to make sure."

Here Koustas paused as he set the booklet against the document. "And I am right. Underwood Special Roman Gothic."

"So you have the size and shape and typeface. How does the computer program know what words to find?"

"Oh, that's easy. We just input the document and those variables. Hold a second while I type it in." Koustas then took just a few moments to input the section with the most promising section of text. 'There is mounting evidence that BLACKED OUT has been BLACKED OUT and on numerous occasions has arrived BLACKED OUT at bombed areas. Despite the train schedule not allowing such distance to be covered. For instance, from BLACKED OUT to BLACKED OUT there is BLACKED OUT and BLACKED OUT.'

Leaning back and stretching, Koustas hit ENTER and watched the screen and advised Faston. "Shouldn't take that long. Maybe two or three minutes."

"Will it possibly give us a name?"

Koustas laughed. "No, no. It deals only with words, not names. Place names, yes. But people names, no. Would be impossible to winnow out the details and the who's who. Ah, here, the results are coming in. They get outputted in the order of the blanks. And there are multiple options for each. So I think it will be like a written Sudoku puzzle. Let's put one thing in at a time and see what else fits the rhythm."

"Agreed," Faston muttered.

"Me, too." Charles solemnly concurred, strolling back in to the room with a vintage WWII newspaper clutched under his arm. "You know, they still put on plays during the war. Quite a few. Most nostalgic, though it seems, from the listings. And all got positive reviews. Would have taken some gusto to pan an amusement during the dark days of bombardment."

"A good time to have been a producer, or actor, then." Koustas extrapolated. "Now, there are 125 options for the first blank section, 97 for the second, 344 for the third, 310 for the fourth, 209 for the fifth, 211 for the sixth and 160 for the seventh. I'll print them out, and we can get to plugging them in to see what sparks."

A few minutes later Koustas returned with rather full documents of words for Faston, Koustas and Charles to divvy up and dive into. "I'll take the first three," Faston offered. Volunteering first was something that Faston believed in to his core. From buying the first round to jumping in the pool first to taking the first bite of unidentified food, Faston went first not to prove he was a leader or some other macho conviction; he just liked to get things going. He liked to be the catalyst. "Let's see," Faston hemmed and hawed. "My section reads, 'There is mounting evidence that BLACKED OUT has been BLACKED OUT and on numerous occasions has arrived BLACKED OUT at bombed areas.' So I would guess that the first blacked out section is a proper name, so I will just put that list aside. Despite it containing words like 'paraphernalia' and 'pater familis'."

"I concur," Koustas said, without looking up from his sheet of words to peruse. Charles also was workmanlike going through his list, using a ruler to run down the words one at a time like an accountant checking his columns before the advent of Excel.

Even by voiding out the first 125 options, Faston still had 97 different possibilities for the space voided in the second section, 97 different options. And 344 options for the third space. That seemed like a Mount Ventoux of words to climb. He thought it easiest to go through and immediately dismiss words that had no real chance of fitting.

The words that Faston didn't believe were possible options for a document from an investigation written during the Second World War included internet, unibrow, biodiesel, agritourism, water boarding, crib death, jetlag, pantsuit and desegregate. Those words were the easiest of the several hundred, as Faston knew they were not in popular use or even existence in the 1940s. Maybe 'pantsuit' was, he thought. But that was just a maybe. It took another hour for him to wade through the words that were in popular use during that epic decade but not appropriate for a memo from the War Department. These included words like Bermuda, blowfish, carbuncle, linoleum, modernist, Stromboli and hepatitis.

When Faston then allowed himself to count the possibilities for each BLACKED OUT section, he was able to breathe a sigh of relief. The totals being 12, 14 and 31. 12, 14 and 31 seeming like very human-scale numbers, options that could be handled by a man of middling intellect and miniscule attention span like Faston knew he possessed.

Before putting himself into the mind of a World War II British investigator, Faston sat back and tried to imagine what someone would be doing with a Blower Bentley during the war. Smuggling? Racing? Cheating on their wife or girlfriend? Or, Faston most believed, just flying along the empty, unlit roads at top speed with the roar of a supercharger whistling at a volume only the driver could hear and that required him to keep his foot pressed into the territory where boost was produced. Yes, Faston thought, the last option had to be it. No matter what time or what country or what social situation, since the turn of the century there had been car nuts. And before that there were bicycle nuts. And before that, wagon nuts. And before that, chariot nuts. Mankind liked going faster than his feet and legs alone allowed. That was a sociological fact you could take to the bank, along with the fact that groups were wiser than individuals and every human carries secrets.

Now Faston was in the mental place of a British citizen driving a Bentley, as well as being conscious of how investigators work. He began winnowing the winning words down to the chosen one or two. Since he had applied such a scientific approach over the past several hours of grammatical archaeology, Faston knew it to be a fine approach to rely on his gut. So he did.

For the first BLACKED OUT section, Faston passed on all options; he was sure it was a proper name.

For the second section, Faston was torn between either 'calculating' or 'aggravating'. For the third BLACKED OUT section, he believed the best options were 'unannounced', 'able bodied' and 'clearheaded.' Not definitive or Bentley-revealing, but combined with what Koustas and Charles came up with, surely significant.

Breaking the heavy silence and not unheavy sweating going on in the room, Faston grabbed his co-searchers' attention. "I've got my words. How about you fellows?"

"Close," Charles proffered.

"Very close," Koustas agreed, then added, "Go to the bathroom. Or better yet, to the store and bring back a few beers so that we can discuss our findings like gentlemen. And a packet of nuts would not be inappropriate, either."

"Done and done." With that, Faston uncoiled himself from his tight sitting position, generating more creaks and pops than a Morgan crossing railroad tracks, and walked down the well-kept middle-class streets of this part of London. In the middle of the afternoon, with sun shining, Faston enjoyed watching the businessmen with rolled up sleeves and businesswomen with bare legs and the newest shoes promenade around him.

Faston let his mind clear enough to catch snippets of their conversations. It seemed as if all the world was trying to solve problems. Faston could not keep track of the "if only," "what if" and "what do you think about" callouts he heard. Faston himself had to solve a problem, but it was almost as if he felt part of the normal humdrum of a business day. It felt good. It felt like his workdays before he won the lottery and was able to quit his job and start searching for cars. An honest day's work, with an honest result. With some snacking in between.

Faston's snack today would be a bit different from those back at home. He wandered the aisles of a small, cramped, stifling store, looking for brands and beers he did not have access to in Connecticut. He eyed the Nestle Aero bar, but chocolate was not what he needed. He saw curried nuts in a pack and thought that was a flavor he would not find at his local Stop & Shop. A quick two steps back to the cooler, and he pulled out a few 500ml cans of Cobra premium, paid the shopkeeper and enjoyed the slow walk back to the stacks.

"Well, I just spent a brilliant 30 minutes clearing my mind outside," Faston told his peers as he walked back in. "Didn't think about the Blower for a moment. And when it is sunny here in London, you just want to move here. Like Chicago. A sunny day there, too, is so captivating and magnetic."

"Yeah, but both places will cuff you on the ears with miserable wind, rain and losing sports teams," Charles said, crushing Faston's quick fantasy of moving his operations from the Nutmeg State to London.

"Exactly, Charles. I was going to leave that unsaid. But, well, you said it. Now, here are some curry nuts…"

"Curry! I knew I should have gone shopping. Hope they are better than the curried chips you once bought," Charles moaned.

"Let me see them," Koustas asked, and Faston tossed a serving over to him. Koustas took a bite. "Not bad, would be good with a Kingfisher or Cobra, though, like eating out at my favorite Indian."

"Let me oblige. Always been a fan of Cobra. A great marketing story, a man saw a need for a beer that matched the popular Indian foods in London and filled that need with a decent product. Marketed by foot at first. Great story." Faston smiled and handed cans to both Charles and Koustas. All three snapped open their can tops at the same time, took equally large pulls and let the aroma of the hops waft around them.

"So, how much of a puzzle do we still have to put together?" Faston asked.

"None, " Koustas said.

"All wrapped up." Charles agreed, looking over at Koustas then at Faston, a large smile creasing his face just as Faston felt one coming across his own visage.

"Why did you let me prattle on about nuts and Cobra? You're done? What does it say?" Faston began searching the room, looking for the document with the blacked-out sections completed.

Koustas calmly snapped a sheet of paper, the noise grabbed Faston's attention.

"Here it is, Faston." Koustas started. "Here it is."

There is mounting evidence that BLACKED OUT has been CALCULATING and on numerous occasions has arrived UNANNOUNCED at bombed areas. Despite the train schedule not allowing such distance to be covered. For instance, from EASTERN SEABOARD to THE ISLE OF MAN there is A FIFTY-PERCENT INCREASE and ABOVE-AVERAGE DAMAGE.

"Awesome work guys. Awesome. Since he talks about someone arriving at places where the trains were not running. That he was involved in the military. Or some other arm. And combined with the gas receipts, I think we need to find out a bit more surrounding the author of this. Time to visit, let me see, one Jonathan Thornley."

"Or his descendants. Bloke could be 118 by now," Koustas noted.

"Or his descendants. Agreed. Now finish your Cobras, and let's dig up the whereabouts of ex-ARP

Jonathan Thornley." Faston didn't even finish his nuts or Cobra. He was too excited about getting closer to the mystery of the big Bentley and an investigation that wasn't closed with a conviction or acquittal.

13
Montreal, Canada, November 2009

"I've spent more time dating you than I have any of my girlfriends," Patrick laughed over an appetizer of foie gras on top of French fries and gravy at a restaurant his contact in Canada had insisted they dine at. He'd been in Canada for 10 days now and was getting sick and tired of being spoken to in French and not understanding, and then having to endure the condescending stares of the locals who were fluent in both languages. Stupid French colony, thought Patrick. He just sulked, gulped down huge forkfuls of the gout-inducing food and stared and smiled at Claude Le Mevel.

"It takes time. It does. To know when to sell something of such worth, such rarity. It takes time, like this dinner." Claude was not about to stop talking about the food, thought Patrick; he was just as bad as Faston when it came to food. "You see, Au Pied du Cochon is that all too rare a dining establishment that offers luxury amid a casual atmosphere. You yourself are eating foie gras on French fries!"

"What is 'fa grah' anyway? It tastes like meat-flavored butter." Patrick pondered out loud.

"It is the fattened liver of a goose."

Patrick felt his stomach turn a bit, and his face went sour. His mouth was at this moment filled to bursting with fattened liver and French fries. Dripping in gravy. Moist with fat and chewy cheese. "Fmmttend limmer," Patrick mumbled, as he swallowed his huge helping of food.

"Yes, indeed. And wait until your main course. You got the duck in the can, no?"

"Yes."

"It is a half a duck breast, root vegetables and a fist-sized piece of foie gras. You are quite the trencherman for ordering a double dose of foie gras." Here Claude raised in salute a forkful of his salad that was made up of more pork than lettuce in a sort of salute.

Feeling as if he had no choice, Patrick raised his own forkful in a return salute. He was careful, though, to have none of that liver hanging onto his fork. The fries, at least, were delicious. With more talk of food throughout the next hour of dinner, Patrick stilled his temper by thinking of how near he was to a big piece of his in-progress puzzle. And to be sharp, he didn't drink more than two glasses of cider, served in beer mugs, despite wanting several more to wash down the rich food. He felt as if he'd just eaten a muffin slathered in a full quarter-stick of butter.

Patrick picked up the check and prodded Claude to get moving. "Claude, how far is your house from here?"

"It is not too far. I think an hour would be fine."

"Let's go then, we can get there by ten."

"I would prefer to discuss this tomorrow."

"I would not, man. I've got a flight to catch tomorrow." Patrick remembered he was courting someone, not just buying something, so he softened his approach. "I mean, I would love to spend more time north of the border, but the flight is booked, and I can't miss it."

"I understand; follow me."

"What type of car do you have? I rented a Mustang. No idea you had so many Mustangs in Canada."

Patrick thought he heard Claude snort before responding. "A silver Bristol Blenheim Three."

"You didn't think it was overpriced?" Patrick hated the newer Bristols. It seemed like anyone who bought one was trying to prove a point. They looked like a Ford Capri with nice leather. And Bristol didn't publish performance figures. Patrick just didn't understand.

"No. It is hand-built. And I don't believe that anything hand-built can be too expensive."

"I do. I had a hand-built burrito this morning, and it was terrible."

"I guess you're right. Now follow me," Claude repeated as he climbed into his silently idling Bristol.

It was not an hour. It was two. For the first of them, Patrick let his mind spin with possibilities. For the next hour, his mind raced with anger. He did have a flight to catch, and he was not going to make it with any sleep. He was losing his edge as he drove deep into the dark countryside surrounding Montreal.

"Eh, not a bad drive," Claude stated when they arrived at his modest house.

"Not bad for a two-hour drive." Patrick did his best to bite his anger. He didn't yell at Claude, which was impressive, as he was even more concerned when they pulled up in front of his house. It was a boring, semi-detached house in a crowded little town. It was brick. It did not have a barn out back. It was, Patrick thought, exactly the type of place where interesting pieces of automotive history were not found.

"Let's go. What you want is in the basement," Claude stated, shedding his coat in the hallway and then descending a cramped staircase.

Patrick followed Claude down the stairs, his track suit snagging on one or two loose nails in the masonry. There was no hand rail, and Patrick stumbled twice, nearly turning his ankle before he was able to stand next to Claude at the landing.

"Mind turning on a light?" Patrick asked, his curiosity and annoyance at equal levels. He wanted to know if this Canadian had the goods he had been talking about via email for the past two weeks. Patrick's partners in this endeavor had ensured him that, indeed, the man was legit. That his story checked out. Now, standing in a dark suburban basement, Patrick pegged the odds at one-in-ten that Claude had what he'd come for.

"Not at all," Claude offered, groping and clanking and clunking his way through the dark, low-ceilinged basement. Finding the switch, he announced, "Ah-hah."

What Patrick saw before him was not disappointing. It was a well-ordered but over-flowing assemblage of automobilia. Hanging from the rafters were grilles for Delahayes, Mercedes-Benzes and even proper, vintage Bristols. Beneath the grilles were neat stacks of wire wheels. Next to these, boxes of labeled knock-off hubs. Near those, brass mallets.

Shifting his eyes to the metal shelving at the farthest end of the basement, Patrick could see exhaust headers that looked to be from a Cord poking into one narrow aisle. He also glimpsed what he thought were Houdaille lever-arm shock absorbers alongside various shifters and dozens of model cars. Old model cars, still in boxes. Patrick's mind spun with numbers of how much all this stuff was worth. Some people thought of the craft. Others the beauty when looking at old cars. Patrick thought of dollars.

"Patrick, over here," Claude beckoned him to a large canvas blanket covering a pile that was too large to be hiding what he came to see. It was fully twice as high and at least half again as long as what Patrick was expecting.

"No need to make this into a magic show, Claude. Show it to me," Patrick demanded, then he checked his watch, already thinking about the drive to the airport, forgetting the piles of old car stuff worth a fortune in this eccentric's hands.

But all those feelings vanished when Claude slowly folded away the canvas blanket. It was the Bentley motor that he had come to see. From blower to flywheel, and it was fully mounted up on what seemed to be a homemade dyno rack.

"Well, shine my shoes. That is a Bentley engine," Patrick boomed clapping his hands together. "I know about it. But I want you to tell me all about it. I need to know all the details."

"As you can see, I am an active collector of rare automotive items. That is not in and of itself unusual. What is rare, though, is that if I cannot find what I want, I source someone to make it for me. From tools for adjusting spokes on a wheel, to the wheels as a whole. If I find a piece of a car beautiful, I want to own it, to hold it. Complete cars really do nothing much for me."

"That explains the Bristol Blenheim," Patrick joked.

"Maybe," Claude conceded then continued, "but I do like the parts. I started as a boy with models, and as money and skill became available I moved onto the real parts. And the blown Bentley four and a half litre motor is one of the most brutal and beautiful ever created. So I had to have one."

"You didn't buy this at an auction, did you?" Patrick wondered, hoping the engine was born from a more novel source. One not so easy to track as items purchased from international auction houses.

"Not at all, not at all. I do not frequent auction houses. I am someone who sells at auction houses. I buy from like-minded collectors around the globe."

"Good to hear. So how did you get all the original parts to build this beauty?" Patrick questioned, trying to get to the bottom of Claude's story.

"First, they are not all original parts."

"What? Not original. It looks as if it is 80-years old. Every part of it. Nothing looks new."

"That is important to me, too. Getting the patina right. Like this Panhard grille," Claude said, reaching over and removing a brass grille from the wall. "Look at those dents, eh? Perfect randomness. The smudges and staining-some new, some old. The edges, see how they are not too clean. I had it made and assembled for me by a few disconnected craftsmen. Craftsmen unknown to each other. Like how the military keeps its secrets secret."

"Not bad. So of all this stuff, how much is fake?" Patrick asked, waving his hand around the basement.

"About half. Maybe a little less."

Patrick could not help laughing. He was impressed. And he thought this was not going to be the last time he made the long drive from Montreal to Claude's basement full of wonderful, valuable things.

"And the motor? How much is real, how much is, let me say, re-created?"

"That is an anomaly. I would say that 70 percent of the motor assembly is genuine. Let us start with the blower itself. That is a real, plain-case Villiers blower. It is one of the early batch, as well. You do know that later on in the run, the second half of the 50 cars had blowers that were ribbed?"

"I did not. Big deal. Why did they change it?"

"Lawsuit. The cause of many things. I think for the better, as the badging is a bit too horsey for a Bentley. Out front of the car. A bit shouty. Most make do with an embossed 'B' in the door-card's leather. Understated, and all that, for the British back then."

Patrick made a note to research which chassis numbers had what blower on them then resumed listening to Claude.

"So, the blower was what I came across first, and it sprouted the rest of my pursuit. It was in great shape, well within spec and delivers the proper boost to the motor. The carburetors attached to the blower are new. As is the plumbing that carries the boosted mixture back toward the intake. The electrics are created from new-old stock parts, even down to the asbestos insulation."

"You mess with asbestos?"

"No, but some of the people I work with in Latvia who specialize in this sort of thing do not seem to mind working with any material. They would probably even make you a hat by dipping it in mercury if you wanted."

Patrick had no idea what Claude meant by hat making, so he tried to get him talking again about the engine. "What about the internals? The crank and pistons, camshaft, you know. They damaged? I imagine those would be easy to have made."

"They would be easy to make, " Claude said, nodding in agreement, "but I didn't have to have them made. They were some of the easier parts to find. The inside bits were had from some spares made back in the racing days. Lucky to have found them. I picked up one camshaft that I thought was right, but it wasn't. Even I get crossed up sometimes. It was the last part that I was needing to make the engine complete. I was about to have one ground when this unit currently installed turned up in England. Most of the original parts have been from England."

"Makes sense. So, the engine number and block. What car are they from?"

"No car. The block is a new item."

"How the hell did you pull that off?"

"Well, remember I was saying that Villiers designed the Blowers?"

"Of course,"

"To do the initial drafting of them, he needed a set of engine blueprints."

"So?"

"So, those blueprints were still in the possession of Villier's relatives. That is, until I convinced them of their value, albeit modest in comparison to the cost of a Blower Bentley, and acquired them."

"And then? Who built you a block?"

"Some very skilled and very underpaid men in China. It is a tricky thing, too. The block and head, getting them right. But the level of skill in China is staggering, and so is their low pay. So when you go over there with some proper funding looking to having something built, there are many opportunities and opportunists. They also don't ask too many questions."

"How long did that take?" Patrick could not believe the lengths to which Claude had gone to create and possess rare things.

"Quite some time. They did not get it right until the third attempt. On the first, the saddles were out of spec. On the second try, they did not get the external finish correct. It was too smooth. Too nice. Lucky in China they just had to go to a different plant that used tooling from the 1930s. Lots of very old and functioning western equipment in China if you know where to look."

"You are a bulldog," Patrick had to admit. The man was intense. It would not be easy to negotiate a price with him, that was for sure.

"If you want, you can look at the other blocks. They are in the corner."

"No thanks. This one here is fine. I would like to hear it run. It looks like it is all hooked up."

"Not a problem. Give me a minute."

Patrick then watched as Claude turned knobs and checked gauges on a dummy instrument panel. After several minutes of fiddling, Claude placed his hand over a bright red plastic button.

"I know, it is odd to start it like this, but I did not want to spend any more time tracking down the original switches. The engine was all I wanted. Cover your ears. It is loud even with the stub muffler on the exhaust."

Patrick did as instructed, removing his hands from his velour pants and covering his ears as the engine barked to life. The entire stand shook for thirty seconds and then settled once the engine found its lumpy idle. But the supercharger itself was silent. Patrick put his hand on it. It wasn't spinning.

"What is up with the blower? Does it work?"

"Yes, it works. I was giving it a minute to warm up."

While waiting for the engine to warm, which it would no doubt do quickly in this barely vented place, Patrick walked around the engine and marveled at how original it appeared. It was exactly what he was looking for, and it sounded exactly like the one Blower he heard run at Lime Rock a few years back.

Claude pushed his way past Patrick and located a small pull-rod. "Now, here is the blower. I can only run the engine for another few moments because of my neighbors. They will be quite disappointed already. Near midnight, and me running my toy. So just a quick run up the rev range, then off."

As Claude engaged the blower, Patrick heard the load increase on the engine. But as Claude gave it some more accelerator the blower whined and the engine didn't skip a beat. Then, in an instant, it was still. Coming to a halt like a ship falling afoul of a shoal.

"That was amazing." Patrick could not help but to be enthusiastic. "I stink like gas and exhaust now, but that was amazing."

"Thank you. I am rather proud of it."

"Now, the price." Patrick was sure it would be steep. But he and his friends had no choice. There were no other blower Bentley motors in existence.

"Why do you want it?" Was Claude's non price-based response.

Patrick then quickly took Claude through the reasons why he was so determined to acquire the engine. He left out no single fact, and didn't try to misguide Claude in any way. He took the chance that Claude was of a like mind. He really needed Claude to be on the same team.

"In that case," Claude quietly responded, leaning closer to Patrick. "I will give it to you on commission."

With a simple handshake, Patrick had acquired the robust heart for his Blower Bentley. That one piece that had worried him the most. Now, Patrick mentally ran through the rest of the contacts needed to put together his Blower. And he did think about it as his Blower.

14
London, September 1940

Stephan marked the 7th of September as a touchstone day in his life. He was not in London that day; he had been driving through the ring of suburbs the previous few nights, checking on the readiness of the towns encircling the city. He was out late every night, often alone with his Bentley, eating up the short distances between town centers.

At night he had to be careful with his turn of speed due to the lidded headlights, but on the straights, and on roads he knew well, he was able to engage the blower and accelerate as fast as many aircraft. It was a warm September, and Stephan enjoyed the cool night air as much as the car. It ran, he ventured, ten to fifteen percent better in the cooler, denser night air.

So it was from quite a distance that Stephan saw London come under an epic level of pressure and terror. The deafening sound of the bombs reached him as the sound of a rock falling into a pond. Waves of sound approaching then ebbing. The searing light was only like a flickering candle, and the chaos was something he could only imagine. He couldn't really hear the screams and cries, but between his ears he heard some of them.

Stephan did take the time, in the dark deserted area between two towns, to pay attention to the assault. He could hear the bombers and fighters before he could see them. He listened as he heard them slow their engines, knowing that they would then unleash their bombs and, when closer to the ground, their guns. Although out of range, Stephan tensed with each wave of attack. The crack of the armaments was a new sound to him and to most of the citizens he was in charge of. He thought that the noise that the German bombs and guns and planes exported with such passion was one of their most powerful weapons. It was the sound of death approaching.

The ARP in London was run by a very senior team, so Stephan thought it a better use of his time to help monitor the outlying areas that did not benefit from such sound leadership. It was a fortunate choice. The bombers that flew overhead, that could be heard approaching the city or returning to France, missed his roving assignments. Stephan had at no time been in danger.

But he did have to break up a series of small-time gangs that tried to control certain shelters and keep them to themselves. Unable to pull his own ARP staff away, he needed to recruit some help. And it came in the form of the more beatific gangs, composed of Catholics and Unitarians. Stephan knew these chaps were always trying to do good, and this time they did good with short clubs not unlike those of policemen. A brief visit by this crew, and all the shelters soon opened and filled to bursting. He left the outlying towns in good order and good nick. The same could not be said for the citizens or city of London.

Stephan made it into London on the eighth to get a first-hand look. In the unflattering daylight, driving into one of the heavier bombed-out sections; he noticed a wall painted with the largest challenge the nation faced, to just 'Keep Calm and Carry On.' But this sign had been half erased as the wall it was painted on had crumbled. Stephan parked the Bentley in a section of street that he felt would be safe even if one of the nearby buildings collapsed. He walked toward the large tube station that served the center of London.

But before he arrived at the station, he came across a large pile of rubble where the Heavy Rescue Squad was digging with sticks and hands through the rubble looking for survivors. Stephan watched as a pair of men struggled with what appeared to be a corner of a small rug peeking out from under a large piece of masonry. He overheard one of them say he could use it at his own home, in his son's room. The men tugged and grunted but struggled to get the rug removed. One of the men finally grabbed a stake and levered up the masonry while the other man, with two hands on the rug, leaned back, and when it came free, he fell backward with it landing on top of him. It took a moment for the worker to realize what had happened. He had not been tugging on a small rug. It was the matted and crushed and bloody body of a man, compacted like an egg that fell off a counter. As the worker screamed and pushed the pulp off him, Stephan walked on and made his way to the tube station.

"Well targeted and well saturated?" Stephan asked the man in charge of the station cleanup.

Taking a break from directing a small crane removing pieces of paving and directing his helpers, the man turned, noticed Stephan's uniform and rank, and stood more upright. "You could say that. Over 70 people were killed down there; a guess, but near a dozen to the real figure I am sure."

"Any problems? Just with prepping the dead. It takes a long time and the men don't like the work. Just look at them." The man pointed a few hundred feet away to a group of three men.

Two of them were slowly washing the faces and hands of the dead with a sponge and bucket of water. The third man, leaning against a large mop handle standing in a bucket of what Stephan guessed was disinfectant water, stared at his feet. The two working men were at the head of several lines of corpses, each at least ten bodies in length, each already stripped of any tattered remnants of clothing. The local in charge was right; at this rate the job would never be done.

It was in Stephan's DNA to abhor inefficiency. Quickly walking over to the line of naked dead, Stephan grabbed the mop and bucket the one man was leaning on and went to work. It was simple work, really, thought Stephan as he plunged the mop into the bucket then roughly but thoroughly washed each body. Front and back. Any charwoman could do it.

Stephan was surprised when one of the men who had been washing the women spoke up. "Hey, don't you think you are being a bit rough." Then hesitatingly added, "Sir."

Stephan decided to give his answer without stopping his work. He was already on his third body. A dead young man of sixteen or seventeen. "Do I think that I am being too rough? No? Because I do not. Not in the slightest. And do you know why? Because the job needs to be done before the next wave of bombers. Did you think this was the one and only large day of bombing? I do not. It is the first of many. We will be under attack for some time to come. These bodies are just going to become blurs of flesh and aches in our backs from taking care of them. The Germans want to kill and maim as many of us as they can, while they can."

"We civilians put up quite a bit less defense than our troops. Sure, we have guns and such, but no fighters at our disposal. Or tanks and mortars. So, we civilians get the barrage. And in between lulls in these barrages, we need to get on with it. Get the jobs that need doing done. No matter how rough they might seem to us because of what we did before these troubles. What did you men do before, for work?"

"I'm a plumber." The first one answered.

"Me and him," Said the man, speaking for the remaining two workers, "we ran a fishing boat."

Continuing to work, Stephan answered while mopping the back of an elderly woman. "You won't be fishing or plumbing or anything else unless you get to work. You'll be learning German. You'll be losers. You'll be slaves. Now, to the job at hand. While we are bomber-free, get some shrouds, wrap them and label them, to get the bodies ready for final disposal. A final rest in a cardboard coffin."

Thrusting the mop into the hands of the man who could only lean on it a few minutes before, Stephan hurried away from the stench of bodies and back to his Bentley. He'd seen enough of the city for today. He had learned enough to strengthen his knowledge and his reports.

15
Near Sizergh Castle, October 2008

Faston had no problem getting Caprice to accompany him and Charles to Thornley's family home, as it was a short drive from Sizergh Castle. Koustas was unable to come along due to some work commitment. All the better, as Koustas had quite a few allergies and would have sneezed his way through the grounds. And remarkable grounds they were. Even to Faston. The usual English overgrown garden, the one that Faston knew Caprice loved so much, was not in bloom at Sizergh. As they walked through the almost abandoned garden, Caprice expounded on what made it unique, filling in the very few gaps in her knowledge of the grounds by referencing the walking guide she'd picked up at the entrance for a few shillings.

"That is Morecambe Bay off in the distance. Quite remarkable, views of that. But what I came to see was the rock garden."

"A rock garden? Really, Caprice. That is one that even Faston could tend to. Slightly cold though, don't you think?"

"Not at all. It is really unique. It stands in heightened contrast to most English gardens. Just look at it." Caprice said, sweeping her hand toward the monolithic creation.

Gazing across at the rock garden, Faston was able, for a moment, to leave behind his thoughts of the Bentley. Huge maples thrust out of a base of limestone. Lesser specimens clung to the surface of the stones. The effect grounded all things and made them seem that much more permanent.

As they walked out of the rock garden and through the orchards and wild flower gardens, Faston lost attention and began thinking about the Bentley and cars and nature. How many cars seemed like flowers, for instance a Bugatti. Others like shrubs, a Mini. And just a few cars brought to mind rocks. The Bentley, Faston thought, was definitely a rock. And one worth turning over every stone in pursuit of. Faston mulled over all the potential stones needing a turn over during their remaining hour at Sizergh, and continued to do so in the car on the way to Thornley's house. He must have looked deep in thought, as neither Caprice nor Charles had bothered him. They let him wander through the gardens silent and focused.

"So, who did you speak to, to get us invited down here?" Caprice asked, as she drove the Lancia B24 that Aron had loaned them in trade for the Jaguar.

"It took a while, lots of Thornleys in the phone book. And lots of cold calls. But we finally reached the son of ex-ARP Jonathan Thornley." Faston answered.

"His son. Excellent. Any other relatives?"

"No, besides some of the son's children. But they will be no help with digging up dirt on Grand Papa."

"No brothers or sisters? Just one son?" Caprice asked, prying Faston for information.

"Just his son. But he is married, so his wife will be around. The kids, probably not. What would they be? In their thirties, I bet. So, we will be meeting with Tate and Maddie Thornley."

"Tate and Maddie." Charles finally piped up from his nap in the passenger seat of the Lancia, "Sounds like a pub supper. Tate and Maddie, please."

"Let's not insult them like that when we get there." Faston answered from the tight back seat. "We should be almost there, huh, Caprice?"

"I think so. I don't have a GPS unit, so I don't have it down to the minute, but I imagine we will be pulling up to the house any moment now." Caprice announced, while scanning the road on her side of the car. "Charles, look at that side, will you, darling? What are we looking for as far as houses go anyway, Faston?"

"Don't know. I don't see too many houses out here anyway. Just tucked into the folds in the hills. I imagine it is some sort of country house, probably not as grand as Toftcombs but probably not small, either. The house is called Moss Rock so I imagine it is made of moss rock."

"Or built on moss rock," Charles thought out loud.

"Or, sited next to moss rock,"

"Everything around here could wear the name Moss Rock." Faston mumbled, peering out the Lancia's windows, looking from side to side, trying to catch the home of Thornley. "How long has it been since we turned onto this road at the last fork? Tate said it was just a few miles."

"I don't know. But I do know that we are here." Caprice announced, swinging the car to the right, past a large Moss Rock, and then guiding it along the twisty, rain-rutted drive towards Moss Rock.

"I guess it comes from the drive marker?" Charles said, as he and Caprice were the first to get a glimpse of the house. As they got closer, Faston too could see the home through the windshield. And it was a rather New England-looking home, low, rambling and white. With some lovely outbuildings made of stone, non-mossy. The roof was slate, and there were at least four doors that looked as if they could function as the main entrance to the house. Piled out and standing by the car, Faston noted that Charles and Caprice were equally puzzled as to which door to use.

"A bit like, Let's Make a Deal. Which door has the owner behind it, and which has a donkey?" Charles, Faston thought, accurately described all their feelings.

Luckily though, none of them would have to guess, as a woman opened the nearest door and waved them closer.

Faston was glad to see that Maddie wore clothes not incongruous to her home. She was clad in Wellingtons, a thick-as-a-pillow sweater and a waxed cotton jacket. Maddie stood with one foot propping open the door and the other on the drive. She spoke with a light accent and winning smile. "Do come in. That was a long drive. And I'm sure you could use a comfy seat and a bit of something."

"We could, for sure, if that bit of something might be a cup of tea?" Faston queried, as he walked up to Maddie and past her as she held the door for all three of them.

"Course. I'll just plug in the kettle and we'll have a hot cup ready for you. And some cheddar and bread. Its not typical, but it is good."

"I think a good cheese is one of those foods that can go from breakfast to lunch to dinner dessert. So why not with tea?" Faston said as a way to make Maddie feel at ease.

"It's made just up the road a bit. So it is a nice, real cheddar. You've heard of the real ale movement, have you? Then this is like that, but cheese."

"Fantastic!" Now Faston got hungry, hearing about a local farmhouse cheddar.

"Now, just walk through there," Maddie pointed through a low door that went into a bright, south-facing room. "I'll bring you your tea."

Charles and Caprice went ahead, but Faston paused to ask one last question, "Where's Tate?"

"Out riding. Don't worry, he should be back with the half-hour ring. He always goes for a ride this time of day. Now go rest up. Put your feet up on the furniture. Pet the dog. Relax."

"OK. OK," Faston said, resisting Maddie no more and joining Caprice and Charles in what turned out to be a large sitting room.

"The view is remarkable. Looks like a damp Kansas," Caprice offered as she sat looking out over the rolling hills, through a large, multi-paned window. Some panes of which were still wavy and bubbly. The original ones. Others were crystal clear. Replaced, no doubt due to some unknown or surely long-forgotten accident.

Faston paused, stretching his body, the Aurelia had been a tight ride in back. Looking out the window he tried to focus and only look out the original panes. It gave the landscape a dreamy, cinematic feel. He let his mind drift for few minutes, while he arched his back, stretched his legs and unkinked his neck.

Limbered, Faston looked around the room to get a feel for who the Thornleys were today, and were in the past. He believed that antiques and possessions tell a story, even if the owners wish they didn't. The furniture was all faded but of decent quality. Nothing was taped or knackered together. Charles was in the finest chair, a rather large, black wingback near the fireplace. Its leather was creased and cracked. Caprice sat on the sofa, in front of the window, stretched out on its pale, yellow-plaid surface. There were no books in the room. A few workmanlike oils on the walls. And just a few pictures were to be found, sitting forlornly on a sideboard and writer's desk.

Walking over to the pictures, Faston bent over to take a closer look. To read their thousand words. The first picture was a black and white of Tate and Maddie on their wedding day, both looking trim and content, on a gray day outside a small church, not a large cathedral. The next picture captured a blurry child riding a bike. A first ride? Faston guessed. The third picture Faston picked up was a sad portrait, very old, maybe the 1890s, of a man in a uniform of sorts. And next, was another man in uniform, standing with his hand on the shoulder of a small boy. And Faston had a feeling that this must be Thornley.

"Charles, take a look. You know the World War II uniforms and insignias better than I do. Is it ARP?" Faston handed the picture to Charles, who pulled a pair of glasses out of his pocket and peered intently.

"And Maddie said that there was a dog. Caprice, did you see it?"

"Smelt it more like it. It's under the end table,"

"A bulldog!" Faston beamed. He loved bulldogs almost as much as his bassets. Bending down, he held out his hand and called the dog. It took a few minutes, but the brindled, compact mass of muscle inched out from the table, sidled over to Faston and flipped on his back. Legs spread, demanding a belly rub.

Faston rubbed the dog's belly for a few seconds then stood up in a shot. "Oh, my. That is a powerful bit of gas."

"It is. It is," Maddie said as she brought in the tray of tea and cheese and hard bread. "But, we do love him."

"How old?" Faston wondered, he was pegging the dog's age at nine or ten.

"Two. He's an old soul. Now, enjoy your tea, let it steep for a minute more, though. You can see Tate far off there, he'll be here in when you're done."

Charles got up and joined Caprice and Faston around low table nearer the sofa. "It is ARP, that is for sure. No doubt. Early 1941, judging by the shoulder markings."

"Well done," Faston thanked Charles.

"Impressive," agreed Caprice.

"Thanks," Charles responded, with a mouth full of bread and tea.

Faston was trying to be easier on Charles these days and let this lapse of manners slide. Instead, Faston watched his loose-leaf tea steep and darken around the strainer. Once that was completed, he put the strainer aside and sat back on the couch, sipping the complex tea, a custom blend no doubt, and watched Tate slowly ride toward home. Following a well-worn path in the wild grasses, the horse and rider looked like they could have been from another century. Thankfully, the cheese was not from anther century. It was sharp and brittle. Well-aged and tannic. So it was a decent foil with the tea. Once Tate was around the house and out of their view, it took about five minutes for Faston to hear Maddie and Tate approach from behind.

Faston got up and went to introduce himself to Tate and shake his hand. As did Charles. "Nice to meet you, Tate. Can't wait to hear about your father." Faston then put out his hand.

Tate didn't respond right away. It took an almost unnoticeable tap from Maddie to get Tate to put out his hand. But he did it in a way that was awkward. He just held his hand out. Dangling, a good foot from Faston's hand. It took just a second more for Faston to realize what caused this odd handshake. Tate was blind.

16

Bombay, India, November 2009

Patrick had no idea that such perfectly shaped pieces of metal could be formed in such imperfect surroundings. He'd reached the building he was in by navigating a narrow, filthy and dangerously pocked alley. Cracked and patched concrete made up the facade, floor and walls of the building. Its roof was nonexistent in some areas. In others it was a patchwork of tin and trees. Exposed electrical wires coursed along the walls, powering equally derelict, pre-World War II machining equipment.

Patrick's other senses were assaulted as well. The shop, Patrick thought, smelled like rags soaked in sweat and then left to fester in a damp, lightless corner. A corner informed him that cats visited often to make a mark. Smoke from tools and filterless cigarettes hung heavy in the air. Almost every worker, Patrick noticed, had a cigarette dangling from the corner of his mouth. Broken wisps of smoke, tickling up toward the workers' noses and into their eyes didn't seem to slow them down. It looked, to Patrick, uncomfortable and inefficient. Thankfully they weren't working with fuel, was the one fact that gave Patrick a bit of peace.

While squinting his eyes, and at times covering his mouth and nose against the acrid environment, Patrick also covered his ears. The noise reminded him of the time he had his concrete patio demolished. Jackhammers. Air compressors. And lots and lots of hand-held hammers wailing away on materials that did not want to give way added to the cacophony. There were random bangs. Thunderous booms. And underneath it all, a constant tap, tap, tapping. As if one person was keeping time with a ball-peen hammer.

A bit stupefied and stunned at the surroundings, Patrick tried not to touch anything or anyone. He scanned the rooms that he could see from his location near the front, or was it the back, entrance to the shop. Looking for a man who could help him with one of the biggest remaining challenges in his current endeavors.

Someone poked his shoulder. Patrick spun around, to be a greeted by man who stood only about five-five but gave off an aura of confidence and competence.

"You must be Patrick," the man said in the Delhi-accented English that Patrick had expected.

"I am. And you must be Minaz,"

"I am Minaz. How do you like my humble shop?"

"I wasn't sure this was the place. But I saw some of the work being done, and figured this had to be it. It's like the Stone Age in here. Haven't you all heard of Craftsmen or Snap-On?"

"Of course. But this is Delhi. We do with less. It may take a bit more muscle, but we have plenty of hard-working muscle. Talented, too. Look at this headlight cowl."

Picking up a brass cone from a nearby table, Minaz handed it to Patrick, who turned the cone over in his hands while Minaz crowed about it.

"Seamless. Can you tell where the seam is? Barely. And that is before it is nickel-plated. That was made for a man trying to sell several Rolls-Royces that have been in his family, but neglected for quite a long time. In families, we often neglect things that are nearby and common, do we not? But that was made by Buomi. Very talented young man. He has been with me for over a decade, and he is only twenty-two. Now, compare it to the other."

Patrick compared the two headlight cowls. To his eye, they were exactly the same.

"As if made by a machine, so similar," Minaz beamed. "But no, they were made right here. And of course, I will never reveal that they were not original Rolls-Royce parts. Even though the owner will probably forget that they were replacements."

"And that," Patrick laughed, "is why I came to see you. My friends and yours are not so different. And I think you might be the man for a rather big, rather delicate operation."

"Well, let's talk in my office." Minaz offered, and then yelled something in a language that Patrick did not understand.

Patrick followed Minaz into his office. Once the door was shut, the smells, noises, and visual chaos that had affronted him ceased. There were candles that Patrick could only reference patchouli as a possible scent for. Whatever it was, he thought, it was better than the shop. The walls were painted a lime green and light orange and stenciled with the same patterns he had seen on the feet of women throughout the city. There was an empty desk between Minaz and Patrick.

"I could talk about what I want, or I could show you. A picture's worth a hundred words."

"I believe," Minaz noted. "the expression is a thousand words."

"Hell, man, either way it could be worth tens of thousands of dollars. Want to see?"

Minaz just smiled and spread his arms across the table, inviting Patrick to show him.

Fumbling for the picture in his bag, Patrick barely noticed the young woman come into the office carrying a gold tea set. Quickly and silently pouring two cups of tea, she soon left. Patrick downed the scorching tea in one sip, placed the cup on the corner of the table and began to unfold the papers he had stashed in his backpack.

"Great tea, my man Minaz. Could have used some lemon or something. But good. Damn, I think I burnt my throat though. But no matter. This is where the rubber meets the road."

"I am very interested, Patrick. You are quite an unusual man. Casual but serious. You wear sweat pants but do not look like you work out. And you travel to Delhi, to see a humble metal smith."

"Hah, you're hilarious, Minaz. I work out every morning. I knock out twenty exercises in twenty minutes. But I didn't battle across the globe to share my fitness regimen. I came to share this,"

Patrick let a huge smile spread across his face. He was shaking with excitement as he unfolded the photocopies of the original drawings for the Phillips bodywork of Bentley SM3912.

"A most impressive motorcar."

"Are you kidding me, Minaz? Impressive! That is motoring royalty," Unable to contain himself anymore, Patrick started walking around the small room. Talking with his hands. Talking with all his energy and excitement. "That is a blower Bentley, SM3912. The only blower missing. The only one that no one knows what happened to. But guess what. We, me and you Minaz, and your crazy pack of barefooted, chain-smoking metal-beaters are going to make it. Some of my historians say the body was fabric, but that is BS. We can make it any way we want. And all the photos I've seen have shown a Phillips steel body. We are all going to make it. And we are going to make a mint when we sell it. A fortune."

"I like fortunes. So tell me what I need to make,"

Patrick pulled out a picture of SM3912, and along with the drawing, walked Minaz through the construction.

"I thought that the radiator shell would give you fits. Tie you up tighter than the rags you tie around your bodies,"

"They are traditional clothes, not rags,"

"Dude. I got it. But after seeing those headlight cowls, you have this metal-beating stuff down like a horse with broken leg. Down!"

"I agree. The radiator is no problem. With the photographs and the drawings we can make an exact replica. It is the windshield frame. What materials? What thickness? Sure, the drawings tell us that. But the finish. How aged? How polished? Difficult questions. I will need to visit a few cars with bodies by Phillips. From the same period."

"Done and done. What about the louvers, the hinges, and all the small stuff? You got that covered?"

"Of course. Not a problem."

"And the big stuff. The angle of the rear bodywork? The thickness of the metal? The edge of the fenders? Hey man, are you going to do the work here? In this shop?"

"I was thinking so," Minaz said as he sat back in his chair.

"I was thinking you and your workers take a trip to the countryside. Be good for you anyway. This place is filthy, man. I mean, shit runs in the streets. Literally,"

"I know. I work here every day."

"It is disgusting. And you have a lot of nosy people around here."

"It is life. Life is short and brutish. That is what Shakespeare said."

"What the hell? You can't quote Shakespeare. Faston is always quoting Shakespeare."

"Faston?"

"The enemy. Now. Here," Patrick reached into his bag and pulled out a rubber-banded wad of American currency. "One hundred thousand dollars. Cash. Move your shop. Take a vacation. Say you don't want to pay rent here. Whatever. Just lie. And just get out of town with the best guys you have."

"A hundred thousand is a start," Minaz parried.

"Of course it is a start. A hundred thousand here is like a million. You can remake Ben Hur for that kind of dough here. But of course it is a start. There is a further one hundred and fifty grand for you and your men on delivery."

"And when is delivery required?"

"Delivered to my warehouse, in Albany, in three months. Delivered. And shipped from different ports in different boxes. Different containers. At least five different shipments. I will come back when you are almost done and check the work. That will be in two months. I check it out as OK. You take it apart and ship it to me."

"And I assume you have a buyer lined up for this. I have an acquaintance who paints the most realistic copies of Monet and such artists. On commission. We are on commission?"

"Don't worry about that. There is a great path to riches for you and me."

"I am at your service. One new but old-looking Bentley coming up." Minaz stood up, shaking Patrick's hand.

"You know the story of Aladdin, right?"

"That is Arabian. I am Indian."

"Doesn't matter. The story ends with a wish coming true. Well, I have a wish, and it is coming true, bro. And you are my lamp. And I am rubbing you like there's no tomorrow."

Patrick swept up his drawings and photos and crammed them into his backpack. Turning back to Minaz, outside the door of the office, Patrick had just one more thing to say. "I'm rubbing you, Minaz. And you look like you're polishing up beautifully. Our wishes will come true."

17
Outside London, September 1940

The only pigeons that Stephan usually sought out were expertly shot, and even more expertly sauced. But tonight, for the first of what was sure to be many, or he hoped to be many, nights Stephan was waiting for a living pigeon.

Stephan had driven the Blower slowly and deliberately over the rough cart path that doubled as a road to the small plot of land he used without permission. A plot of land that just happened to contain a derelict brick building. With glassless window frames and nooks and crannies in its roof. It would be a perfect place to have his birds roost. And for the past year he had trained his birds to return to this place. And this place only. He'd tested them many, many times, and they never failed to show.

Stephan had begrudgingly given the birds some respect. They could fly enormous distances at impressively high speeds and with impressive accuracy. For just a warm place to sleep and decent kit of food, the birds were the cheapest men and women in his service. But he still liked them better browned and basted.

Parking the Bentley near the makeshift coop, Stephan shut it down and sat inside it as the night was cool and the leather of his car had almost transformed into a custom-fitted lounge over the past months. It was the most comfortable seat he had ever sat in. Even more comfortable than the Bibendum chair that he had perched upon years ago at a London club. With the top up and the heat from the cooling engine still able to leak into the cabin, Stephan sat and watched for his birds, letting his own mind fly over the many details and duties he had to execute. And had executed.

Pulling a small Dunhill flask from the hollow compartment of the Bentley's leather-clad door, Stephan took a long pull, relishing in the warmth that spread from within. Warm inside. Warm outside. What more could you expect to have during a war, Stephan thought. The cherry schnapps also helped to loosen his mind. And shake off the things he had seen.

Another long pull of the schnapps, and Stephan could put into perspective the dead bodies he'd mopped. The crushed legs he'd seen amputated at the local hospitals, wrapped in previously white sheets and casually brought to the incinerator. To look past the day-to-day damage on a small human scale and see the good he was performing on a large scale. On a scale good for his country. Those were the benefits of the schnapps.

After his third draught of schnapps, Stephan could relax. He felt his shoulder muscles relax. His eyes could stop searching side to side. And most importantly, he could focus on one thing, listening for the flutter of his birds' wings disrupting the night air. The scratch of their feet on the wood and brick. And their cooing. That always sounded to Stephan a bit like bragging, the pigeon version of a hunting dog's baying.

Stephan's eyes remained open just enough to avoid sleep. A sleep that came too rarely these days. And when it did come, it was hard to stave off. Listlessly relishing the leather of the Bentley, Stephan could listen to the quiet of the woods for a solid half-hour, until he heard the first disturbance on his right-hand side. It sounded as if his birds had buzzed him, like a fighter pilot buzzing the troops after a victorious battle.

Stephan soon spotted the athletic, mottled bird. And got a very good look at it when it settled on the radiator cap of the Blower. Stephan had liked that this car had not had a mascot. No 'B'. No ridiculous French,

Lalique, blown-glass abomination of deco decadence. Nothing except the honest, functional knurled-edge cap.

But now he had a pigeon as a mascot. And he thought that was a better mascot than any he had seen. It was functional. Stephan recalled that Thomas Jefferson wanted the turkey to be the symbol of America instead of the eagle. Stephan would have sided with Jefferson.

Getting out of the Bentley, leaving its warmth and comfort, Stephan felt the chill of the September English evening. He turned up his collar and peered closer at the pigeon proudly perched on the hood of his car.

The bird fluttered its wings a bit as Stephan approached but it didn't fly away. When he saw the small, metal tube crimped onto its leg, no larger than the cap of a pen, Stephan knew this to be one of his birds. Just as he was about to reach out to this message-bearer, two more pigeons flew into the small, brick house, somehow signaling to his mascot to follow them in. The three birds were now in the rented cabin, converted to a coop, and that is where Stephan stepped.

As Stephan put each bird into the small cages he kept up in the low rafters, he undid the small light-metal capsules and pulled out the pieces of paper that each contained. Pieces of paper that, because of what was written on them, seemed to weigh more than the birds that carried the messages to him through the darkness, flak and chaos of a London night.

Thinking about the journey of these pigeons, Stephan was always amazed at their resilience. Their ability to orient and get to a destination. And arrive, unruffled. Stephan thought about what it must have felt like to be crammed in the fetid quarters of a U-boat and then be released in a rush, when the captain had gotten as close as he dared to the English coast. As close as was needed to let the pigeons see, or feel or whatever they did, to locate land and head towards their home.

When he read the messages and understood their orders, Stephan imagined what the birds did when the hatch was unlocked on a stifling U-boat and they were thrown into a saltwater heavy night sky. Chilled and dangerous. Wide-eyed and nervous. But confident, because you had been bred to do a job, and you were going to do it.

Read in order, the notes clearly laid out what was expected of Stephan over his effective operating tenure, a tenure that could be one more day or ten more years:

3454: The garbage is full and will need to be taken out over the next few days. It is a rather toxic mix of refuse; so do be careful where you place it. Do let us know what you plan to do with it so we don't step in it or trip over it. Nothing quite like putting something like this where you don't want it to be. Who knows who might find it! A simple highlight as you know, is enough for us to know where to drop it!

To his superiors, bosses and handlers in Germany, Stephan knew he was viewed as one of their most potent, most effective, most destructive weapons. He was a number to them, just as many of the fighters, tanks and bombers were. If they could have minted more of himself, if the mighty German industrial infrastructure could have pumped out more German-born, English citizen, Nazi-leaning, whip-smart, insidious men, they would have. But they didn't. They had him. He was the only spy that had any effectiveness at all.

The incompetence of the others they sent to England just solidified his inviolable trust among the English. Like the dolt who, landing in a small town on a

Sunday morning, inquired about the hours of the one local pub. He was picked out as a questionable sort inside of an hour. Stephan shared a laugh with the locals who told him the story, and showed him what to look out for in his own perambulations.

Thinking about that poor German sacrifice, Stephan knew he would not be caught. No one he knew was more British than he was. For heaven's sake, Stephan thought, I drive a Blower Bentley.

18
Thornley Residence, Moss Rock, October 2008

"My father was, it has to be said, one of those men who died disappointed," Tate began to answer Faston's general question about what sort of duties the elder Thornley carried out with the ARP, "Not that he went on and on about what he called... his greatest failure as a man."

"Right not to do that," Charles piped in, "Those are the crazies you meet at the pub and bars. Going on about some conspiracy theory. That they know where Elvis is living, or that they wear a tinfoil hat to keep the government from reading their thoughts. Wouldn't want your old man to be the town crazy."

Faston just stared at Charles in disbelief, at his interrupting Tate, who was beginning to speak about his dead father.

"What Faston, What? So sensitive. Just getting to a point." Charles responded.

"Unseen truths are often unbelievable until they are revealed," Faston hated it but needed it when Caprice and Charles joined in making him calm down. Caprice continued, "Like when researchers found out it was a virus, not stress, that caused most ulcers. Remarkable really. Unbelievable to most."

"I think I'm getting an ulcer right now, from you two," Faston joked, "Sorry, Tate. Let's get back to hearing about your father and the ARP."

"I haven't talked about my father in a long, long time. I think about him quite a bit. Especially when I'm out riding. So, you coming, just as I was returning from a ride, was a good bit of timing. I am feeling a bit nostalgic, and the memories seem to be a bit fresher than usual. A bit clearer."

Seated with his back to the window, Tate was facing no one in the sitting room. Faston, Charles and Caprice were huddled on the sofa. Tate, in a chair alone. It disquieted Faston to be seated and listening to Tate. He seemed almost animatronic. Disembodied. Like some game you put a quarter in to hear your future. Or in this case, the past.

"The crux of the problem was that my father was in the ARP," Tate continued, "not in the service that hunted down spies. So when father first had an inkling that someone in the ARP was playing for the other side, he had no direct path for resolution. No access to top-down support. He was an investigation team of one."

"How much do you know about his inklings?" Faston asked, anxious to discover how close they were to finding a verdant pasture or barren escarpment of information.

"Oh, I think enough to know what he was thinking. But the details, not too much. Father passed when I was a youth, so we never dug in to this. I would overhear things. He would talk to me about how he felt."

"Let me get this straight," Charles interjected, "Your father believed that there was a German spy working for the ARP."

"A Japanese spy would have been picked out rather easily, and they didn't bomb us." Tate responded in a way that showed he was warming up to their presence. And their mission.

"Obviously," Charles muttered, "But this would be an ulcer medicine-type revelation. The British, to this day, are quite proud that they foiled every attempt by the Germans to have effective spies embedded in the UK. They believe that there was not one functioning informant on the isle."

"That is what they taught us in school. That the homeland was not violated by the Germans. Well, except

Jersey. But that island's invasion is a like a drunken aunt; you just don't talk about it." Tate concurred. "But that doesn't mean it didn't happen. So, looking to discredit a national point of pride is not high on most scholars' lists."

"Were the Shroud of Turin debunkers Catholic? I think not." Charles noted.

"That is a point of pride, that father was a beacon searching out what he felt was a wrong. Not just toeing the line. He would always reinforce that to me, when we would be out in nature together. We'd go fishing, as I could always fish, even as my eyesight was going south at around thirteen. You can cast and wait for the nibble. I got rather good at it. You lose one sense, you develop others. Not a myth, that."

"Would your father just talk about generalities or get into specifics?" Faston wondered.

"I was just a child. So he spoke in generalities and big themes. Looking back, that is. Then, I just thought it was fatherly advice. He would often tell me that being different and thinking different were fine things. Things to be proud of. And that helped a boy going blind. One of his favorite ways of telling me about these things was with stories. Like the mistaken idea that following the herd is a good thing. He told me about how they would hunt buffalo in the Western states of your country. How they would run the leader off a cliff, and the rest would follow."

"A bit harsh for a boy to hear. How old were you when your father died?" Caprice asked.

"I was fifteen. And I didn't think it was harsh or scary. The lessons stuck. And I do like answering all these questions about my father. But why are you here again?"

"To find a car," Charles answered.

"To find a Bentley. And to help find answers to any other mysteries intertwined with the car."

"My father never had a Bentley. He was a Daimler man. A family man. And a man who was disappointed that when the ARP disbanded, and even while it was functioning, that he did not catch this spy."

"Or prove that the spy even existed in the first place." Faston stated, wanting to keep the facts as clean and real as possible and not to get caught up into what Charles referred to as 'the crazy ramblings of an old man'.

"Hah!" Tate burst. "Just look at the facts and locations of bombings. And their effectiveness. They had to have a spy. Those Germans had to have more knowledge of our country than the tourist books most historians say were the guides they used for planning bombing raids. The Baedeker raids were not that effective, while other bombing missions were. They knew a lot about our country."

Faston felt he was agitating Tate, so he brought the conversation back to the Blower. "Sorry, Tate. I'm no war historian. I'm a car historian. Didn't mean to offend. So, let's talk about the car. We think there is a link, maybe, between your father and the only missing Blower Bentley."

"A Blower." Tate repeated. Drawing out the name. Even non-car fanatics felt a connection to the Blower name, and Faston noted that in Tate's voice. "I don't believe he ever mentioned anything about a Bentley to me. Like I said. It was more about being true to a cause. And being able to have the courage to follow what one knew to be right, in the face of disbelievers."

Faston remained silent. Although Tate had evolved from an animatronic to an animated person in their chat over the last half-hour, Faston felt this rapport was slipping away as a chance to get closer to the

Bentley. That they would finish their visit shortly. That they would cram back into the car and head back to their base at Toftcombs. Reinvigorate themselves with good food, and better Scotch, and go after the Blower another way. Find a new way into the history of SM3912.

"You know what I've been thinking?" Caprice wondered out loud. "After all that passion. That effort. After having such strong feelings. I'm surprised he didn't put any pressure on you to take up his quest. Or that he didn't keep the search going on his own time."

"No secrets passed along from father to son?" Charles enjoined.

"Not exactly. He just left Maddie and I an enormous collection of information. Boxes upon boxes of stuff. Shelves wilting and closets expanding and all that. In fact, Moss Rock has a whole room dedicated to father's cause. Would you like to see it? I obviously haven't *seen* it for years."

19
Portsmouth, September 17 1940

The last-minute knowledge. The startling things that became relevant as the clock ticked forward. All reasons why Stephan was in downtown Portsmouth. Back close to where he bought his Bentley six months prior. Stephan was near the confluence of major hotels, running along the shore and its feeder streets. Finding out who would be where. And when. The great and not so great of the British military suppliers were there, ostensibly, Stephan learned, to find ways to cut costs, innovate and profit from the whole experience. Stephan didn't hold a grudge about them trying to make a profit. He did, however, find the whole idea of the British being better supplied than the Germans wholly inappropriate.

Stephan parked the Bentley on a spotting station near Craneswater Park, so he would better remember where it was located, and where he could signal incoming planes. With a flick, the Bentley chuffed to silence while Stephan and his passenger got out of the warm leather seats.

"You drive like an absolute terror," Thornley laughed, pretending to sway a little bit, like a sailor fresh off a long sea journey.

"I took it a bit easy, too. I didn't even engage the blower except on the longer straights." Smiling back at Thornley, Stephan wrapped his arm around his superior, and the two walked up Parade Street toward the snuffing lights of the small Beaufort Hotel, looking to all the world like close chums. Which they were. So that is it, The Queen's Hotel, Stephan thought.

"Now I know why you chose that car. Remarkable way to blast across the country. Must be a point-to-point champ. Just don't ever take Sir John Anderson for a ride like that."

"Why's that?"

"The man has a driver older than Moses. Must be seventy. He dulls around London at no more than fifteen miles per hour. Any faster, and his lordship gets apoplectic."

"Good to know. What sort of car does Anderson own anyway? Not a Bentley? Seems too sporting."

"Too true. He, of course, has an opera-roofed Ghost."

"That car is well-built, though. Probably take a direct hit and just have minor scratches to show for it."

"Lets hope we never have that happen. Anderson has been the driving force behind keeping the homeland safe."

"You're right. Now, is this the hotel, Thornley?"

"It is. Let's go in and see what these businessman want, eh?"

"Let's. I've got a bit of Edradour Scotch to get us through." Stephan said, giving Thornley a glimpse at his flask.

"You do get around! Edradour! Rare stuff, that."

"I didn't drive all the way to that tiny distillery. Been once, a while back. The small peaked-roof mash rooms. Just a few fellows make all of the stuff. They alternate chores, too. One day they are the cleaner, the next the distiller. But I've got a few connections. And they pay off sometimes."

Stephan and Thornley paused outside the three-storey hotel. The double bay windows, stacked on top of each other, were blacked out, as was the four-panel window in the peak of the roof. The door to the hotel was off to one side, through a small tile-roofed entranceway that had a glass-windowed door, also blacked-out.

Inside, the hotel was dimly lit and ploddingly designed, thought Stephan. "You think they'd be able to spring for a better location. One right along the Parade. Maybe one," Stephan added, patting the back of a threadbare armchair. "that didn't have the appeal of a state home for the elderly."

"I don't know about that. Money is a bit tight these days. And along the Parade is a prime location for bombings. Let's go in, and I can press my case for some better spotting equipment with some of the optics manufacturers."

Stephan and Thornley walked back toward the low, muffled sound of lots of people talking on top of one another. Opening the double doors and stepping into the packed room, Thornley broke off, leaving Stephan to bump and bounce around the crowd. There was lots of laughter and lots of stories about gross profit and reduced quality. Finding a lone, limping man in his thirties, Stephan stepped up to him and struck up a conversation to pass the time and to try and gather more information.

"How's your war effort going so far? Anything that the ARP is involved with?"

"No, nothing the ARP is involved with. And my effort is just behind a desk. The leg kept me out of the fight. But that doesn't mean I can't help our boys."

"So, how do you help them?" Stephan asked, hoping he was a weapons manufacturer of some kind.

"I make chocolate cake."

"That does sound tasty. But how does that help?"

"Quite simply. One and a quarter ounces of my chocolate nut cake are provided in the emergency ration of every soldier. In that little tin that most men tuck into their breast pocket or into their helmet. Would you like to try some? I always carry around some samples."

"Why not," Stephan unwrapped the hard cake from its wrapper and bit off a corner. It took some chewing, but he made his way through it. The aftertaste was rather pleasing, too. Lots of cocoa flavor. "Not bad."

"Thanks. And if you ate that in the field, you'd have to report the fact to your commander. It really is to be eaten as a last resort. Along with the sugar cubes and tea packed in the tin."

"Well, thanks for the sample. I might have to grab some more before I leave. What time will you be here until?"

"Oh, I say about eleven. These things take time. Catching up with all the chums. Figuring out our supplies. Catch me up before you leave and I'll go to my case and give you as much chocolate nut cake as you like."

"Thanks again," Stephan replied, patting his new friend on the arm. He began circulating around the party again, pausing to take the time to write some notes on his always present scraps of paper with his also never-left-behind diminutive pencils. The next person Stephan was able to have a conversation with made personnel troop gear.

"You make binoculars?" Stephan tried to clarify, as he broke the man away from another conversation.

"Oh, no. Not the binoculars proper. The cases. Leather. Actually, the same cases my company made for the last big war. Patented in 1903."

Before Stephan had a chance to respond, or ask the case manufacturer about the binoculars his leather carryalls were designed to fit, a man thrusting a shoe between them interrupted.

"Feel these, gentlemen," said the small, impish man wearing a pair of funny shoes, even though the rest of his outfit was pure Saville Row. "That sole is soft and comfortable. The ankles don't chafe. Oh, I see that you are with the ARP."

"I am," Stephan said, as cool and uninterested as he could.

"Your people do a lot of standing. I think these would do them good. Raise morale, even. A good fitting shoe can do as much for morale as a letter from home."

The canteen man who had been fingering the shoe added his opinion. "I see lots of soldiers out at night wearing these. Creeping around brothels and such. That sounds quite wild. You could call them brothel-creepers."

"I think I will keep calling them desert boots," the small man snipped, grabbing back his shoe and turning toward Stephan. "I'm sure you could put in a good word for the shoes with your boss, right."

"I'm not in procurement, so I've no idea if I could or not. I'm just chauffeuring my boss around. And he's over there," Stephan pointed out Thornley, and the two men made all haste to cross the stifling, buzzing room to reach him. Stephan then continued to meet the big and small of the British war effort, taking notes all along the way of what they did and how he could exploit it.

20
Thornley Residence, Moss Rock, October 2008

Faston, Charles and Caprice tried to keep up while following Tate, who walked around his own home as if he were fully sighted, on their way toward the supposed deposit of information about potential German spies. Walking past several bedrooms and just one bathroom, Tate paused at a small door, grabbing the knob and opening it. There was a narrow staircase behind the door that Tate began climbing with ease, keeping one hand on the richly stained wood walls. Not tripping at all on the narrow, differing tread-width steps. This was more than could be said for Charles, who kept slipping as he climbed the stairs.

"Father liked to be in a quiet part of the house while working," Tate explained as he arrived at the top of the staircase and stepped aside to let his visitors past.

Faston's pulse began to climb as Caprice was the first to see the room and gasped, "Oh, my!"

"What?" Faston asked.

"I can't explain it," Caprice whispered.

"Everything can be explained," Faston began, but stopped trying to explain his logic to Caprice when, surmounting the top step, he took in the full expanse of the room that Tate had brought them to. Faston didn't even chastise Charles, who bumped past Faston when he got into the small room and immediately began going around its perimeter like a hound dog on a confused scent.

Faston, standing next to Tate, grasped his shoulder, "Tate, you undersold your father's collection and dedication just a bit, I think."

"I did say it was his life's biggest disappointment, didn't I?" Tate offered, in just as laid back a tone in which he spoke earlier.

"You did say that," Faston concurred, "but you didn't say it with much enthusiasm."

"We are known for our restraint," Tate smiled out. "It's why we think 'its just a flesh wound' is about the most humorous thing ever said by an actor. Ever."

Faston would usually have loved to discuss his favorite Monty Python sketches, but he was far too overwhelmed by the room he was in. It looked to Faston like a combination of a World War II planning room and a serial killer's hideaway. The room itself was dominated by a table; Faston figured it must have been built in the space because it was too large to fit up the stairs. The topographical map of England on it looked like something a model train enthusiast would build. From north to south, it must have been six feet. And the width was proportional. Markings, points of interest and highlighted road routes overlaid the map. In the totality of its first impression, this was the type of room that seemed to inspire both bold action and quiet contemplation.

The rich wood paneling of the stairway was barely visible behind innumerable scraps of paper, maps and images taped, pinned and stuck to the walls. Full broadsheets, from newspapers across the UK, covered enormous areas of the walls and jumbled across the floor in knee-high piles. One area of the walls seemed to be just faces of ARP employees. Row after row of men in the same uniform, staring earnestly at Faston. Imploring him, no doubt from their graves, to find the man Thornley was after. A draftsman's table was loaded with writing instruments, old cameras, binoculars and diary upon diary. The information still seemed to course around the room from document to document. Faston just wanted to jump in and start researching.

And, then, in the corner of the room behind Faston was the space that brought a sense of calm and contemplation to the room. A classic, round-arm, tobacco-colored leather club chair claimed this corner. It was in the smaller European scale, not the enormous chairs Faston hated to find in McMansion living rooms. The arms were burnished from easy, long-time use. A simple, mechanically moveable lamp aided reading in the dark corner. To complete the area of calm was a steamer trunk, laid on its side, as a table. Approaching the table, Faston could see water rings where a glass had often been set. Faston could practically see Thornley, glass of liquor in one hand, document in the other, trying to solve the biggest mystery of his life.

"None of it in Braille, I am sad to say," Thornley noted, walking down the stairs, "so I can't help. But take your time searching. Mother will make dinner for you in a few hours."

"Well, Faston," Caprice began to ask, "I get to see the great Mr. Hanks uncover another automotive gem. So how does he go about it?"

"Like a death-bed Catholic, grasping at grace, if you ask me." Charles piped in.

"You are all too kind." Faston laughed, standing with his hands on his hips surveying the room slower this time. Looking at individual headlines on the papers. Looking into the eyes of one photograph. Five minutes must have passed before Caprice broke in.

"Well, you both seem overwhelmed."

"Gob-smacked, would you say?" Charles asked.

"Gob-smacked," Caprice parroted in her best English accent, "is for sure what you two are. This is what Faston must have looked like in college before a big paper was due. Standing in the stacks, confused and quiet."

"I would have been drunk as well." Faston atoned.

"Thank goodness you're not drunk. I would have left this fanciful flight ages ago. So, to brass tacks. Don't you think? I will start perusing the newspapers on the wall. Each has some sort of marking on them, so I will try to figure out that system. Charles, why don't you take in all the photographs? See what links them to each other. There are the ARP chaps, then some bombing photos, and it seems in that far corner a few pictures of cars. Cars, imagine! And the table as well could use some documentation. And Faston, you tackle the man's work zones. The drafting table with the diaries and the contemplation corner. Maybe take the diaries and go contemplate them in the chair."

"Driver. Organizer. Humanizer. Thanks, Caprice." Charles lauded.

"Charles," Faston stammered, "as if I would have allotted the work differently. Just get on it. Caprice, thank you for showing me by your enthusiasm how little enthusiasm you actually have for this task."

"Touché."

With Caprice having given the assignments, and neither Faston nor Charles fighting against them, all three got to work. Caprice worked like a graduate intern; she was off like a shot. In moments she had stripped the newspapers off the wall, only to be confronted by another batch of newspapers. As she tore these down, Faston saw her encounter another layer.

"This is insane!" Caprice all but screamed. "There are one, two, three…six layers of newspapers."

"Don't forget the ones on the floor, Caprice." Charles piled on.

"Deep breaths, Caprice." Faston said trying to soothe his wife. "We have only been at this for a few minutes."

"You're right. I'm not into the whole car hunt thing, but this is a challenge I can help solve."

"Quite so," Charles agreed while standing by the topographic map of Britain, "quite so."

The trio got to work, and Faston didn't stop for what must have been several hours. His neck ached from being perched on a stool at the drafting table; he stupidly did not take Caprice's advice and move to the leather chair. Looking up from the table, Faston saw that Charles and Caprice both had glazed eyes and were rubbing their necks. They must have been feeling, as Faston did, that this was overwhelming. That Thornley was a man obsessed. A man who could not bear to throw out a single bit of information that *might* lead to his quarry. Just as he was about to suggest that everyone take a break, Faston heard from Tate.

"Hope you're all ready for a smoky dinner." Tate announced. "Be down in five, will you?"

Five minutes later, hands washed of decade-old dust; Faston and his co-searchers were seated at the dented and polished wooden table, which had seen generation after generation eat dinner at it. At such a table, Faston felt predisposed to like the food. Pleasant surroundings always dulled his critical tendencies.

Maddie walked in carrying a rough-planed wooden charger at least three feet in length. Setting it on the table, she described what was being laid out.

"Tate did tell you it would be smoky. And he was not being understated. We just recently acquired a smoker that Tate and I have been getting used to, so there it is, smoked duck. Shot by our neighbor. Maybe not quite up to the subtle smokiness of Bottisham's duck, but quite good. There is a ginger and quince jam to cut the fat of that, eh. Next on the board, a smoked trout. Tons and tons of smoked trout we get. We have a rather nice beat that Tate can fish. Then, most unusually, I think, we have some smoked peaches. A bit of the local honey on those will make it a true dessert. So eat up.

There is lots of bread, too. Another loaf in the oven if you take that one to task."

Faston jumped at the platter and loaded his plate with all the offerings. He noticed that Charles and Caprice did so as well. They must have been just as hungry as he was. Ripping the loaf of bread - it was not cut - Faston felt the saliva build in his mouth as the crust cracked and the warmth of the loaf carried the aroma to his nose. At least the bread would be good, he thought.

As Faston, Caprice and Charles tucked in, Tate spoke up. "I snacked as Maddie was putting this board together, so I am not too hungry. But I must ask, how goes the search?"

Caprice answered, as she was the one Faston noticed polite enough not to gorge herself. "I have been working on the newspapers, Charles the map and photos, Faston the diaries. How long were we up there?"

"Near to three and a half hours," Tate accounted.

"And, in those three and a half hours," Caprice said, "I have just been uncovering more and more stuff to look at. Like peeling back an onion."

"Rather a cliché, that. Peeling back an onion," Charles piped in, "How about, like turning pages in a Stephan King novel."

"Or pulling ticks off a coon hound."

"Endless, all of them. I get it. And that is what it has been."

Faston, having swallowed a perfect bite of bread, duck and jam, spoke for his experiences, "The diaries are fascinating and maddening. Full of cross-notes to a system that seems simple but is not because of rabid use. He notes his words, with the newspapers and pictures and of course, the map. Like modern day hyper-links on the web. But not as easy to follow. Truly, I am overwhelmed. But this duck amazes me. Really well done. I have not mastered my smoker yet."

"Pfft," Caprice let slip through her lips. "Not mastered? All your food tastes like $4 chardonnay. Over-oaked and one-dimensional."

"Thanks. But back on point. Charles, did you have any luck with the map or photos?"

Charles was not ready to answer. He was busy dicing a bit of the peach, dicing the duck and trout and putting this crude salsa on the bread.

"Charles, please answer. Most people let their stomach do the mixing of foods. Glad you saved yours the effort."

"Nothing. Really overwhelmed. I think I need a fortnight here." Charles answered in a staccato fashion, and then got back to work on his smoked mixed plate. And Faston thought, Charles' eating was workmanlike.

Tate broke his silence, "Charles mentioned something there, between bites, that I think I made out. That he needed a fortnight to go over the information."

"At least," Charles concurred with flakes of fish falling from his mouth.

"Faston, I'm afraid the newspapers alone would be a couple of fortnights. Months." Caprice softly concurred.

"And," Faston began, "I am not so certain that I could get through one of the diaries, let alone the half dozen or so I saw, in a fortnight. Ten days is just not enough time."

"Ugh, Faston you must read some more British literature, a fortnight is two weeks. Fourteen days, at least a contraction of that." Charles corrected.

"Thanks. Four more days would not help me. No wonder that chair, which I dumbly refused to sit in, was so well worn. The information in that aerie is staggering."

"Well then," Tate said between bits of honey-drizzled smoked peach, "why don't I ship the lot of it to you in the States?"

21

Selsey, South East of Portsmouth, September 17, 1940

An hour after leaving the Beaufort Hotel, and moments after dropping Thornley at the train station, Stephan stoked the Bentley along the B-roads toward Selsey. He made his way around Langstone Harbor and further on, past Bosham Channel. Turning south, he pressed on through the silky, dark and clear night. All the way from Appledram to the outlying homes of Selsey, Stephan found the Bentley willing and able to go as fast as his courage allowed.

A full moon and modest cloud cover allowed decent speed. The low-geared steering kept the car from being fiddly on the cambered and crack-crazed roads. While the long travel of the brake pedal inspired confidence and let Stephan dive deep into turns that he both did not know and could not, in reality, see through to the exit. And accompanying his thoughts of the mission was the whistling of the carburetors from the front and the whirring of the crown wheel and pinion from behind.

Stephan felt as busy as a pilot. Thinking of the mission. Minding gauges. Trying to stay hidden and effective until the last moment. And the minding of gauges was always a joy and chore to Stephan. The Hobson telegauge was where he kept his eye most often. It told him how much petrol the Blower had in its tank. At times, when getting along at over sixty miles per hour, Stephan swore he could see the telegauge show a real-time decrease in his fuel reserves. While at times like this moment, with judicious use of the accelerator, Stephan was able to keep a decent amount of fuel in reserve for his run back to his hotel.

The final instruments, of the many perforating the dash, that Stephan made sure to glance at were the water temperature and oil pressure, the basics for running a high-performance car. But this night, and for many nights to come hoped Stephan, the most important of his gauges was the ammeter. The ability to call on ample electric reserves was critical.

Stephan slowed the Bentley and ambled along in first gear as he made his way off the secondary roads of Selsey and onto what were more in line with cart tracks. Stephan hunted along the twin-rutted tracks in search of a location near the shore. After what he guessed was a quarter-mile of putting around the darkened lane with dimmed headlights, he came upon the channel. Turning his car into a position that would allow him to head off back toward the main road in a moment's time, Stephan parked. He then set about his work.

Stephan had briefly tested his system months ago back in Scotland. His signals helped the Junkers attack the Firth of Forth. It was not a devastating attack, but it did prove that he could signal locations to German planes without being detected. If he was careful. And lucky. And committed.

Stephan scooted forward on the leather seat, reached under the dash and grabbed the controls of the headlights he had installed himself. With the Zeiss lights off at the moment, he checked the operation of the linkage. He pulled back one rod, and the lights pivoted up ninety degrees. He pushed and pulled the second rod and watched as the wood disc passed over the headlight without catching or seizing. Now he just had to wait for his cue to signal.

Stephan's cue was the roar of the BMW and Bramo engines from the Dornier Do 17 bombers that would have left Cormeilles-en-Vexin airbase in the north of France. Stephan knew they would be loaded with 500 kilograms of bombs. And under the command of Oberst

Stefan Frölich, he knew the bombers would be on time. On target. And ready to fight.

As Stephan waited in the warm, English-leather confines of the Bentley, he thought about how this operation came to be. From being in touch with his German ancestors, although he had lived in England for most of his life, and on to the fact that one small bird, often a symbol of peace, had helped arrange this meeting and future meetings. Stephan felt that victory was destined and that the German empire would triumph over the world. And a big step in that triumph would be the fall of England. The bombings had started in earnest. And now that his commanders felt comfortable employing Stephan on a regular basis, he hoped the bombings would become more effective. More deadly.

A little before eleven, Stephan heard the drone of the bombers. They would be sweeping across the channel on a northwesterly run. Stephan's training had told him to not signal until two minutes after he heard the planes. To count the time down, he turned to the Smiths clock set in the machine-turned dash. The time passed quickly, and soon Stephan got to work.

Stephan pulled the knob that controlled the big Zeiss headlights. Working quickly, as even with bigger batteries he could not run the lights very long, or they would completely discharge the system, Stephan set out to give the target's coordinates.

Using signal languages sent to him months ago on the wings of his trusty pigeons, Stephan began flickering aloft the location of the Beaufort Hotel. This would have been a surprise to the pilots who, no doubt, left their base believing tonight's target would be the naval shipyard. Stephan had made the decision to override that after learning about all the suppliers gathered at the Beaufort. The signals were unique to the operation at hand, and Stephan concentrated on the lights, making sure he got his signals correct. Only after the last coordinate had been blinked into the sky did he risk a look up himself.

Stephan turned just in time to see a tight formation of four Dorniers above the clouds. The sound of the planes muted the sound of the Bentley as Stephan fired the big four-cylinder. Letting the engine idle, he worked the rods under the dash and repositioned the headlights in their stock location, facing forward and mostly shielded, just the regulation slits meekly illuminating the dirt roads, Stephan set his jaw and made for his removal from this strip of land.

Orienting himself along the B-roads wending toward Brighton, Stephan set a sedate pace, the telegauge hinting he would not reach Brighton if he used the force of the blower. Ahead, was the warm bed of an ARP barracks used by officers. Behind him was, if he'd done his job, a much damaged British supply chain.

22

Litchfield, Connecticut, January 2010

"Faston, I'm coming up," boomed Charles over the intercom at the gate to Faston and Caprice's inn. For the one thousandth time, Faston thought to himself that he had to take away the security card he had given to Charles. But today there was nothing to do about it, so Faston just went to grab his vintage Shell Gasoline jacket. Every time Faston slipped it on, he imagined smoking in the pits at LeMans. Not that he smoked. Or thought it wise around race fuel. But that is what was done when this jacket was produced.

Opening the slab of metal that doubled as his front door, Faston waited to greet Charles. He could hear Charles before he could glimpse him. And he knew that Charles was not driving his Triumph. No way. No how. What Faston heard was a V8. And then he saw it. A Series III Maserati Quattroporte. Blue. With Rust trim. And it sounded to Faston like the car had glass packs. And, it had a distinct tilt to the starboard side. Odd, as Charles was port. And to Faston, it felt right to refer to the sides of the Maserati as port and starboard. It was a seventies boat. No doubt there was cocaine residue in the plush folds of the leather seating, the interior being the only redeeming quality of these Maseratis. That, and you might be able to purchase one cheap enough to run in a 24 Hours of Lemons event. But what were all the boxes in the car, Faston puzzled.

With a groan and graunch from stem to stern, the Maserati came to a rest and Charles came bounding out. Carrying a box, Charles walked over to Faston, "There's a U-Haul full of boxes and crates at the bottom of your drive. And guess where they are from?"

"The Maserati parts manufacturer. So you can keep that three-ton decadence running."

"No, Moss Rock!" Charles exclaimed. "Moss Rock!" He repeated, thrusting the box he carried into Faston's arms.

The arrival of Thornley's entire research archive was about the only thing that could keep Faston from giving Charles and the Maserati a thorough dressing down. "Fantastic! Let's go get them. And I guess this car will have to do as our conveyance for the packages. Fire her back up."

With lots of cranking and a bit of sputtering, the Maserati farted to life. Faston and Charles emptied the boxes that Charles had brought up with them, then Faston jumped into the passenger seat. But before they took off, Faston noticed something extremely disturbing out of the corner of his eye, "Are you wearing driving gloves?"

"Rather fetching, eh?" Charles peacocked, as his hands glided over the honey-colored, sweat-stained steering wheel.

"You know how I feel about driving gloves. You look like a cycling tourist."

"I do. But I do not care."

Faston had a deep-seated hatred of driving gloves. To Faston, the idea of driving gloves sounded good. But in practice. In 99.5 percent of execution (excluding Nomex racing varieties while racing which are 100 percent OK) were so ridiculous as to cause sad aversions of one's gaze when in the presence of a dandy who dons these grippy historical remnants, and he would tell Charles his feelings as they drove to the gate. "

"Driving gloves were a necessity, Charles, when you owned a Bugatti with a cord-wrapped wheel and needed to keep the beast on the bumpy two-lane tracks around your Southern France or Northern Scotland manse. You would chafe your lilly-white, unworked hands if you didn't. And we couldn't go around shaking the hands of Ladies with a capital 'L' with hands as chafed as the gardener's, could we? No. So the invention of the driving glove in both cold and warm weather varieties. The rope-backed warm weather versions being the most offensive. This open back always seemed to Faston like a woman who wore a too low-cut blouse. A bit showy. A bit garish. This peek of flesh is just not fashionable or proper. A hand either needs to be fully protected or not."

Charles responded with a simple, "I disagree."

Faston was about to continue his speech but saw the stack of boxes and crates that needed moving up to the house, then unpacking, and fell silent. Silent being Faston's default mode while encountering a physical job. At times like these, thought Faston, it would make sense to have a practical vehicle. A pickup truck. Or at least a classic Jeep Grand Wagoneer. Something that hauled more than his current stable of cars. That stable being the SWB 911 race car. His recently repaired Bugeye Sprite racecar. The recent swap he made of a track-prepped 1982 Targa for his lovely, stock 944 Turbo. The only reason he traded the Turbo was because of the Targa's high-compression 3.0 liter bark. With 2 in 2 out M&K muffler and SSI heat exchangers it made every trip the aural equivalent of a blast around track. That and its 201,000 miles made every mile added guilt-free. The fact that Caprice loved driving it more than the laggy Turbo also helped him make the swap. His 6.3 Mercedes and Jaguar XK 120 rounded out his collection.

"Just grab the keys to the 6-3, Faston, and get on with it. I think it will only take a few trips."

A mere 23 trips later, Faston and Charles were loading their extremely impractical cars for the last time. Faston was determined not to make a 24th trip, so he was loading the large Mercedes carefully and aggressively. Thinking about it like a giant Tetris puzzle, and forcing the boxes like a Tokyo subway employee. With just one box to go, Faston thought he could open the sunroof on the Mercedes and balance the last package on the roof of the car by wedging in the cardboard box.

Without turning around, Faston heard the 3.0 liter of the Targa being shifted from third, to second, a brief wail and then almost silence. Caprice loved the no-power-anything Targa. She did not take it easy, though, on the old Stuttgart hand-assembled money maker for Porsche. She gave it no quarter. And despite all the miles on the clock, the car didn't seem to care. Though it was rather thirsty, giving Faston and Caprice only about 15 mpg.

His ears never lied when it came to cars, especially Porsches, and Faston soon saw Caprice pull up beside him. The top was off, Caprice's hair was held back with a blue silk headband, and both looked perfectly, effortlessly beautiful. Pretty.

"What in the world are you trying to do?"

"Be handy."

"Hah! Seriously, what are you doing?"

"Packing up the last of over twenty trips that Charles and I have made to bring the boxes Tate sent us."

"My. That is good news. And just one that seems to not fit. I just have one bag. Filled with muffins for breakfast from Trent's. So let me take that."

Not wanting to abuse his Benz anymore, or make this task last any longer, Faston tossed the lightweight box to Caprice, who set it on the passenger seat and spun the Targa up the gravel drive. Before driving his Mercedes up to the house, it struck Faston that Caprice's aggressive driving on the gravel had caused the premature flaking of the Targa's rear fender flares that he'd noticed the other day.

Once Charles, Caprice and Faston were back at

the house, Faston thought it best not to get into a 'how to drive the Porsche on gravel' conversation. Instead, he tried to keep the flagging energy of Charles up, get the boxes into the house, then get them unpacked.

"Room 5567 is not booked for a few months, Faston,' Caprice announced while chewing on a spelt cookie she must also have picked up at Trent's, "so why not recreate Thornley's room in there?"

"Why not recreate the room in Maine, it is so far." Charles panned.

"You don't want to just redo the library?" Faston asked.

"Uh, no. I don't. Last time you brought a project into the library there was a Cosworth DFV in there for over a year."

Faston blanched but responded, "It is a rather complicated engine. And I thought I had the skills to put one together effectively. And in the garage, I am too messy. I thought I would have kept a 'clean room' atmosphere in the library."

"You kept a clean room for sure. But the mechanics you had to hire to come in and complete the engine did not."

"That engine did go on to power a Tyrrell that has run quite well in vintage Formula 1 events."

"Remarkable. 5567. Let's go."

More than two hours later, after more hauling made difficult by trying not to trip over the Bassett hounds, the boxes were installed in room 5567. It was two o'clock. Too early to start dinner and too late to extend lunch. So Faston fell back into his silent mode and began turning room 5567 into a facsimile of Thornley's second-floor detective room.

Pictures went up rather quickly. Faston making sure to use white paper tape so as not to leave marks on the walls when the pictures would be taken down. The newspapers were quickly ordered into stacks by publisher and date. The journals, of course, were stacked carefully by an Eames Lounge that Faston had also brought to the room, an extra bit of effort that Charles questioned.

"Do you really need to move that assemblage of bent wood and aluminum?"

"Yes. I do."

"I find it repulsive. Why not get a proper club chair like Thornley had?"

"I am quite sure that if Thornley had ever set eyes on an Eames Lounge he would have purchased one. You do know, Stirling Moss bought an Eames Lounge in 1958 with the winnings of a race. He took payment in cash instead of the silver trophy, for the sole purpose of buying one of these chairs. And the ottoman. He still has both to this day. Almost every interview at the great champion's house for the last five years has shown him seated in it. It is the same rosewood and black leather as this version."

"I just asked, Faston." Charles said holding his hands up in the air. "No more lectures today, please. The driving gloves rant was one thing, but this is another." Charles ended then sat down in the very chair he had been chiding. "Quite comfortable, though."

"Quite."

All that was left was for Charles and Faston to reassemble the topographic map of England in the middle of the guest room. Faston thought it would take no more than a half-hour, the same time it took to assemble his vintage Scalextric slot car track. He was wrong. It took another two hours to assemble the table and get the 30-odd pieces together, their first attempt having created an island that was more reminiscent of Australia than England. Charles tried on numerous times to strike up conversation about WWII, giant Flemish rabbits, celery, paper clips, Lyme disease, Old Lyme Connecticut, strumpets, blower Bentleys, Mondial Ferraris, moths, flames, Necco wafers, Voltaire, the Wesleyan Universities, megapixels and of course, Triumphs.

Faston didn't speak a word, he just kept working and fitting and thinking about the Blower. About where it was. About how all the information needed to find it was now in one of his guest rooms, just a few hundred feet from where he slept. It was now completely taking over his imagination. Faston worked and thought until the table was done. The map resembled England. And he could no longer ignore the growling in his stomach.

23
Brighton, September 18, 1940

"....At any moment a major assault may be launched upon this island. I now say in secret that upwards of 1,700 self-propelled barges and more than 200 sea-going ships, some very large ships, are already gathered at many invasion ports in German occupation." Stephan read Churchill's quote about the impending, or formerly impending, Operation Sea Lion with disgust. Although Churchill did not know it yesterday, Stephan knew that the operation had not gone as planned. That it had no doubt been terminated. Although this fact had probably hurt the morale of his fellow Germans, it just inspired Stephan to do more with less. And more often.

Stephan had not picked up *The Argus* this evening to read up on Churchill and the man's liquid-courage filled ramblings. He wanted to know if there was an impact on the Beaufort hotel. It took until page 7 to find out. Stephan scanned the article entitled, *'Industrialists Drink, Dine and Dive for Cover.'* With a headline like that he thought the results could be sunny-side up or ineffectual. By line three, he had learned which it was.

'The few bombers that approached Portsmouth this night, after such heavy bombings just two nights ago, seemed out of place and out of sorts. The bombs they dropped did not target the several ships in port, or the munitions depot. For some reason, and lucky too, for the pilots and us, the bombs honed in on the Beaufort Hotel. Striking around it in a near full circle of explosions, no one bomb hit the hotel. The concussions did cause much blustering and chaos at a meeting of war suppliers, but no one was hurt. Random bombs also fell miles north of the Beaufort, landing harmlessly on an unused fish

smokehouse.'

What the paper didn't describe was the communications tunnels buried 166 steps down under the old Fort Southwick. This was the secondary set of coordinates that Stephan had beamed to his bombers. Yes, Stephan thought, the bombers were his. Although he was not sure the bombs would damage the tunnels, he was sure they could shake up things, maybe break the confidence of the Wrens and coders who worked in the cramped conditions. Sending, receiving messaging and watching the toys moved around a map of the English Channel were what kept the staff undergrounds busy. It would have been nice to rock the peace near there, but all the bombers chose to attack the primary target. Remarkably, they all had missed. It left Stephan feeling as ineffective as the gunners of Cap Gris Nez who hurled their dumb metal rocks across the channel at Dover. The projectiles had been making lots of noise but no real impact so far. Stephan had even heard that the mail had yet to be late in Dover.

"Damn!" Stephan shrieked, thinking of it all, crumpling the paper and tossing it into the fire that smoldered in the corner of his mean rooms. The only reason to stay in these rooms was that they were near where he housed his Blower. The owner of the inn was a pre-war motor racing photographer and amateur hill climb participant. His mechanical knowledge more than decent. And he promised to keep quiet about the style of car being kept in his premises.

It was to his car that Stephan went after having received the poor news from *The Argus*. The only downside to this car-friendly arrangement was listening to the owner's pro-English ramblings.

"A bit quiet last night, eh?" Kinlan quipped as he approached the carriage house silently. "I saw the lamp on. Had a sure hunch it was you working on the Blower. Came to see if you needed a hand."

"Quiet or not, the war never ends for me."

"But you had to get a peck more sleep last night?"

"Hardly, I slept less than usual."

"Gossssh. So serious. Here, I brought a couple of pints of Guinness. And a chip butty, as well. And you are elbow-deep into it, aren't you?" Kinlan added as he chomped into his bread and chip sandwich.

Despite his disposition, Stephan had developed a love of Guinness. He liked that he could drink quite a few pints and not feel dulled. Not like most of the German beers he preferred. For a beverage that could rough one's edges up but not tear them up, he found Guinness to be perfection. He never took a liking, though, to the starch on starch combination presented by a chip butty.

"Cheers," Stephan said, taking one of the mismatched pint glasses that Kinlan had carried out to the carriage house. "Pass on the chipper, though. Even with it being cool out tonight, I've been working up a sweat tending to this car. The autovac seems to be a bit weak."

"No doubt it is one of the cork washers." Kinlan opined before, and after, a large sip of Guinness.

"No doubt. Would be a quick replacement. If replacements were available. So, I've made do with hand-carving one."

"Hah! A proper craftsman in uniform. Best get it right, or the suction will never be enough to keep up with Blue Seal's prodigious thirst."

"Blue Seal?"

"I always called my cars after their colors. Red Dragon was my Amilcar. White Chocolate was my MG. See. Blue Seal is the name I think of when I think of your car. It is dark blue and slippery and quick. And, especially hard to spot at night. Like a seal."

"I've always thought of cars more as tools than as persons."

"Oh, mate. You have it all wrong." Kinlan said while shaking his head and sitting down on one of the Blower's wing-shaped step boards. "I have a very strong opinion about this. I think I even spoke too softly. I don't just believe my cars have personality. I know they do. They're alive, mate. I'm sure of it."

"Go on. Convince me." Stephan asked while he sanded away at the cork blank to make a replacement for the worn seal that could have stranded him on the road. Or somewhere more troubling.

"Whether a racing car, a Sunday car or a lorry, they all got a personality. That's what I tried to capture when I was taking my photos. It's the spirit of the car. It is powerful and real. It is part of what the blokes who built it, the ones who maintain it and of course, the ones who drive it put into it. You're telling me when you walk past a row of cars they all seem the same to you?"

"They could be different marques. But they'd all be cars."

"I can't believe this! Do all women look like different ways to make a baby?"

Stephan couldn't help himself, so he let out a laugh. At least Kinlan was not talking about the British war efforts tonight.

Pointing at Stephan, Kinlan winked and continued, "I got you there. My mate sees ladies for what they are, unique and curvaceous creatures. Some a bit pointier than others. Some curvier. Some like it rougher than others. Some like to be showered with attention. Some like to be ignored a bit. Right?"

"I guess. Some."

"Right it is. Right it is. And cars are just the

same. Are you saying that this Blower here is just a bit faster and louder than a car you had as a learner?"

"Those are the facts."

"The facts are for a little box in The Motor that tells me what a car does on test around Brooklands' banking, not what it feels like. You got to get in tune with your car on a deeper level, or you will never get the best out of it. Just look at the way you are sanding that piece there. Looks like you are trying to strike a match. You've got to caress it, put some attention in to it."

Kinlan took a large pull of the Guinness, draining half the glass, and continued. "Cars, trains and aeroplanes are machines that can rise above just being parts together. The Americans get this. Have you ever chatted an American up and asked him about his car? They all have a name. Usually a girl's name. But still, they know if their car is a beauty or a brute. Betty or Broom Hilda. Trains are legion with great names. None greater than the 'Flying Scotsman'. How brilliant a name. Not quite as dynamic as the four and a half litre supercharged Bentley. Pssh. Give it a name."

Without knowing it or wanting it, a smile had creased Stephan's face. "A name. I think something like 'efficiency' would do nicely."

"Efficien…what? Really?"

"Why not. Or 'clockwork'."

"Neither. Something with some blood pumping through its veins. If petrol were blood, what would be the name of it then?"

Although Stephan was giving Kinlan a bit of a go, he was warming up to the idea of giving the Blower a name. A name that he'd only keep to himself and Kinlan. "Blue Seal. Fine name you gave there, but it's not quite me. And not quite the car. A seal is a quiet thing. This car is not exactly quiet."

"Not loud either. These days at least with all the

explosions around. She seems to be quiet."

"In a city, quiet. On a country lane, not so much."

"Maybe you got something there. A bit of a split personality. By all appearances that car is a doctor's sedan. One thing. But in reality, it's the transport for an important war officer. Something totally different. Split personality. I like that. You should go with it."

Stephan laughed to himself at the absurdity of it all. "I do, too. A split personality. How about just initials though. J.H.?"

"J.H.?"

"Jekyll and Hyde."

"Perfect. And perfectly British." Kinlan nodded and walked back to his rooms, leaving Stephan alone.

Stephan spent another hour getting his replacement cork gasket to fit properly. He'd once heard that drawing a perfect circle was one of the most difficult skills an artist had to learn. Sanding a well-sealing cork washer, then, was one of the most difficult skills a mechanic could acquire. Once fitted, the washer did its job, and Stephan took the Bentley out on one of the rarest things in wartime England, a pleasure ride. No signals to give. No destination to arrive at. Just a man enjoying his machine. And he had to admit it; tonight, he thought of the Blower as more than a car. J.H. was, for the time being, his best friend.

24
Albany and Bombay, January 2011

Patrick was beyond pleased that he had not had to travel to Bombay a second time to meet with Minaz. He thought that he would need to travel and see the progress first hand that Minaz and his talented team of metalworkers had wrought. But he needn't have worried. Minaz had not only set up a special workshop away from the prying and peering closeness of his urban garage, he had equipped this suburban factory with a live video feed so Patrick could watch as much or as little of the work as he wished.

Patrick, in front of the computer at the moment, waited for Minaz to join him so the two could have their weekly conversation. While he did so, Patrick surfed around the Internet hitting his favorite sites including bringatrailer.com, rennlist.com and hemmings.com. While he was making a sarcastic comment on yet another early Datsun on bringatrailer.com, he heard his phone ring then saw Minaz's smiling face peer up at the camera while he waved hello.

"Double Patrick. How are you?"

"Good man. Good. You guys are cranking."

"I think that is a compliment. Thanks. What do you think?"

In the past week, Minaz's workers had begun shaping the fenders of the Blower. First, they had built wooden bucks to create patterns on which to pound and shape the metal. And then they got to it. Trial and error. Patrick had the few remaining pictures of SM3912 in front of him as he checked the work to reality.

"Hey Minaz, take the camera down and walk it a bit closer to the left front fender."

Minaz jumped up with surprising vigor, snatched the camera and did as Patrick had asked. "Is this better? You have not seen finer work, eh?"

"I've seen finer. But not in such a short time. Top-notch stuff. Man, is it close to these pictures. You have an army working on this thing."

"Just 24 men who work 70 hours a week, not an army. But the body is close to the scale drawings I had made," Minaz announced, panning the camera to show the full-size drawings of SM3912 taped to the wall which acted as blueprints for the workers.

"Right there, man. That is solid. Sol-id! Really. It's a big car, huh?" Patrick asked as he saw the slight Minaz standing next to the growing bodywork. A tall, upright car looked to Patrick like a two-door Packard with a chopped soft top.

"Any trouble I need to know?"

"Some of the fittings and hinges are taking more time than I thought, but nothing to delay our ship date. We should be done in another two or three weeks. And then, like you instructed, I will box it up into many different boxes and air-freight to you."

"Well done, man. Later." Patrick hung up his phone and closed the browser window that looked into what he felt was his workshop halfway around the world. Everything was coming into place. Patrick even thought to himself, 'The Japanese aren't the only ones who can build a car with just-in-time suppliers.'

25
Litchfield, March 2011

"I feel like I smoked a garlic cigar," Faston told Caprice and Charles as the three of them sat in the guest room rebuilt as Thornley's war room. They had just finished a late lunch and were all arrayed with their choice of research documents. "I told you not to get those two clam pizzas to go from Sally's." Caprice reminded Faston as she closed the last of three boxes of pizza the group had managed to finish and took the last sip of her Pilsner Urquell. This was the second of their now twice-monthly Bentley hunting days.

"But, we rarely get to New Haven anymore, and I can't help myself. Like a gambler in Vegas, I have a hard time knowing when to say when. I should know to only get the regular. But the clam is soooo good. Only made on a couple of nights a month, too. And you know I am a sucker for limited-edition things."

"I prefer the potato pizza from Bar," Charles added.

"They're upstarts. And you ate two whole pizzas alone yesterday. So, your stomach rumbles govern your palate. Not vice-versa." Faston fell quiet and had to admit the conversation between the three of them had become catty and petty at times as they all hunkered down and tried to pull out clues to the whereabouts of the Blower.

The complexity of Thornley's system was not quite Enigma Machine-like, but it was robust. There were colored dots, numbers, initials, carats and double carats on almost all the pieces. Popping a piece of gum into his mouth, Faston stood up and went to the whiteboard that held the keys they had all figured out over the past several months. As the gum lost its battle with the potent garlic, Faston chewed away on the puzzle in front of him.

Blue dots - connoted ARP officer pictures and office locations
Black dots – noted known Bentley dealers and repair facilities
Orange dots – were pre-war racing facilities
Yellow dots - ?
AS initials – of which there were many on the map, Air Strikes
SS initials – at least two dozen on papers and map ?
VS initials – concentrated on the east coast, Buzz Bombs
Carats and double Carats – these criss-crossed routes on the map with no apparent order. Some yellow carats were unknown clues.

These were the main categories that dominated Thornley's system. And it had taken years to get to where they were. There were still dozens of one-off marks, pushpins and annotations that had been red herrings and black holes of time-wasting attempting to figure out. Faston popped another piece of gum into his mouth, trying to tame the garlic, and turned to the corner of documents that had not even been dusted off after being deposited here.

"Caprice, you're the one who is good with the numbers. What percentage of docs do you think we have even delved into?"

Arching her back and stretching from being hunched over a stack of aerial photographs bearing both blue and orange dots, Caprice placed her reading glasses on top of her head, an act Faston always found attractive, then finally answered, "30 percent. Maybe 35. Simply Byzantine."

"Hah, you modified Byzantine with simply.' Charles laughed, 'Well done. Opposites those, but they do work well together."

"I think we've been approaching this in far too organized a manner." Faston opined, "I mean, my greatest finds have always been these odd eureka moments. I'm not Bob Ballard with sonar and maps. I'm more Inspector Closeau."

"Stepping in a pile of it is no way to go about things. It is not a very replicatable process." Charles said.

"Not for a scholar. But for an artist it is the only way of going about finding something. And I think of myself more as an artist than a historian or scientist or scholar."

"An artist?" Caprice smiled, which Faston knew meant she was intrigued to see where his logic would take him.

"Yeah, an artist. Think Christo, that wacked set of flags in Central Park, pure organized beauty out of a random idea. Basquiat, the energy of youth pasted on whatever scrap the man had at hand. Dada school? A freaking bicycle wheel on a stool. Dali? Dale Earnhardt?"

"Did you just say Dale Earnhardt?" Charles coughed.

"I did. The man drove like an artist. Not like the scientists that are behind the wheels of the Cars of Tomorrow. The man had passion and drive. He was nuts. I would never drive in a race that he was in. I mean the artistic ideal of going on emotion more than science. I know some artists are systematic, but in the end those sort of artists bore. Like most renaissance painters, cotton candy colors, they were the network programming of their day. A few rose above, but not many. I like the get in the car or the studio type of artist, grab what is at hand or stop at what catches your eye, type of artist."

Faston then knocked a few inches off the piles that the team had yet to look at, randomly grabbed a file and tossed it to Charles, pictures falling out as it sailed across the room. He then flipped a leather-clad yearbook of sorts to Caprice. And for himself, Faston grabbed the next document that was in the pile, a pamphlet about deep-level shelters in London.

"We're artists now." Faston encouraged, "So, let's make some discovery art." Faston tore into the pamphlet titled, *Unsafe Use of Deep Level Shelters*, trying to shake the initials and carats and annotations that swirled in his head. After just a few sentences, he was struck by the strong *against* sentiment that this piece put forth. Skimming along making discovery art did not necessarily entail being totally thorough, Faston jumped to the last of its seven pages, while en route picking up facts about the immense size and complexity of these pill-box entered tunnels filled with bunk beds.

'So, we have at Goodge Street, Clapham North and Belsize Park a number of shelters that can accommodate upward of 10,000 citizens apiece. We might as well say that these shelters are capable of housing in perpetuity and death the bodies of these citizens. From risk of fire, to lack of adequate ventilation and potential blockages of sewage and potable water, these shelters are unsafe, unfit and unnecessary. They are the product of an overzealous wartime developer looking to make a profit without regard to true safety. These underground tunnels are better suited to storing documents than defending our brave people. If you are a

citizen, avoid these shelters. If you are in the ARP, avoid directing people to them.'

The document was attributed at the end to a Stephan Sidlow of the ARP.

"Did either of you know about these unused tunnels, deep-level tunnels in London?" Faston asked Charles and Caprice. "Built for air raid protection purposes but not sure if they were ever used."

"No," Charles said looking up from his file, "I thought they used every shelter that was at their disposal. Why wouldn't they? They suffered lots of citizen casualties. Seems like they would have used everything available to put a stout roof over people's heads."

"I know, a bit odd that someone would write this diatribe against these deep-level shelters."

"It could have been a political play. Politicians never resist an opportunity to score points by invoking the safety of their constituents." Caprice noted.

"Could have been," Faston agreed while beginning to shape the pamphlet into the one special paper airplane shape he knew, the squared-off stunt style. "But, this pamphlet was written by a man from the ARP."

While wrinkling his nose and scratching his head, Charles offered up his thoughts. "Hmm. That is exactly the group who you would think would be lobbying for such a structure."

Faston, having finished folding the pamphlet into a paper airplane, launched it toward Charles where it fluttered, fell and awkwardly skidded to a halt at his feet. Then he went back and sat down in his chair and dug into another piece of sixty-year old paperwork.

Picking up the topmost document in the pile, a collection of dispatches from the ARP to various suppliers, Faston eased down in his chair and chewed his gum, skimming the letters and glancing up toward the flat-screen tuned to a delayed broadcast of some World Rally Championship broadcast. The sound was turned off, but that didn't dim the wild action as Finns and Frenchmen tossed their machines through the hard-scrabble landscape of Portugal. Despite the dearth of such activity in the United States, Faston had long been a fan of vintage rallying and was a growing fan of the WRC now that the Discovery Channel was carrying the action. One good outcome, Faston thought, of so many Subaru WRX drivers clamoring for the coverage. The indomitable Sebastian Loeb was once again leading the race, his silent, suffering co-driver next to him, head down, reading off the pace notes as the rally car flicked from right to left. Swallowing huge bumps, getting huge air, which caused the crowd to roar, and chattering out of tight corners, rev limiter bleating and tires digging into the hard-packed soil.

"You know, Charles,' Faston spoke while still watching the television, 'Everyone of these rally drivers is an artist. F1 guys are surgeons. But there is real passion in the way they attack these courses. And the partnership and trust they have with their co-drivers is remarkable. Remember when you and I did the Targa Newfoundland?"

"How could I forget?" Charles responded as he picked up and began to examine Faston's paper airplane.

"We did the touring class, finished with the second-most penalties. Got lost. Bent the struts on the TR4 loaned to us by Vintage Racing Services and overall just argued relentlessly."

"Don't forget the cold, too."

"I know, I should have had a heater blower motor added back in to the car. Regardless, passionate artists these guys. That, and the fact Citroen is a powerhouse in the sport, make it worth watching. Agree?"

Faston watched as a car sponsored by the country of Dubai rolled down a hill, flipping at least five times, and then coming to a halt against a tree. The replay included footage from a spectator who caught the action on a small camera as well as the operator's joyous laughter at catching this spill on film. "Charles, you don't agree about Citroen. Come on, they aren't that bad." Faston asked as he noticed Charles had completely unfolded the paper plane and was looking at the back cover.

"Sure, Faston. Citroen. You know, this plane that you made, did you read the author's brief bio?"

"Nope."

"It says that Stephan Sidlow was 'Eastern Counties Liaison and assistant to the ARP Director'."

"So?"

"Come here." Charles asked Faston as he walked over toward the map built in the middle of the room. "You, we all, have noticed that the eastern parts of the map have almost 75 percent of the markings. We've seen that for quite a while. Really obvious."

"No arguing there."

"I'm just saying that maybe we should dig into this fellow Sidlow a bit more. He seems to be criss-crossing our facts more than most."

Caprice had joined Faston and Charles at the table and picked up the pamphlet which Charles had put down on the map.

Faston shrugged his shoulders, popped a third piece of gum into his mouth, and had to agree with Charles. "Sure, why not. If the guy was a bit high up in rank in the ARP, I am sure we can find out more about him."

"Guys," Caprice said a bit louder than usual, "Maybe you should take a really close look at this guy. We have all these SS markings on the maps and documents."

"No idea what those are." Charles noted, "Can't be the SS we usually think of. No German troops made it to Britain."

"No. But Stephan Sidlow. His initials are SS."

Faston felt a surge of energy course through him. He just had that Clouseauean feeling that this was the key to finding the Blower. "First things first. Dig through every scrap of paper in here with the initials SS that are signed or stamped or noted Stephan Sidlow."

And that is exactly what Caprice, Charles and Faston did for the next 13 hours straight. Not eating. Barely drinking. They all felt the energy and opportunity to put away this mystery. Faston felt like he did when racing with a lead. It was, admittedly, a rare feeling. And when leading, Faston never coasted to victory. He tried to extend his lead, to win big. Like the uncompromising athletes who would rather crash out or crumple in their pursuit of a truly great performance.

It was past 2 AM when the trio felt they had finished a vast majority of the search. All blazed through the materials looking for the initials, markings or actual full name of Stephan Sidlow. Forty-three. That was the tally of documents that included some reference to the mysterious Stephan Sidlow.

Walking back to the main house, Faston looked over at Caprice and waited for her to speak.

"Wipe that smile off your face."

"Was I smiling? I hadn't thought so."

"Were you smiling? You positively beam when you get this close to finding a car. Whether it's a $3,000 parts car or a $3 million Voisin."

"What? Are you jealous of the cars?"

"Not really, I see you smile at me the same way. And as long as cars and myself are the only ones who elicit that boyish grin, I'm fine."

"Don't worry. So, you are more the scholar than me. Do you think this Stephan fellow is the character who owned the Bentley? I feel good about it. Just too many records that lead to one man. And Thornley doesn't seem like a chap who would have gone off on some sort of misled prosecution."

"Tell that to the guys whose convictions are overturned every year due to DNA proving the clues and hunches wrong."

With that, Caprice took a little of the wind out of his sails. Made him trim in his expectations and reef his goals for finding the Blower.

26
Newcastle Upon Tyne, April 5, 1941

What was it the Americans said, 'Like shooting fish in a barrel', Stephan puzzled over his morning tea and paper at the Newcastle ARP regional office. Two days ago he had looked at North Shields as a representative of the ARP. Today, he read about it as an enemy of that same organization. But he no longer felt like a lone assassin. He had his birds. And his Blower.

Stephan and his flock had arrived at a rhythm of operation that was ruthless, efficient and most importantly calm. It was a rhythm, a song of destruction that had at its first chords the soft fluttering of wings. Several nights ago, the last night of March, Stephan had spent a few therapeutic hours at his pigeons' stone house. The Bentley's top was down, the air crisp; Stephan had stuffed his hands deep into the pockets of his ARP uniform and waited for the sound of his message carriers.

As always, the birds did not disappoint. Stephan had slowly exited the Blower, not wanting to spook the birds, and walked into their stone home. It never failed to bring a smile to his face, and didn't this last time, when he was able to hold one of the softly cooing birds and unhook the message from its foot. Tucking the proud carrier - they always were unblinkingly proud when they arrived at Penshurst - under his arm, Stephan read the message and tried to take it all in.

The Luftwaffe wanted to make another large raid on North Shields. Stephan had helped coordinate the six-hour attack on April 9th and 10th, when 70 bombers dropped over 5,000 fire bombs on the city. The raiders also tossed down over 250 high-explosive bombs. But the main target to cripple remained elusive as the King George V shipyard still progressed on their projects.

And the citizens still paraded around the town with smiles and energy, revolt and intent.

North Shields and the surrounding areas were known by the British to be tempting targets. That is why Stephan was needed to help the bombers navigate the near-decathlon of obstacles laid in the way of successful bombings. There were the barrage balloons flown at 3,000 feet to deter the lowest level, and most effective, bombing runs. Stephan could always hear the balloons before he saw them. Their tethers shrieking and singing under the strain of wind and loft. The beaches at Tynemouth, Cullercoats and Whitley Bay scared away landings and bathers equally with barbed wire and mines, with a good ration of light anti-aircraft guns sprouting from the tops aimed by skilled operators aided by immense spotlights. This cold breezy part of England seemed colder and harder than ever before. Stephan needed to soften it.

The final bit of defense these North East targets employed were the screen generators, huge, noisy machines that were only started and stoked on moonlit nights. Spewing a cloying and odiferous smoke that stuck to your clothes and permeated the nostrils, these smoke machines were, Stephan knew, a palliative for the people versus an effective defense. Finally, the sirens that warned everyone that an attack was coming were the most potent sensorial assault that helped to engrain wartime experiences of passive and active participants. The pulsating sound struck fear as it warned of approaching enemy planes. The constant tone was the collective exhaled breath, as that tone signaled the all-clear. Sirens, thought Stephan, were the soundtrack of the war. From the stink of new rubber gas masks to the feel of rough-woven uniforms, everyone on both sides was constantly on high alert, well out of their previous comfort zones, with all their nerves buzzing.

And on the night of the 3rd, Stephan had once again gone out of his comfort zone. A zone, that he had to admit to himself, that was growing bigger and bigger. Not too much seemed to fall outside of what felt normal these days and nights. But taking the Blower up to the lapping waters at Seaton Sluice north of the main targets of North Shields was one of those things that had felt out of the ordinary to Stephan.

The coastal defenses, and their defenders, were within viewing distance of Stephan's Bentley when he had parked and turned his headlights into signal lights at 1:40 AM. Getting out of the car, Stephan had walked to the edge of a bushy hillock and scanned the coastline for wardens and patrols that might be walking along. For this process he had used his powerful Hensoldt binoculars. While concentrating on avoiding the foot patrols, Stephan heard the low roar of the approaching aircraft and had to scramble back to the Blower to signal in time.

Stephan had decided to try and damage both morale and machines with the locations he signaled. For the latter, he signaled a prop foundry along the Tyne. For the former, Stephan chose to direct bombs on the Wilkinson Lemonade Factory, as it was one of the largest shelters in the area. And after inspecting it first-hand, Stephan thought the aging factory was poorly suited to being a shelter; he of course had not told the local authorities his feelings.

Musing about almost being caught and wondering what he did with his binoculars, he couldn't find them last night, passed the time but Stephan was soon interrupted.

"What are you thinking about, Sidlow?" one of the older wardens asked Stephan, bringing him out of his contemplative state.

"What's that?"

"Ah, you were just staring out the window. It does get to you, I know, sir." The warden said, pointing to the headline of the newspaper folded across Stephan's knee.

'FUNERALS TODAY FOR WILKINSON DISASTER', read the reporter's line. "Ah, it does weigh heavier some days than others." Stephan lied.

"Three whole families were totally wiped out. The end of the line, so to speak,' the warden pondered, rubbing his craggy, weather-worn face that stood him out as a fisherman in calmer times.

"What was the total of the deaths again?" Stephan asked in his best caring voice.

The warden took a deep breath before answering, "128 killed, 250 wounded. The entire factory collapsed."

"I was there, man, I saw the damage."

"Yes sir, you are never shy to see the hard stuff. Would you like a bit of information that might be hard to take?"

"Sure."

"A patrol on the coast has found a pair of German binoculars lying on the beach. As if they sprung up from the ground. Says a German must be on the ground. Maybe signaling ships."

Stephan could feel his eyes dilate. He stared at the old man and responded, "Not likely. How many bombers fly overhead? Hundreds. I bet the binoculars fell from the sky as opposed to springing up from the sand, eh?"

"You're most likely right. Most likely."

"As you can tell, I didn't get too far into this paper, and you seem to know more news than I. I heard that the prop foundry was hit. Any word on its level of operation?" Stephan asked the man who might have more up-to-date information than the paper carried anyway.

"About 80 percent; they think they will only be a week behind schedule."

Mustering his best stiff upper lip understatement, Stephan answered, "Good news. But the workmen won't be refreshed by any of old Wilkinson's lemonade, though will they?"

"What was that, sir?" The warden puzzled.

Getting up and donning his ARP cap, Stephan walked past the warden, patting him on the shoulder as he spoke, "Nothing chap, bad joke."

Stephan slammed his feet onto the sidewalk as he walked back to where the Blower was parked, punishing himself for his mistake with every step. Avoiding such mistakes was how he was able to be so effective. And damn the Crown, he was going to be effective until the war ended, on his country's terms. Germany's terms.

27
Albany, New York February 2011

Patrick found himself thinking of the international space station. How the Russians, Americans and dozens of other countries spun through space at thousand miles of an hour in equipment built across oceans, and it all clicked to together like a Zippo lighter flicking closed. *Yep*, Patrick thought, *I am a ground-based NASA. A BBRA. A Blower Bentley Recreation Administration.* Standing near the freight dock of his faux company, Drift Boat Services, Patrick looked around at the great living forgery he had created. He was just a couple of months away from debuting his forgery that would cost him in total around $800,000 of his own money. Heck, he had near $20,000 in warehouse and fake boat company props. But, he figured to at least triple his investment. And a nice bonus that you could not put a price on, thought Patrick, was the grief that would come to Faston when he got trumped on one of the biggest automotive finds ever. To the world it would be a find, even though to Patrick's small group it would be a creation. Walking around the warehouse, compulsively checking his phone for tracking updates, Patrick, was soon brought back to Albany from his daydreams of a pouting Faston by the ringing of the freight delivery buzzer.

As the large freight door spooled open with creaks and groans, Patrick couldn't wait to find which of his shipments would arrive first. He had coordinated it so that the motor, the body and the interior would all arrive on the same day. Already in the warehouse were the gearbox, front and rear axles, brakes, wheels, boxes, bins, and plastic bags of other miscellaneous parts that Patrick had acquired under various names and through various means. And if a couple of small parts missing were from the completed car, great! What seventy odd-year-old car has all its parts?

It was this blend of genuine, authentic Bentley parts with his re-creations of the unobtanium bits that had Patrick thinking that this ruse would actually work. One other thing had Patrick convinced that the auto world would believe him. It was the fact that in general, when it came to things people wanted, they wanted to believe you. It was the secret of a thousand cons. Just act natural, state your case, and most people will believe you. The errant person who raises a red flag is usually drowned out by the masses who agree with the con. From reporters making up sources to job applicants making up degrees, this sleight of hand was what made the world go round. And, if the lie delivered on the promise in all but fact, who was hurt?

While arriving last night were the 14 craftsman from India, acquired with the help of Minaz, who would do the final assembly. Flown in for just this task, boarded on the premises, they would be flown back to their homes when the Blower was assembled and running. Patrick couldn't help but think of them as his oompa loompas.

Walking in the door, the freight driver looked for help, "Hey, who is Patrick Patrick, uh that must have been a typo. But I need a Patrick from Drift Boat Services."

"That's me. Custom drift boats for me. Build them right here. No better way to go fly fishing. That's what my friend Faston says. Now, let me sign that."

"Just one box, from Canada. Rather heavy."

"Well, it does say it is from Habitat Plane Company. It's my new planer. It's a stocky machine. Small and heavy. You put boards in and out they come to the desired thickness. The workers love it. Saves a lot of hand time."

"Here you go. It's yours now. Just leave it on the dock?"

"I would prefer…"

The driver interrupted, "I'll leave it on the dock."

Fifteen minutes later the engine created by Claude Le Mevel in the deep, wooded suburbs of Montreal was uncrated. Since Patrick last saw the engine, Claude had done a masterful job of making his new engine look old. There were scratches in the aluminum, stains on the leads, tarnish on the copper and your general wear and tear from wrenching and upkeep on an engine that had supposedly covered at least 50,000 miles and been involved in one wreck of decent impact.

Happily, the engine had been shipped on its stand and dyno combination. While waiting for the rest of the parts to arrive, Patrick thought it a good thing to start up the motor. He followed the same procedure as Claude did in Montreal. Added fresh gas and ignited the 4 ½ litre blower motor. It chuffed to life with sounds and smells that filled the warehouse. The 14 workers all stopped chatting and milling about and came near the engine and huddled over it. Patrick noticed the men exchanging hesitant smiles and nodding in approval. When he gave the motor some more throttle, the men clapped. Patrick kept blipping the hand throttle rigged to the motor until it coughed to a stop. The less than half-gallon of gas he had put into the machine had been used up in minutes.

"Well, it works, men." Patrick announced to the group, knowing that not all of them understood English. "Now, get back to getting ready."

The team of workers went back to organizing tools and plans while Patrick whiled his time away by staring at the engine, checking his phone and pacing the concrete floor.

By the time the freight doorbell buzzed for the second time it was near noon. Patrick's stomach was growling for food, and his mind was growling for a glimpse of the Blower's chassis, body and leather.

When Patrick Patrick raised the door he was hoping to find the mass of shipments that would mean the body had arrived. Instead, there were a half-dozen boxes sitting outside and a FedEx truck already rounding the corner off to its next delivery. It was the interior, Patrick was sure of it. And the South Africa return address confirmed it.

Patrick had been put in touch with some leather bootleggers in South Africa who faked purses and Herman Miller furniture. High-end forgeries. And this was one of the highest-end forgeries ever. Cracking open the heavily stapled boxes, he was soon amidst the heavenly scent of vintage leather. That heady, almost female scent of aged skin was intoxicating. Pulling what he guessed to be the rear trim panel out of the box, Patrick examined the wonderful black hide. The 11 vertical sections of leather had been stitched together wonderfully and puckered at odd areas in truly random pattern. The bottom and top edges of the panel were worn differently. The bottom was heavily scratched. The top was more faded, as it would have been exposed to the elements, even the rare British sunny day. There were some damp stains as well. Patrick could even find a couple of oil stains and one rather large cigarette burn. Brilliant. There was no shine. The filling was plump in spots, sagging in others. The same level of detail held true for the bench seat and the door cards. The carpeting would be non-existent. Patrick had salvaged some old Bentley carpets and was going to use them to have bits of carpet remaining. But the floor boards would remain bare.

Patrick's team unpacked the rest of the interior and laid it out as it would appear in the car. Included in this group was the concealing hood. A piece the craftsmen had created and tagged but left unassembled as final fitting would only be able to be done once the body had been bolted together. The men placed all these pieces behind the engine. So, like a Maisto model car appears when you first take off the box top, the Blower was starting to come to life as a 1 to 1 scale model on the floor of Custom Drift Boats' warehouse.

For the next hour, Patrick sat on the seat that would soon be in the 50th Blower Bentley. The only one not known to the all-knowing Blower Bentley community. He reveled in the comfort and warmth of the patinated leather. The high back on the seat offering enough support. Patrick even entertained the thought of having another one made for a sofa for his home theater. About the same time he realized he would never spend that much money on himself, Patrick heard the shipping door buzzer ring for the third time. *The body!*

"The Body!" Patrick bellowed as he scrambled to the door, his sweat suit billowing, his sneakers squealing on the concrete floor. His excitement elicited not so much as a murmur from his workers, who were still fiddling with their own tools and the remarkable engine.

"The Body!" Patrick repeated to the delivery man as he greeted him and shook his hand up and down as if he was a vintage NASCAR jack man lifting Richard Petty's winged warrior off the tarmac.

"You need to sign here. Twenty-six crates."

"Right man. Twenty-six crates. Perfect. Boys, come help the man." Patrick asked of his men, working on the Bentley parts but hidden from the delivery person by boat props. There was no reaction from the men.

"Oye, guys. Twenty-six crates." This time Patrick waved his arms, beckoning the men toward him in an internationally understood sign.

The men ambled near the door and within twenty minutes had unloaded all the crates from the delivery company's semi-trailer. The largest crate, was for the chassis, the box was nearly fifteen feet in length and almost eight feet wide. Its weight, Patrick thought Bentley might say, was adequate. It took nine of the workers to heft the huge, heavy crate into the warehouse. Patrick, of course, did not touch the crates. He let his workers get sweaty with exertion, even in the chilly Albany air.

The uncrating was a different matter. Patrick had his crowbar and screw gun at the ready and went at the crates like a four-year-old goes after presents under the tree. Attacking, uncrating, inspecting and moving on to the next one. Only when he had finished taking the lid off each of the packages did Patrick go back and start removing the pieces from the crates and laying them out on the warehouse floor.

The first piece that Patrick fully removed was a front wing. Patrick marveled at the light grey paint. Minaz had shown no fear in preparing the car with a cellulose paint. Fully authentic. The builder then took the time to chip and bend the fender to believability. Minaz had even sent a picture of the two fenders strapped to his own car, roaring up and down the dirt and loose tarmac roads near the shop to get an authentic chipping effect. The same was done for all the panels.

Patrick took this fender, it was surprisingly heavy, and walked it over to the left front of the parts heap on the floor. Its proper place. He balanced it so the fender stood upright. This first bit of bodywork flushed him with pride of a job well done. Patrick was self-aware enough to know what he was doing was against the law, but he did take pride in how well he was breaking the law. Any cad could fake an early 911S on a 911T. But it took a real genius to fake something of this magnitude. The next pieces excavated from the robust wood and padded crates were the engine covers. Minaz and his men had done a sterling job of getting the louvers right. Some even bent in a bit on their edge; others were straight. The three latches that held the sides to the frame were beautifully wrought. Patrick even noted a stress crack rendered into one of the tabs, a nice touch that might have occurred on a high-mileage, hard-driven blown Bentley 4½ litre.

To complete the diorama of body parts coming together, Patrick wanted to see the chromed grille. He tip-toed around the scattered wood of open packages and huge crates yet to be opened. Finding the smallest crate, Patrick and one of the workers cracked it open. Tearing away the cotton wadding that encased the snuggly bound grill, Patrick laughed at his own distorted reflection in the curvaceous, bulbous leading edge of his re-creation. Here he was, holding a brand new grille housing that looked exactly eighty-years old. Scratched but buffed, heavily plated but worn at rub points, this was a grille Patrick would have felt comfortable showing at Pebble Beach or Villa d'Este.

Patrick stayed at the warehouse until all the parts for the Bentley were uncrated, unwrapped or otherwise brought into the work area ready to be bolted onto the chassis. He felt as if he was looking at a Hollywood set for a historical film. Every detail was right. The only thing a note off-tune was the accent of the workers. It was the lilting sounds of India, instead of the hearty sounds of the original British workmen that echoed off the floors and walls. Patrick was not bothered at all by this; if they could make a convincing Royal Enfield in

India, making a convincing Blower Bentley was not that far of a leap.

Driving back to his apartment, rented under a different name, Patrick considered the best way to announce his find to the automotive world. A video? A press release? A picture leaked to Octane magazine? All enticing. But whichever option he picked, Patrick made a note to himself to do it in a big way. A way that Faston would be unable to ignore or be ignorant of, even if holed up in his prissy Connecticut bombshell of a house.

28
Litchfield, CT, March 2011

Faston had that peculiar feeling of sitting on the gunwale of history, taking a last few calming breaths before rolling backward into the depths of time. Faston, Charles and Caprice had slept for only a few hours after their research marathon, but all rushed to get back to it. Just the first step into the room where all the materials were laid out had enveloped Faston in the smell of history. That peculiar smell of all deteriorating old things. The group was discovery-drunk. Faston himself was humming with that feeling he knew he shared with explorers who disappeared in the jungle, divers of Spanish Galleons and the first Westerners to drive into the heart of China at the turn of the century.

"This is completely intoxicating, the way all the pieces are falling together." Faston said.

"It is a bit Cusslerian." Charles agreed.

"Yes. Clive Cusslerian." Caprice asked.

"Now." Charles demanded, 'Let's get back to connecting the dots."

Forty-three references to SS, Stephan Sidlow. That is all they had to work with. The references were in pamphlets, notes, scribbled on the back of sepia-stained photographs and even on a tag taped to a pair of binoculars. It was rich pile of leads. Most of it would probably have been more at home in a bric-a-brac shop. But instead, it was here, in the guest room cum 'war-room' of Faston and Caprice's inn. Faston felt like it was an episode of Antiques Roadshow sprung into being.

Looking over the information, Faston began to talk out loud, "What is the most important piece in this room?"

"Who knows, they aren't given a rating." Charles clucked.

"Wish they had one." Faston whispered just loud enough for Charles and Caprice to hear.

"No, they aren't numbered," Caprice began, "but I think it is pretty clear that this huge topographical map that is dominating the middle of this room is the most important piece. Why else build it? It would have been easier to mark up a paper atlas, so why build this unless it was the piece that Thornley spent the most time on. Many people are more visual. They need a real thing to react to. Faston, you remember when you were in advertising? Your clients couldn't buy an idea unless you made it real for them. They didn't think creatively. They couldn't just assemble a few ideas in their heads and roll them around until they became a fully formed idea. You and your fellows have that ability. I bet Thornley built this to better understand his quarry."

"So you're saying we should start with the table?" Charles asked.

"I am saying we start and end with the table. I think it is the hub that we plug all this information into. Before we narrowed it down, the quantity of information kept me from thinking that the table was more than a map on a table. But now that we're down to a more manageable number of pieces, it just feels like the amount of references to SS we have is nearly equal to the amount of markings on this table." Caprice explained as she walked around the table, Faston watching her to see if she latched onto any one bit of the model.

Getting up off the low lounge to take a closer look at the map, Charles joined the group in thinking out loud. "Caprice, that is a solid plan. Better than just flitting about the information. I've one extra thought that I am shocked we haven't considered yet. But I guess that's what a lack of sleep will do to you."

"And what's that?" Faston encouraged Charles.

"That we use our own modern networks and contacts to find out all we can about this Stephan Sidlow.

"Well, your idea, you get on it." Faston smiled, "I'll stay here and work with Caprice. Or maybe I will go get us lunch, the fiddleheads are just coming to market."

Caprice interrupted Faston, "I think we have plenty of snacks to eat here. Let's see; there are three types of popcorn, dark chocolate and cherry granola, pitas and hummus, cornichons and some sort of Italian bread. You'll stay out here with me, Charles, and make some calls or click some keys hunting down Stephan."

Settling down onto one of Faston's precious library chairs, Charles wondered whom first to call about Stephan Sidlow while he nibbled off his plate. Taking one bite for every two that he gave to the dogs, Charles ran through the potential helpers he knew across the globe. Koustas was a natural option to reach out to, but he had another source in the UK he thought he'd try first.

Alberto Zapata was a Mexican national, son of a Cancun real-estate tycoon, educated at UCLA in the fifties, and a specialist in spies. His published works covered the dealings, plots and backgrounds of the shadowy figures from the USA sent to South America in the sixties. But Alberto's second specialty, his minor in life, where he spent his time, was the work done by England to keep counter-intelligence officers out of their country during WWII. Currently, Alberto was a tenured professor at UCSD.

Charles had met Alberto at the Carrera Panamericana. Alberto was participating in the race because, besides being a first-rate historian and researcher, he was also wonderfully rich. And Alberto had a predilection for two types of vehicles. Huge, enormous trucks capable of hauling as many family and friends as possible and split-window Corvettes. He owned eight of them, all race vehicles. His favorite being a low-revving, 429-powered 4-speed model in vintage Sherwin-Williams livery, an absolute beast on the Carrera Panamericana course. Charles was sure that if Alberto spent more time behind the wheel instead of behind his books, he could be a winner of the events he entered. Instead, Alberto was a joyous participant. The slight driver with the heavyweight smile. The man to buy the first round and motivate everyone around him, even his competitors.

Visions of Alberto buying a round, then another round, and another round of tequila for all the first-time finishers of the Carrera Panamerica swirled through Charles's head and stomach as he dialed up his friend. *Could never stomach that Agave-derived poison, even the good stuff,* Charles thought while the phone rang.

"Charles," Alberto enthused into Charles's ear, "so nice to hear from you."

"Well, Alberto, so nice to hear your voice, as well. How are the Corvettes?"

"Healthy, for sure. Healthy infusions of money ensure that."

"Cars are funny like that. And you know what else is funny about cars."

"What?" Alberto played along.

"That they sometimes go missing and that some people want to find them."

"That is odd but not necessarily funny. And it has made quite a name for your friend Faston."

"And that name came into good use years back." Charles teased.

"How is that?"

"Because he was approached with a job to find the last, the only, missing Blower Bentley."

"That is a good use of one's name." Alberto retorted through a laugh that Charles interpreted as disbelief.

"I'm serious. And we have some serious leads. And that is why I am calling you. You better have a pen." Charles said as he tried to settle in, rather than upon, the crisp leather of the Barcelona chair. Unable to get more comfortable on the chair, Charles laid on the floor with the dogs. He propped up his head with a couple of Caprice's gardening books and began to cast his request across the phone line to Alberto.

"First, you might be wondering why I am calling you. You know very little about finding missing cars. Even less about Bentleys. But you do know quite a lot about spies. You know how they operate. You know their backgrounds. You know their motivations."

"You flatter me." Alberto interjected.

"I don't think I am flattering you." Charles stated while petting the dogs and staring up at the mahogany boards that made up the ceiling in the library. "I think I am telling you the truth. Now I am going to give you the Cliffs Notes of the information that we have. And, like Cliffs Notes always do, they will give you a C on a test and, in the more intelligent sort, they will elicit lots of questions. I am counting on you to ask me lots of questions."

"You want me to ask you lots of questions?"

"Yes."

"But why?"

"Because it would be helpful."

"How would it be helpful?"

"I think the questions could crystallize some of your inklings."

"But what if my inklings are wrong?"

"Well, in that…" Charles finally understood that Alberto was putting him on, asking lots of questions, "in that case, you can ask just a few good questions."

Alberto's infectious laugh again crossed a few thousand miles and tickled Charles's ear. "You got it now. Just smart questions."

"You have that pen handy?"

"I do."

"The Cliffs Notes then. The Blower was last heard of in 1939. It was repaired for some crash damage. A British car collector contacted Faston with some rather far-fetched clues. Mainly that a car used by one of the ARP employees had to be a Blower due to the amount of petrol that war records showed that it used. But we did not know the owner of the car. So, we came across a man named Thornley, the aide to the royal head of the ARP. We went to his house. The man was possessed. Lots of records. Lots of stats. Lots of nonsense. After months of plowing through these records like a homesteader breaking Oklahoma sod, we have one potential lead about who owned the car. And this person was also, according to the notes of the late Thornley, a German spy who spent the entire war in Britain."

Laughter was the last response Charles had expected to hear. But that is exactly what Alberto did, letting loose a huge laugh that seemed to come from his toes on up through all five-foot five inches of him and erupt into the phone.

"Alberto, Alberto," Charles tried to talk over Alberto's waves of laughter. "What is so funny? I don't think any of this is very funny."

"You don't? Really, you don't see anything funny in this?"

"I don't."

"I think it is one of the most ludicrous things I have ever heard. A couple of car people have come up with information about an active German spy based in the UK during WWII. Car people are jokingly myopic on their subject. So, to hear a dyed-in-the-wool car man talking about what would be one of the biggest historical discoveries of the past century is pretty funny."

"I'm also a historian, Alberto. It should not be too surprising coming from me. And Faston and I did not find the information; we just stumbled upon the man who found out about this spy." Charles offered, trying to defend his mildly wounded pride.

"That does dull the surprise a little bit. Coming from you was the only reason I didn't fall out of my chair laughing."

"Thanks, Alberto. So what do you think? Any basis to this?"

"Maybe, but tell me a little more about this Thornley," Alberto asked, Charles imagining him rubbing his chin as he constantly did when thinking deeply.

"Not much more to say. He had a blind son who took us through his hoard of information on the mysterious subject. Poor Thornley himself is no longer with us. Son didn't know more about the object of our pursuit than we do. Just glad he didn't sweep all the information into the trash. Faston would have; the man is too neat. In the end, you are about as up to speed as we are. We did the leg work, but now Faston, Caprice and I are passing off one of the batons to you to run with."

"I haven't run in a while. But being part of the team that brings this sort of mystery to a close, to rub in the noses of those know-it-all WWII historians, will have me lacing up."

"Good. Good." Charles smiled and talked while massaging his bare feet into the rug that provided the only splash of color in the room. The pleasure from the feeling, as well as from the knowledge that Faston would despise this act, was his reward for having added a high-energy member to their expeditionary force. 'We don't exactly have a hard timeline to find this car, missing for seventy-one or seventy-two, or seventy-three years. What's the difference? Right?"

"Right. Time just adds a little more dust that we have to blow off. I'll email you my updates as soon as I have anything." Charles was about speak, but Alberto spoke in a softer voice than he had at any previous time in this conversation after a long pause, "I know you are ready to find a car Charles, but are you ready to change history?"

Charles stopped rubbing his feet on the carpet. That electric shock of being on the verge of something big tightened his chest, like jumping into an under-heated swimming pool. It took him a beat to let the fear of history-changing be replaced by the excitement of finding an historic car while making history. "I do think I am ready Alberto. And, here's to sticking it to the know-it-alls." Charles signed off.

"Here's to it, Charles."

"Get off me." Caprice said while hip-checking Faston's attempts to turn their few minutes of alone time in their room into carnal action instead of the needed research. Caprice then gave Faston a kiss, which he knew was meant to soften the blow of rejection.

Surveying the table together, both he and Caprice assumed the position of a beginning billiard player lining up a shot. Two hands on the rail of the table, while lowering their gaze to something about thirty degrees above the map.

"Brass tacks, Caprice, how the hell do we move forward? I'm a people person, not a research person."

"Faston, there is no one right way. Just a few wrong ways that we have to avoid. So, throw something out...."

"Clusters." Faston blurted, then being confronted by a hard-eyed stare from Caprice, he smiled back, "Clusters of markings."

"Good. I see clusters on the east coast."

"Then by Newcastle." Faston narrowed.

"And in London," Caprice tapped the map by the dark ink-ringed area that was London, "But we don't have specifics of his trips within London. Which side of the Thames? Which parts of the city? Which seedy parts?"

"OK, so we discovered three clusters. How about we go to the opposite bit of information. Those yellow dots on the map?" Having previously identified different colored dots as locations of Bentley repair shops, racing facilities and ARP office locations, there were just two yellow dots on the map, two lonely paint splotches. And both were on the far eastern edge of the map, almost in the sea.

"I like the don't bite-off-more-than-you-can-chew approach, Faston." Caprice offered.

"Me, too, especially since it is something that Charles never does. Literally or figuratively. A mouthful of food or an Aegean stable-load of work on his plate is what he is all about."

"Which towns was he trying to identify with these dots? Thornley seems to have gotten the yips and put the dots in the Atlantic, not on the land." Faston thought out loud.

"I doubt he got the yips." Caprice puzzled.

"What makes you think that?"

"Just the perfection of the rest of his notations." Caprice spoke while pointing out the crisp edges of the coastline on the table map. "Do you think a man that would build a near-perfect scale map would then go around sloshing on his notes and thoughts?"

"Eh, probably not. So, could he have meant the ocean?"

"I don't see why not. I don't know all that much about the maritime history of England during WWII, but I think that there was plenty of activity along the coast."

Exhaling audibly, Faston paused, letting his feelings of frustration and the mounting scope of exploration settle. "Ugh, Caprice. We narrow the search in one way, we broaden it in others. Now we have to search out locations off the coast of England. Why? What the hell was our guy Stephan doing out there? Fishing? Broadcasting pirate radio?"

"Settle," Caprice all but whispered, "we'll find the guy, or the car, or both, or none. Does it matter?"

"Yes, it matters," exclaimed Charles, who had come back to the guest room.

Flopping back onto the Alto chair, Faston took the bait. "And why does it matter, Charles? Just another old car."

"It matters because we have been missing the point. We have completely and utterly skimmed over the importance of the search we have been undertaking. To be so ignorant of the bigger picture is really staggering. Even for us." Charles paused, then picked up the pace. "Speaking to Alberto just moments ago was the splash of cold water to the face that woke me up. We are talking about a car. Alberto was using the words 'change history' when I spoke with him. Really, we could be the crew that proves the Germans did have spies in Britain during WWII. So, really, whether we find the car or not, we need to get to the bottom of this. This is fantastic; I've recalibrated expectations and raised my enthusiasm. Are you with me, Faston? Caprice?"

Stunned by the old guy's energy, Faston took a second to gather his thoughts, glance at Caprice for advice in the form of a raised eyebrow and answer Charles' question. "Of course. You're right. I mean, we've been looking at only one positive outcome, finding the car. Now there are two potential positives. Finding the car and finding the truth about Stephan."

"So you're with me?" Charles enthused.

"Yes," Faston replied.

"Unflaggingly," Caprice winked.

A wide-eyed Charles, who looked to Faston to be drunk on outcomes that might never come to fruition beamed, "Awesome."

"But Charles," Faston wanted to temper, not put out the group's enthusiasm, "let's not get too excited or tell any more people about what we are doing. We could be laughing stocks. After all, the information we are going on is from a man we never met. Thornley could have been as convinced of this spy being active in England as a woman suffering from hysterical pregnancy thinks she is carrying a baby. And in both cases it is a pretty big disappointment when the truth comes out. I'd like the four of us to be the only disappointed ones, not the entire academic and automotive communities."

"Party Pooper," was all Charles added before walking around the room a bit and flipping through the paperwork that was lying about like so much historical flotsam and jetsam.

"Charles," Faston huffed, enthusiasm turning to frustration that Charles was not staying focused on the pieces earlier identified as relating to Stephan. "Please. Will you stick to the notes at hand that relate to our guy?"

"No. You two seem to have that covered. I am going to dive into the documents again, with an eye toward finding a spy. Not just a car. Should give me a refreshed perspective."

Faston was going to try once again to convince Charles to stick to the sorted materials, but, quickly concluding that such a conversation would only delay both their work, he stayed silent. For the next few hours, Faston and Caprice searched hardcopies and online sources looking for what was happening off the English coast during the war.

The results they came up with were generally interesting but not, it seemed, specific to their task. Throughout the war, many small engagements took place with German boats. Many were small gun ships and mine-layers. There were no large battleships in the Channel. There was however - and it only came out after the war - an enormous amount of German U-boat activity between and the coast of France. Many submarines coming to view within sight of the coast. Faston thought about the hard men who piloted the leaking submarines in service at that time. Minimal charts keeping their pulse high, and the need to surface often caused tense situations on an almost daily basis. No way could he have served on one of those boats himself, thought Faston. Heck, he got claustrophobic just lying under a car on jack stands, let alone being sealed in a metal coffin where you had to practically live hunched over.

Silenced had settled on the group for over an hour. The only sounds being the slurping of Coca-Cola by Charles and the off-key humming of Caprice as the two of them joined Faston in getting to work. Faston felt it must not be going well, as no one had made any connections or new solutions for how to get their quarry. He was just about to ask everyone to call it quits and go out for a gelato at a new place in Litchfield opened by a graduate of the gelato university in Italy. Americans have McDonald's Hamburger U, and the Europeans have a school dedicated to gelato. That about summed up the differences between continents, Faston considered.

Before Faston could throw out the invite, Charles took off his glasses and posed a question, "What do you use binoculars for?"

"Oh, my god. Seriously?" Faston fumed at the simple question.

"Let me finish, Faston." Charles calmly continued, "In war. In war, what do you use binoculars for? A bit different than bird-watching."

Caprice threw out some options first as to what uses binoculars might be put to in wartime, "Hmm. Spotting troops. Scanning the horizon. Looking for the enemy. Judging distance."

"Impressive," Faston noted. He was never surprised at Caprice's facility in subjects usually considered the purview of males. He couldn't even remember how many times his wife had humbled or corrected men at car shows or auctions who tried to impress her with their knowledge.

"Good thoughts, Caprice," Charles said, giving a slight bow in her direction to show his respect, "and those are all the things that the local paper thought when a set of Hensoldt binoculars were found near North Shields."

"Hensoldt? So, German binoculars," Faston said, walking over and taking the clipping that Charles had been reading.

"The article makes no mention of Stephan," Charles noted. "But they did make the connection between submarines and the potential for spies. The article actually thought 'Nazi sympathizers' were more likely than spies, they could have been looking for boats. Or signaling boats from a location so close to shore. And a location that seems to be awfully close to the off-shore marks on your map."

Faston was feeling both excited and disappointed. They had been making great progress in finding out more about Stephan. More about spies in England. More about WWII history. But not more about the Blower. He surveyed the room and all the clues spread around and wished for a set of binoculars that could look back in time and find out exactly where the Blower was. In lieu of that, a gelato would have to suffice.

29

September 1944, Newcastle

Driving the Blower was one of the few, if not the only, pursuits that gave Stephan any bit of joy these days. And tonight, after his most recent actions, he needed to clear his head with speed, danger and the damp air, all of which had his eyes watering and blood rushing to his face. Digging his hands around the cord-wrapped wheel, Stephan let the effort of driving the Bentley at ten-tenths envelop him. Take over his body. Overwhelm all his senses. Focusing his eyes far down the road, Stephan was able to get into a rhythm after a few miles that allowed him to have an almost out-of-body experience. It was a sensation of watching himself drive, as if he were being chauffeured around by himself. A sensation that allowed him to keep moving physically but slow down mentally.

Stephan was more desperate than ever these days to keep his motivations and actions secret. He was constantly pushing into situations that, years earlier, when the war was turning in Germany's favor, he would not have attempted. Stephan had been forced to become a driving force of his country's final moves, the star player of a wartime endgame. It had come to this after a disastrous eighteen months for the Third Reich, a time when the Russians and Americans had stopped, disrupted and even pushed back troops on all fronts.

Stephan and the Blower were a pair of the rare weapons that had not been made less effective recently. His targeting duties, while waning, were still effective. It was while looking for new ways to aid the cause that he decided to take upon the rather risky task of sending Allied Force offensive plans to his superiors. Using pigeons was still the only method available and riskier than ever due to the dominant British Navy presence in the Channel these days. The receiving submarines made ever fewer, but ever bolder, trips to receive these missives.

Making this new line of work more dangerous was the fact that Stephan had to insert himself into meetings and offices where he was not totally expected. To gain access to these planning meetings and strategy sessions, war rooms and smoky back rooms, he had to begin to lie. "Why would a senior ARP officer need to be in a meeting where invasion plans were being made?" Stephan had to answer that question and many, many others. And his answers were filled with lie after lie. The half-truths, white lies and one-hundred percent fibs piled up as quick and fast as did the miles when the Bentley's blower was at full boost. It was this Aegean stable full of lies that had, Stephan had to admit to himself, almost soiled his perfect cover.

It was only by committing a filthy act that Stephan kept himself clean.

When Stephan awoke this morning, the first thing that came to his mind was the pair of binoculars he had left at North Shields years earlier. That time he had not been found out because of his mistake, but at the time he swore to himself that he would not make another. Or if he did, he would make the mistake go away. He'd sooner kill himself than be caught and pilloried by the English. By the French. By the damn Jews. Not a chance. Never.

Stephan's convictions and monastic commitment to his cause and course of action were tested with the rapping on his apartment door that woke him and caused the memory of his previous error to shock him into consciousness. It was not a quick knock from a deliveryman. It was not the gentle knock of a neighbor looking to borrow a nothing or notion. It was the knock of a person looking to wake the dead. It was a knock that wasn't going to go away.

"Sidlow. Come to the goddamn door," was the rage-filled bellow that accompanied the knock. Stephan recognized it immediately as the voice of the young Captain Hawley. A man who he had spent eight hours with the previous day in an offensive briefing.

Stephan never met rage with rage. He knew the best way to try to diffuse the situation was to act as if there was nothing in the world that could possibly cause Hawley to be so upset. So he tried to greet Hawley with a joke.

"It is a stout oak door, Captain, but it is also over three-hundred years old, so do show it a bit of respect."

"Respect? As if you knew what the word meant." Hawley answered, barely able to make eye contact with Stephan. The man looked to be vibrating with anger. Stephan glanced at Hawley's one remaining hand, which was clenching and unclenching into a tight fist. Stephan had learned yesterday that the man had lost his right arm while parachuting into France. And he lost it of his own accord. Coming down in a tree, Hawley's arm had become irrevocably caught, then with his company leaving him for dead, Hawley had to make a decision; cut off his own arm below the elbow or die stuck in a tree in an apple orchard. He chose the former. The story had been relayed to Stephan with reverential awe by the Captain's own superior.

One arm or two, this was a formidable challenger.

Barging past Stephan, Hawley stormed into the small room, scented of waning fire, that was the one public space in Stephan's lodgings. "Where is it?" was all Hawley asked.

"Let me put the kettle on, then I might be able to help you." Stephan said, turning toward his kitchen, acting as if there was not a care in the world and that Hawley's demands could not possibly involve himself.

"The gall, man. Come back here and listen to me." Hawley demanded, this time in a more gentlemanly, but no less threatening, voice.

"After the kettle is on." Stephan repeated, then took a few beats longer in the kitchen than needed before returning to the public room. "Now, sit down. How can I help you?"

"I'll stand."

"I'll sit. I'm still half asleep." Stephan sat down in his flat-spotted second-hand sofa from circa 1920. Rubbing his eyes with the exaggerated movements of an infant waking from a nap, Stephan motioned with both hands for Hawley to continue.

"The briefing. Get it. Give it. Now." Hawley demanded, while opening the briefcase he had been carrying, and once open, pointing to where he wanted the missing document placed with his half of an arm, the folded-over uniform sleeve taking the place of an accusatory finger.

How the hell did he know he had not returned his copy of the document which detailed several plans to invade Berlin, thought Stephan. The man was tough and smart.

Still standing, Hawley responded to the question that Stephan had only thought, "There were twenty documents for the twenty attendees. You were the least likely attendee there. I don't know whose ass you kissed to even be able to stand in that room, but that is beside the point. I've known all the other men for years. I've barely met you. Simple. Give me the document, I'll write my report of this incident and leave it to the powers that be to take care of the matter as they see fit."

Thinking as fast as he could to come up with a believable answer, Stephan was relieved to hear the kettle steam in the kitchen. Walking to retrieve it would give him a needed minute to solidify his thoughts.

"Enough with the tea, Sidlow. Enough." Hawley frustratingly stated when Stephan left the room.

In the kitchen, Stephan took the kettle off and started clanking about looking for cups and saucers. He didn't want Hawley to think he was stalling. While getting tea together, he stuffed the documents he'd taken beneath a drawer that he then slid back into the cabinetry. Quickly after, he thought that the best course of action to gain additional time would be to push Hawley's attention to someone else who had attended the briefing. But who?

Backing into the sitting room so he could open the door and carry a tea tray, Stephan took one last deep breath and turned to Hawley, with a smile as he set the tray down on the table that stood between the chairs Hawley had seated himself in and the sofa.

Taking a seat on the sofa, Stephan leaned over the table and poured a tea for Hawley. Handing it across the space, Stephan held up the cup, but toward Hawley's disabled side. Looking puzzled and angry, Hawley gave in first with a huffed 'fine' then took the cup, but only after having to shut the briefcase.

"Now that we have a warm cup," Stephan began, "I need to tell you why I was at the meeting."

"Surprise me."

"I was there to find the man you think me to be."

Huffing, Hawley had to wipe the tea that dribbled out of the corner of his mouth, "You've got to be kidding me? On whose authority?"

Relaxing back, rubbing his eyes for effect, Stephan explained to Hawley how he came to be at the meeting. And the good thing about wartime communication that benefited Stephan right now was that withholding information in name of secrecy was seen as an asset, not a liability.

"Hawley, you know I can't tell you on whose authority," here Stephan dragged out the word authority to emphasize its importance in military circles. "If I told you that, you would have a real reason to be livid with me. As of now, we are two men after the same quarry. And right now, you feel like a hunter who has stumbled across a tiger who tells him that they are on the same side and how he will help the hunter go after an elephant."

"Pff, enough with your Kipling. Facts. Who. Where. And you are coming with me."

Hawley had played into Stephan's hand, because he had no intention of letting Hawley out of his sight while until he convinced him one way or another that he did not steal the papers. "Now you just said something I can agree with. I was just about to suggest you accompany me on a little trip to the man who I am sure took the missing papers."

"Really?" Hawley sarcastically drawled, finally able to set down the tea cup and regain some of his regal bearing.

"Really. I was sent there, as I mentioned I can't say who I was sent by, but sent to the meeting to look for precisely the sort of anomaly you stumbled upon."

"Who?" Again Hawley pushed for details.

"I think you will be surprised." Stephan warned, acting superior in every way to Hawley. And right now Stephan felt that he had Hawley believing he knew more, was better connected and of higher rank.

"Major…"

"Major!" Hawley exclaimed, already disbelieving, "there were only two Majors in attendance, and I have known each for going on a decade."

"And that is why I am sure I was tasked with ferreting out the interloper and you were not. What is they say, 'hold your friends close and your enemies closer?'"

"Quite."

"As I said, I was tasked to find this man," Stephan slowly repeated, refilling his cup, "and just as you are now, I was surprised when getting this assignment. All the more so when I tracked the traitor down to Major Clarkson."

"Clarkson! The man has more medals than most. And wounded several times."

"Some look at those accomplishments as reasons to not suspect a man. Another angle is to look at that soldier as a gentleman who is angry about sacrificing so much and still being only a major."

Hawley didn't respond. He just looked coldly at Stephan, who took a moment, then continued to explain why he thought Clarkson was the traitor.

"Really, men have killed over much lesser promotions. There was the clerk at a department store in Leeds who was upset that he was passed over for a move from housewares to menswear. So this is nothing unusual? And a bit of digging on my part into all attendees of the meeting before the get together had me gather some interesting bits about Clarkson."

"Namely."

"Namely that he is near to being broke. And would you say that Clarkson on top of being brave was also a bit of a peacock? Fond of the finest and all that?" Stephan asked Hawley, knowing what the answer would be.

Hawley's eye twitched at the corner, a sign that Stephan took for the stress of starting to believe that his friend Clarkson was responsible for stealing the documents. "Clarkson had a fine estate, always under renovation. And some fine cars, too."

"Cars that he raced. And racing costs a lot of money. He spent a fair amount on his Bugatti Type 57. And his oft-crashed, oft-repaired Riley TT Sprite, a car whose penchant for blowing holes in its block either due to driver error or manufacturing error would have almost anyone's balance sheet bleed red. Then there is the art, the trips, the bespoke uniforms, and the petting zoo. The man has a petting zoo. And his club. Speaking to several employees of his club, it seems that Clarkson is not only a generous buyer of spirits and food and entertainment, he is also a lax payer. His account is in arrears for near to four-thousand pounds. And that is just one example."

"I'd no idea. He just treated me to Bollinger and roast beef at his club a month ago. No idea." Hawley shook his head from side to side and seemed to slump his posture.

Stephan exhaled. The glazed look in Hawley's eyes reminded him of the look that many people shared when they found out a loved one had died during the war. Utter shock, to the point of crying was an understatement of their duress. And the one thing that Stephan knew would make Hawley feel better about having his trust supposedly broken would be to get revenge.

"Hawley, I know where Clarkson is lodging. So how about we go pay him a visit?"

"And where is that?" Hawley asked, perking up a bit.

"About three-quarters of an hour from here. Let me change into my uniform, then let's go confront Clarkson. Was looking with a bit of dread at having to do it myself. So, glad you came along."

"I'd say I came along in a funny way. So let me apologize first, and second, hurry up man. I can't wait to talk to Clarkson."

The apology. That is when Stephan knew that Hawley was completely on his side in believing Clarkson was more likely the spy than himself. Stephan dressed quickly in his ARP blue uniform. And before leaving his room, he tucked a blackjack into his left-side jacket pocket. Thumbing the worn leather to remind himself of its weight, curves and capacity to do damage.

"That was quick, Sidlow. I'm ready." Hawley said, standing near the door, briefcase dangling from his left hand. His right coat sleeve tacked up on itself.

"Agreed." Stephan followed Hawley closely out of the house, only turning to quickly lock his front door. Then, catching up to Hawley in a few steps. Only to direct him toward where the Blower was parked. "My car is right in here," Stephan said stopping by the doors toward his alley-based garage.

"Ah, your Bentley. You have quite the reputation for this car. In fact, might say your car is better known than you."

"Really?"

"One of those things that everyone is amazed you get away with. Driving that petrol-devouring beast. And it is a tad showy."

"I think I've gotten away with it because it isn't just fast transport for me. It's fast transport for my superiors as well. Although they wouldn't be caught dead owning the Blower, they seem to like the fact that I own it. I think after our quick blast out of town, you might be different. You might want to be caught dead in it."

"Let's see."

Five minutes later, Stephan and Hawley were negotiating the tight streets of Newcastle, meandering north, heading for the house in the dark, quiet countryside that Clarkson had set up as his lodgings.

Fingering the dash of the Bentley and in general looking around at the cockpit, Hawley was silent while Stephan got the Blower started and up to temperature, but he finally stated his opinion about it to Stephan. "This is not as lairy a car as the boys think it is. Might even say it is cozy in here."

Stephan laughed, because he had not even used a quarter of the accelerator pedal's travel and no boost. The coachwork and interior fittings had lulled Hawley into a relaxed attitude. He had even slid down in the seat, visibly relaxing. But a smooth downshift from third to second inspired by a clear stretch of road had Hawley quickly bracing himself against the increasing speed as Stephan began to exploit the power of the big four.

Stephan noted that it was Hawley's turn to laugh out loud. "Incredible. Feels like a Spitfire. So much torque. Maybe we should give all the motor pool gals these. Speed up the dispatches some, eh?"

As the speed increased, Stephan needed to concentrate on the road ribboning toward him and the plethora of information on the state of his car being displayed on the myriad gauges. Instead of turning to talk to his passenger, Stephan spoke to the windscreen. "I'd say it would. Some of those gals have said the same thing to me. And they drive like pilots. I think we will see a number of ladies get into motorsport once this business is over with. Once you get a taste for speed, it is hard to go without."

To illustrate his point, Stephan whipped the Blower even harder. As the road cleared of most traffic now that they were twenty minutes from Newcastle, Stephan found it impossible to resist the sensation of the twisting, sliding, bellowing Blower. To put Hawley even more on edge, Stephan had asked him to pull out some of the documents he had brought in the briefcase, and they were now slopping around on Hawley's lap.

"Hawley, what say you and I memorize a few details of one of the other attendees? Take a lesson from our conversation this morning. Instead of coming in blazing accusations, we can come in and ask Clarkson for his help in finding the traitor. You do have some of the CVs from the attendees, right?"

"I do."

"Good. Just pop out the list, and let's run through it, find a lesser known of the group and bone up before grilling Clarkson." Stephan stole a glance over at Hawley who returned his look with a sly smile. Stephan thought that Hawley might even be developing a bit of kinship towards him.

Digging out the document from the briefcase was not easy for Hawley as the Blower roared around bends. Stephan knew that Hawley would be struggling to keep upright in his seat, fumbling with the clasp of the briefcase and trying not to get motion sick while doing so. Stephan just pressed on, passing a dawdling Austin at more than three times its speed and scanned the road ahead. A tight stone bridge provided Stephan with what he was looking for.

Stephan nudged the gearbox into neutral, knowing the speed he had would keep them still at around fifty miles per hour as they crossed the bridge. Reaching across the dash, he tapped one of the instruments, wanting to see if he could get a better reading. But that was a ruse to get close to the door.

Without a right arm to protect himself Hawley was a bouncing, off-kilter prey. Stephan unlatched the door with his left arm, keeping his right on the big, cord-wrapped wheel. Thankful for the straight tracking of the Bentley, because a wandering car would be disastrous at this moment.

Hawley was too shocked and disorganized to re-latch the door before Stephan acted. Leaning up against his own securely latched door, Stephan swung his left leg around and kicked Hawley as hard as he could. The first blow sent Hawley halfway out of the Bentley and the papers and briefcase fully out of the car. Feeling the pavement change beneath the Blower's tires, Stephan knew without having to take his eyes off Hawley that they were now crossing the bridge. One more sharp kick, and Hawley slipped out of the coasting car. His foot tangled for a moment in the narrow footwell of the car as Stephan heard the bone-cracking rasps of Hawley's head meeting the bridge's stone border. One larger bump in the road dislodged Hawley totally from the car.

Reaching back across the cabin, Stephan swept out the rest of the papers swirling in the car and then pulled the passenger door shut with a click. Snicking the lever from neutral to third, he eased his pace and rifled through his mental road maps of the area. He wanted to take the long way home today. One more mess averted. But killing one Englishman at a time was not the way to help his country turn the war. Stephan needed to urge his superiors to use him in a bigger, bolder way.

30
Albany, NY April 1, 2011

It had taken in total almost four years from moment of conception to birth of the Blower. Four expensive, frustrating, tortuous years. Patrick had all but dropped out of the collector car scene as he worked with his global network to create what was sure to be the sensation of the decade, SM 3912. The last Blower not accounted for. *Well, Patrick Patrick laughed to himself, it was accounted for now.*

Walking around the Blower in his rented warehouse, Patrick ran his hand along the long hood. Rubbed the perfectly scratched windscreen frame. Flicked the soft, stained-just-so hood. Opening the door he inhaled deeply and relished the remarkable sensation of smelling something old that he knew to be brand new. A combination of genuinely old Bentley interior padding and time spent with a French perfumer in creation of an 'old car scent' had created a fully sensorial experience. The Blower seemed like the genuine article in every respect. Even a peek underneath reminded Patrick of the lengths the team went in creating the car. A crease in the rear chassis replicated the supposed accident damage. And a generous amount of time with slingshot and stone had readied the rest of the undercarriage for close inspection by the most educated experts.

Patrick slid across the seat of the Bentley, his track suit gliding across the creased and aged leather, knowing that at this very moment the world would be learning SM 3912's story. A story he had worked on creating with the president of the auction company who would be handling the sale of this creation. RM. Gooding. Coys. All of the big players in the collector car world were established and Patrick thought, would lack enthusiasm for his project. Faston dealt with the big three of the classic car world. Faston felt comfortable with them. They always seemed to give Patrick the cold shoulder. Somehow, every year, his invitations for cocktail parties went missing. What Patrick knew he needed was an underdog who wanted to be top dog. And in the auction world there were a couple of choices.

There was Vintage Iron the American upstart. While across the ocean there was the three-year old company Pneu. Patrick hired a private investigator to look into the companies and the owners of the companies to see if there was one or the other that leaned towards being less truthful in any respect. The investigator told Patrick that both companies seemed on the up and up until he started looking at Vincent Fornel, the president of Pneu. A little tax evasion so he could afford a country home. A little trouble at University trying to cheat his way to the top of the class. A whole lot of marital infidelity with women prettier than his wealthy wife. The investigator conducted a few interviews with people who knew Vincent and concluded that here was a man who would do anything to get ahead. And that was the type of man Patrick wanted.

Patrick flew to Paris and met with Vincent almost a year ago to the day. Patrick brought along photographs and video of the various pieces of the Blower, which at the time were peppered across various parts of the globe. Patrick had gone into that meeting knowing that besides being a bit of a cheat, Vincent was also quite a showman. A brash upstart who believed any attention to his company was good attention. Pneu had launched with a decidedly un-auction like pricing structure that included no sellers premiums, a practice that got him lots of top flight cars all the while infuriating his competition. While his marketing prowess came in a form Colin Powell referred to as shock and awe. From a "Channel Crossing" auction in which Pneu sold 17 cars in the quick ferry-ride from France to England to hiring Elton John to play at another auction, Vincent was causing a stir in the staid auction industry.

The one downside to his behavior was that it put off some of the blue-blood buyers and sellers. Many of those people would rather hold onto to their cars than have Pneu sell them. And that was Patrick Patrick's way in. Besides bringing in a windfall from buyer's premiums, there was no way the Bentley collectors would be able to shun bidding on SM 3912 just because it was being flogged by Pneu. So Patrick was bringing Vincent and Pneu apparent respectability as well as profitability.

And that is exactly what Patrick had laid out over a lunch of pea soup, grilled shrimp and white wine. Vincent had come to the meeting having done his homework on Patrick Patrick as well. A fact Vincent laid out right after sitting down. Patrick gripped the cord-wrapped wheel of the replica Blower and felt a smirk tighten one corner of his mouth. It had taken all of two minutes for the two men to feel comfortable enough with each other. Comfortable enough for Patrick to tell Vincent he had created a perfect replica of the only missing Blower. And comfortable enough for Vincent to enthusiastically say he would sell it. And switch their white wine for a bottle of champagne. Then another bottle of champagne as he and Vincent had sat and talked for hours about how to announce the sale of the Blower.

Ideas that he and Vincent had kicked around at the hangover-producing lunch included having a special one-car auction near the Bentley factory, creating an auction and orchestra at the Paris Opera house or even getting the word out by placing the car on Wheeler Dealer's as a car to repair or Chasing Classic Cars as a car Wayne could find in Connecticut. But in the end, the two decided to sell the Bentley in a way that would give the classic car world the biggest one-finger salute. They would sell it at Monaco. They would sell it from the remarkable Espace Fontvieille space overlooking the harbor. And they would sell it with no reserve. Patrick whooped out loud from inside the Blower and pounded his fist on the seat he was so excited about pulling off the biggest con in ages. This was as big as the Black Sox. As big as the JFK heist. As great as the great train robbery.

The most important part of working with Vincent was crafting a believable story of how the Blower was found. This, Patrick soon found, was as hard creating the replica in the first place. The story had to be just as bullet-proof, authentic and carefully crafted as the replica itself. With that in mind, he and Vincent quickly came to the idea that the best, most believable story would be one of the most obvious. And that would be that SM 3912 had been tucked into a garage during the war and forgotten about. Simple. Believable. The only hard part of this story was whose garage it had been in all this time. They needed a real person. Not an actor.

The search for this final partner in Patrick's classic car cabal took five months to find. Eccentric, minorly royal and all around crazy, Sir Torance Borland fit the bill. He was reclusive. He was cash poor. He was nearing 100. And he had all but holed up in his sprawling holdings after being shell-shocked as a Captain during the war. He hadn't let anyone on his estate to catalog his houses, art or other property. Ever. All of that was good. But the real score was in learning of Sir Borland's epic hatred of people who tried to fool him out of property he knew was worth much more than he was asking. "The gilded-tongue gypsy pickers" was how Borland had referred to any antiquarian who approached him wishing to review his possessions in a rare newspaper interview.

So when Patrick and Vincent approached Sir Borland, in itself a hazardous intercept while the old squire was walking his property, he quickly agreed to hear more. Once inside the main home on Sir Borland's property the negotiations had gone quickly. Patrick recalled almost every word of the brief but fruitful conversation.

"You want me to say I've had this Bentley parked up for decades?" Sir Borland had clarified.

"Right. And for that, you will get five percent of the sales price." Patrick and team had settled on five percent as a generous offer for Sir Borland's rare gift to the project.

"And all the men from Coys and collectors from Carmel will think the car is real?"

"Of course."

"Then you have an owner of the car to put in the catalog." With that, Sir Borland had pushed up out of his chair and using his cane as a shepherd would his crook, he had guided Patrick and Vincent out of the house. He may have been game to join the sale of the replica, but Sir Borland was not about to let Patrick see all his possessions.

His phone erupting with contacts, calls and text messages brought Patrick back to Albany and the present. He scooted out of the replica and paced around the now all but empty and antiseptically clean warehouse. And because it was April Fools Day, as he scrolled through the texts the same question, "Is this real?" kept being asked. With a reply to all, Patrick simply answered, 'Real. Details at Pneu.fr".

As the hours passed, friends, customers and most important of all the media were now simultaneously trying to be among the first to talk with the man who had found the Bentley. Although he didn't get a text or call from Faston, Patrick knew that he had to have heard about the Blower. And that thought was the second best one that kept coursing through his mind right now. The first was how much money and fame he would be getting come the Monaco Grand Prix week at the Pneu auction.

31
Litchfield, CT April 2, 2011

Aron Stores, the man who put Faston on the hunt for the Blower was not the first, but it was the only call that Faston had the stomach to take after finding out about Patrick announcing the auction for the Blower in less than two months time.

Aron's tone was good-natured but pressing. "Faston, I guess I should have contracted your competitor."

Faston could feel his cheeks getting red and his mind racing about how Patrick had beaten him to the Blower. "I guess so. I hope you can accept my apology regarding spending so much time and money trying to find the car and coming up empty."

"So, you're sure that Patrick has found the car? That it is not an April Fool's joke?"

"I think so."

"That sounds a bit defeated."

"We, Charles and I, were talking, we're confident that we were getting somewhere. But nowhere in our work did we find a mention of this Sir Borland. Or even come across a remnant of time that would have shown how the Blower would have crossed paths with him. For the last few hours it is all we can think about. We can't stop asking ourselves, 'how did we go so wrong?'"

"Maybe you didn't."

Faston couldn't tell if Aron was playing the benevolent coach or what. He should just throw in the towel. At least that was what he and Charles were going to do. They were going to pack up all the records, ship them back to Thornley and get on with the rest of their lives. But Aron's questions did stir that one percent of

Faston that felt there was no way that Patrick could have plucked SM 3912 out of thin air.

"Aron. I love your confidence. And to be truthful, there is a small, tiny part of me that thinks something is fishy here."

"Then throw a line in the water and find out for sure. When's the auction again?"

"The end of May."

"This project has a timeline finally. Seven more weeks. I can spring for that to have total peace of mind. Think you can put in the time chasing every Red Herring and loose string?"

Faston took a deep breath trying to pump up his waning energy for the project physically and mentally. "Seven weeks. I think I can do that." Covering the mouthpiece of the phone with his hand Faston yelled to Caprice and Charles who were sulking in other parts of the house, "Think you two are good for a few more weeks? Until the auction?"

Hearing a positive grunt from Charles and a committed 'yes' from Caprice, Faston answered Aron. "The team is in Aron."

"I was never a man to follow false prophets. Good luck." Aron signed off.

If they only had approximately seven more weeks to find out if the Patrick Blower was the genuine article or not, the team had to get moving. Faston called a meeting, "Everyone to the kitchen, I'm hungry and angry."

When Faston and Caprice arrived in the kitchen Faston had already set out a Baltimore Bracer cocktail on the table. Faston had been on an egg-white drink kick for a couple of months now. And this bracer was one of his favorites. Applejack, Pernod and vermouth shaken with an egg white. All of these flips had a silky smooth mouth feel that Faston loved and his friends tolerated.

Besides, Faston thought, if at any time he needed a drink called a bracer it was now. Something designed to steel the nerves.

To compliment the bracers they were sipping, Faston was quickly blending an asparagus and shrimp spread with leftovers of each. Chopping each ingredient finely, Faston tossed them with olive oil, crème fraiche and salt and pimenton. For crackers, Faston eschewed all the fancy ones available at Trent's gourmet store for a guilty pleasure. Ritz. Sometimes buttery comfort food was where it was at.

Placing the bowl of spread and the box of Ritz on the counter, Faston leaned across the table and raised his glass in a toast. "Here's to seven more weeks trying to solve a seventy-year old mystery."

"Cheers."

"I hope we catch the bastard in some fakery. Otherwise I won't ever be able to be in the same room as him again." Charles bemoaned.

"You bring up a good point. The only option to having actually found the Blower was to have created a replica of it. Right?"

"Right." Charles concurred.

Caprice just raised her glass in silent salute and took another sip of her bracer.

"But the car could not be the only thing fake. The story. The ownership history. Everything that went along with the car would need to be fake."

Charles downed the last of his bracer with a scowl and spoke while working a Ritz deep into the bowl. "There have been some pretty spectacular fakes made of cars. Really sensational stuff. Especially race cars. What with the FIA passport debacle and all trying to prevent them. That leaves us two ways. We either find the real car. Or prove that the one Patrick has is a fake."

"I want to find the car more." Faston gritted. "I really don't want to go to Patrick Patrick and get into a pissing match about whether his car is real or not. That will turn out badly. What I want to do is find the car. Go on a blitz regarding any info we have. Then I will be able to sleep knowing we did our best. And did it in a way that kept the higher moral ground."

"You could send someone else to check out the Patrick Patrick Blower." Caprice suggested.

"Now, that is an idea."

"We could send Peter." Charles suggested while grabbing a Batch 19 lager out of the fridge.

"Hey hand me one of those." Faston demanded. He was thrilled that Batch 19 was now available in Connecticut. After tasting this beer on tap in San Francisco over a year ago he couldn't stop thinking about it. Besides the hoppy, malty taste, Faston loved the story of how it was a beer brewed from an old recipe found in the Coors brewery from before prohibition. A lost beer for a finder of lost cars.

While taking deep sips of his beer, Faston swirled around the idea of somehow getting Peter to view the Blower Patrick supposedly discovered. Peter was the author of two books on Bentley history and had been the Bentley judge at Pebble Beach and dozens of other international concours events. He could be counted on to be impartial and precise.

Faston scrolled down to Peter's number in his phone and rang him up. Peter picked up on the third ring. "Peter, this is Faston."

"Faston," Peter answered warmly, "how are you? Last time we met it was at the Mitty."

"Ugh, another of my less than stellar driving outings." Faston replied, remembering how he was off the pace by at least six seconds in his Bugeye.

"What makes you call today?"

"I am sure you heard, that Patrick is going to be auctioning off SM 3912. The fiftieth blower."

"The only one we didn't know about until now." Peter interrupted Faston, "And get this."

"What?"

"I got an invite to test drive it."

Faston couldn't believe it. Patrick had by himself reached out to the premier vetter of Bentleys. "That is incredible. It is why I was calling you in the first place. Because me, Caprice and Charles have been tracking down that very car for the past year."

"You're kidding." Peter sounded to Faston genuinely surprised.

"No. I am not."

"Find anything?"

"Just enough to keep us digging deeper into the past. We have some pictures. Some leads. But none of them led us anywhere near Sir Borland. Not even close. So we have a pretty odd feeling about Patrick's car."

"Well, I've seen twenty or so of the other Blower Bentleys in existence, so I think I will be able to tell the real from a fake."

"I hope. But this one is different isn't it? With its Phillips coachwork, if that indeed is still what sits on the chassis. Rather different than the usual open leather four-place seating."

"That is true. But I have judged a couple of Isotta-Fraschitti by Phillips. So, I feel pretty confident about the details of that coachbuilder."

Faston had just one more question for Peter, "So when are you going to look at the car?"

"April 11th. So a little over a week."

"Well, be sure I am your first," Faston emphasized the word first all but begging to switch places with Peter, "call when you have inspected it and given it the thumbs up or thumbs down regarding the legitimacy of its birth."

"Will do, Faston."

While Faston had been talking with Peter, Charles had received a call from someone that he was in an animated conversation with. After eavesdropping for a few minutes, Faston realized he was chatting with Alberto. Faston didn't like eavesdropping, besides he was too anxious to await Charles' download of Alberto's findings, so he asked Charles to place him on speaker.

"Al, we're on speaker," Charles yelled louder than necessary, "Faston wanted to listen in. OK. And Caprice just walked in too. The whole team is here."

"Hey, everyone." Al began. "So, this Stephan Sidlow has a thin trail. Just a weak dotted line back in time across a couple of different personas and lives. Not one constant thread. Quite a unique pastiche of people."

"And Al was telling me," Charles said while turning towards Caprice and Faston, "that one of these lives was spent in Germany. Before the war."

"Yes," Al jumped back into the conversation. His pace and excitement crackling over the cell phones tiny speaker, "And his name at that time was not Stephan Sidlow. It was Franz Kohl, son of the baron of Saxony. He was one of the earliest to join up with the Nazi party, when he was not even a teenager."

"That's promising."

"Promising for sure. Plus, something fascinating is that he had a hoard of English tutors and did his secondary schooling in England."

"So, how did you find out about Stephan, nee Franz?" Faston asked.

"Because of the rather large, showy funeral held for Franz Kohl." Al answered, his tone leading Faston to ask a simple question.

"So?"

"So? There was no body. This was in 1933. While Franz, was here at school."

"Franz supposedly dies." Faston spoke out loud, trying to work out the puzzle of information that Alberto was laying out in front of them. "But he is enrolled at school here, so it would seem obvious that Franz Kohl was not dead."

"It would, except that he was enrolled as Stephan Sidlow. And this Stephan Sidlow never returned to Germany, as you know, he became quite a high-ranking, well-connected man in the ARP."

"How did that happen? Tough for an outsider to rise up at that time in England." Caprice asked Alberto.

"Good question, Caprice. Don't know exactly, but he did get chummy with some of Sir John Anderson's family at school, so imagine he got the foot up from that."

"How did you find all this out, Al? I mean, you would think that a person with these connections, no matter how loose, would have been discovered by historians before now."

Al, paused for a moment before answering, "I would like to think historians would have, but a small name is small potatoes. Sure, all these events seem promising but there was never the first moment that would overcome the inertia to look into a somewhat odd funeral from a German lord. And you were the people who put the object in motion, so to speak."

"And I got some help in making the connection between Franz and Stephan being the same person from a colleague at Dresden. He was one of several German scholars I reached out to. His specialty is tracking down missing soldiers. So, it was a stroke of luck that Franz Kohl was on his list, because although listed as dead, there were records of communications, letters to his parents. Letters that when he looked into them had the content one would expect of a son. The letters were written over a couple year period but stopped in late 1938."

"And these letters were written by Franz?" Caprice asked the question that Faston was just about to ask himself.

"No. They were signed with a set of initials. S.S."

Slapping the table, Faston knew they were closer to tracking down where the owner of the Blower was spending his time in England. "Where were the letters from?"

"They were postmarked Newcastle."

Faston, Charles and Caprice all looked at each other smiling. Faston could tell that Caprice and Charles were both twitching with the prospect of finding out what happened to the Blower they had been tracking. Not the Blower that Patrick had pulled out of a hat.

"Newcastle then." Faston stated. Caprice and Charles nodded in agreement. Al wished them luck from over the phone and told Faston he would be emailing along transcripts of the SS signed letters in case they provided any information they might need.

32
Newcastle, October 1944

Despite not wanting to. Despite trying to avoid it. Despite his best intentions, Stephan had formed a few close relationships. Relationships first formed to help cover his intentions. No quicker way to get undue attention than to be viewed as a loner in the community. Nothing so prying as neighbors or coworkers who wish to find out what a person they encounter daily is all about. And even worse, if they didn't know the truth they often made up their own fantasies about a person and spread them around as gospel. No, better to have some people you could call friends.

This task of acquiring some close bonds was one undertaken with false beginnings but now there were two people that Stephan truly enjoyed the company of. If they were Germans, they would have been some of his closet friends. But as it was, Stephan felt a bit like a farmer's child who formed a close bond with a new calf, knowing that someday they would have to kill it. Or at the very least, acknowledge that it had been killed.

All these colliding emotions were smashing into the back of Stephan's eyes as he looked across the table at his neighbor Ms. Hennepin and her boarder Colin Gardner as they chatted about the state of dress of most citizens in England, the poor state of reportage and which personal possession would be the hardest to lose in a bombing. This sort of banal talk was what dominated at the table of Ms. Hennepin. And ever since the retired theatre director had been forced to let a room from her over two years the wide-ranging conversations stretched from Euripides to recipes for turnips. Rarely did it stretch to the war. But when the conversation did touch upon the war, like it did tonight, it was always on a philosophical level. When nationalistic prejudices were removed from the conversation, Stephan thought the war was actually a challenging, vibrant topic.

"It is completely crazy to think that one type of culture can gain control over a population that has evolved a rich culture of their own over the course of thousands of years." Colin was talking while waving his butter knife around like a conductor. "Think about it. Changing how one talks, what one eats, is at the core of a person's belief. You can only tolerate it for so long."

"But the ruling government would only have to make it through a rough first few years. Removing the troublemakers. Eradicating the history. Slowing the birth rates and killing off the old people who would be most knowledgeable and passionate about losing touch with a culture." Ms. Hennepin responded. "What does a three-year-old know about rules and right from wrong? In short order, the schools could have the children working to convert the parents to a new way of thinking. Stephan, what's your take? Possible to change a country's way of thinking?"

Pouring himself a second cup of tea brewed for a third time, Stephan joined the conversation at Ms. Hennepin's urging. He relished this sharp exchange with his neighbors. "I think it is hard to wipe clean a population. The test I believe will be in the recovery. If the subjugated are making money, if the elites of that country become the elites of the new country, I think there is a good chance. But if you remove all the top people and replace them with foreigners, the shock would be too great. And nothing will help if the people are starving."

"Let them eat cake won't fly this time around." Colin quipped.

"I don't think that it flew last time." Ms. Hennepin laughed. "But the idea is right. I think that the new ruling party would need to be partial to helping the masses first and themselves later. If the leaders sit back and smoke cigars…"

"Like Churchill?" Stephan couldn't help himself.

"Oh, he just doesn't smoke cigars." Colin noted, "he drinks like a hound after the hunt."

"I miss cheap, plentiful liquor." Ms. Hennepin whined.

All three dinner guests exchanged a knowing smile at that and went back to savoring the apple tart that Ms. Hennepin had been able to make with fresh apples and rationed butter. Stephan finished his slice of tart with ever smaller bites, trying to make the treat last. In his mind, the world swirled and looped around the dinner table at Ms. Hennepin's home when he was there. The respite was complete but always short-lived. Just like it was tonight.

"I want to put on some Puccini?" Colin winked, getting up from the table and placing the worn record on the phonograph.

"Ugh." Stephan groaned. "No more Puccini. We need to find a new record for you. But, that is not the reason I'm leaving. I've got work to do."

"Do it tomorrow." Colin chirped.

"I will. But I have to get to where the work is tonight."

"Drive safe. I know you won't drive slow." Ms. Hennepin suggested as she brought over another slice of pie wrapped in some reused paper from the grocery for Stephan. Sliding it into his uniform coat pocket, Ms. Hennepin gave Stephan a quick hug and turned back towards the living room and the toe-tapping Colin.

"As always," Stephan said while doffing his cap, "it has been an enormous pleasure. Now, out into the real world."

"Nothing is real for long anymore, Stephan. Nothing. Not me. Not Ms. Hennepin. Not even you." Colin yelled over the Puccini. "Once it has passed by your sight, it is inconsequential."

Stephan pulled the door shut behind himself and tried to take Colin's observation at face value. He began the process of forgetting about them being real friends. Forgetting about them being real people. Forgetting that they were really quite alike except for where on the globe they were born. He went through this process in order to carry out his job. And with his job in mind, Stephan slipped into the Bentley and began winding his way towards tonight's destination. Penshurst's grounds and the birds he used to send his communiqués.

Stephan had for some months been thinking about how he could help win the war for Germany. How one man could help to break the ridiculously tempered resolve of the British people. Punching the gear selector from third to second and back again along the country roads brought the boxing analogy to mind. As a boxer himself at university, Stephan had learned that the best way to break someone's will is to first let them think they have the better of you. Let them think that you are tired and about to go down with their next punch when in reality you are weathering a mild storm and ready to strike back.

Germany, Stephan's Germany, had been weathering more than a mild storm. The allies had been gaining ground and victories at an alarming rate recently. Only the Japanese had proven able to cut down huge swaths of soldiers in the recent months. From what he read, received in communications and distilled himself, Stephan knew that despite official German broadcasts, times were getting desperate.

So if Germany was really down, Stephan thought, what it needed was a powerful right cross. That loaded knockout punch from the arm of a fighter that had until the moment it was released just dangled impotently at his side. As luck and the fortunes of war would have it, Germany had just such an undeployed weapon under production and rapidly being stockpiled. And Stephan knew that Hitler had been under duress to find the best way to deploy his newest most fear-igniting weapon.

That was the whole point of leaving behind his old friends tonight, winding his way deep into the English countryside, and getting in touch with his countrymen. Stephan had, like the seemingly beaten boxer, figured out a way to counterpunch.

Ever since he heard of the Vergeltungswaffe program over two years ago, Stephan would often return to thinking of how to use it to end the war whenever he had a moment's peace. The V2 rockets were monsters at 46 feet long and weighing in at 27,000 pounds fully loaded with fuel and a 2,000 pound warhead. The sound they made when flying was like that of the Valkyrie.

Stephan had even marveled at the technological specs of the V2. Graphite vanes in the engine. Motor-controlled vanes on the outside of the weapon. An accelerometer that controlled engine cutoff to determine the distance of the weapon. And they reached a height of fifty miles in the air before plunging rapidly into the target zone. It was beautiful to Stephan.

Add to that the plans to possibly launch these weapons from U-boats and Stephan envisioned a weapon that could reach the United States. And to the feedback he had heard that how much damage can 1-ton of explosives do, Stephan wanted to implore the Fuhrer to look into enabling the V2 to carry sarin, tabun or some of the other biological weapons that Germany was creating.

It was a deadly weapon both in actuality and in its effect on the psyche. And it was the later that Stephan was convinced could win the war for Germany against England. Stephan knew if they could terrorize the English with these long-range bombs in a big enough concentration, they could have a chance to negotiate a treaty with the English. Stephan knew they couldn't build the V2s fast enough to make so many that they could destroy England. But they could build enough that they could fool the British into thinking that Germany had an unlimited quiver of these deadly devices. And it was this message that Stephan wanted to get to his superiors.

The grounds of Penshurst were upon Stephan after a drive that seemed to be completed without him. His mind was on the message. Slowing the Blower, Stephan pulled off the tarmacadam and wended his way through the trees and ruts that led to the roost. Careful not to high-spot the Bentley on a deep rut or scratch a fender on the dense forest components.

Shutting down the Bentley was simpler than starting, and a twist of the ignition had the low compression four bump to a stop. Stephan increasingly loved the solitude of being with his birds. He was able to pretend he was in his own country, surrounded by his countrymen. Not, as was the case, a lump in the pudding that was Britain. His pigeons were his countrymen.

Before attaching his message to his chosen carrier, Stephan tended to his flyers. Sweeping away the hay at the bottom. Spreading some new hay he had stockpiled months earlier. Feeding them. Watering them from the nearby stream. Stephan inspected a few of the couple dozen birds he still cared for. Checking their feathers. Looking for signs of petulance or injury. All the big-chested birds were healthy. Strutting and cooing about the beams and perches, they looked like toy soldiers. Waiting for their captain to lead them into battle.

But only one bird could go. Stephan thought of the bird that got to deliver his message as a lucky one. The messenger trusted with delivering instructions. The war messenger was a noble, ancient battle participant. One that could feel the weight of his duties as he trudged or drove or flew through night and day. Through enemy and friendly territory. Through tiredness and hunger. The messenger was the link. With the advent of radio, Stephan felt the job of the messenger was going away. This was a shame because the radio could deliver words. But it could never deliver the face of a situation. Deliver the hard to swallow fact that men were in the field dying.

Before folding the message into a size small enough to fit into the metal tube clipped to the bird's leg, Stephan read it one more time.

I hear the newest fashions are all the rage. That some people many counties over are reacting to what happens in your neighborhood. Remarkable! What with all the rationing going on. I should like you to wear your best and brightest. And bring me something to wear as well a few Fridays next. I should think a trip to the Woolworth's on New Cross Road would be in order.

Stephan never threw the birds into the air once he clipped on his message. He always let them rest on his forearm until they left of their own accord. It was what he would want his superior's to do, to trust him enough to act once given an objective. And he was sure this present decision to implore a new more dominating; more civilians crushing approach was the right one.

Returning to the Bentley, Stephan fired it and retraced his route back to his apartment. When he arrived back at his house, Stephan uncurled his hands from the steering wheel. The cording had reddened his palms. His knuckles were raw and cramped. Stephan rubbed his hands on the leather of the seat to soothe them and get the blood flowing again. His mind was free and easy, but his body was reacting to the stress that he never let enter his thoughts. He'd been here too long. Away from his home for too long.

33
Albany, NY May 22, 2011

Patrick Patrick had stopped thinking of his replica of SM 3912 as a replica. Every time he thought of the car now that it was complete, he thought of it as a the real deal. In his mind, this Bentley was built in England over seventy years ago. Not assembled by a global network of shady automotive profiteers. The best liars were the ones who believed their lies. And Patrick fit that bill. He believed the car was real, and he would portray that emotion and feeling to all who asked.

The car was, Patrick was sure, faultless. But today would be the day that proved that. Today was the day everyone in the collector car world would soon hear about the missing Blower. For the event, Patrick had rented out the parking lot of the NFL Bills' stadium. He needed a suitably grand expanse of tarmac to run the Bentley out on. And it was here in a tent, with no Bentley in sight, that Patrick wandered around glad-handing the most famous names in automotive writing, history and one very special racer who all in attendance would meet later.

Patrick surveyed the crowd, noticed a large knot of people gathered around the barista he hired to make lattes, espressos and mochas for everyone, and headed in that direction to get the pulse of the audience.

"Hey man!" Patrick boomed, clapping the first person he came upon on the back. It was a representative from the German magazine *Auto und Sport*. "I wish we had the autobahn here to let loose the Blower. She runs out like a freight train."

The writer nodded, took a sip of his coffee and answered. "It would be good to at least see the car." Patrick noted a bit of suspicion in the man's tone.

"In due time. In due time." Patrick repeated while repeatedly clapping the man on his shoulder. "The Blower is here. Now, eat some of these bagels and lox. Or get a waffle made. You can get any topping you want. They even have Nutella. Kid you not, man. Nutella."

"Nutella is what my kids eat." The man deadpanned.

"Hey, then be a kid for once." Patrick encouraged and further walked around the room. Scanning the space he saw that the room was somber despite the massive amounts of food, coffee and money Patrick had spent on flying everyone in first class and putting them up at the Morgan State House Inn.

While walking over to talk to the editor of *Octane*, someone tapped Patrick on the arm. Turning, he noticed it was Grant Mura, former editor of several classic car magazines and currently head of the Bentley museum.

"A bit bold even for you, Patrick," Grant paused a while, "Patrick. Ey? A Blower. This has to be seen. I've been talking to a lot of the people here. And there is quite a current of skepticism coursing through this room."

"Hey, man. I wouldn't believe me either if I were you. But, you will. Crazy story and all. That Sir Borland character was hoot. Hoot!"

"I've heard he was, as you say, a hoot." Grant nodded. "But the natives are getting restless. Isn't it about time that you showed us all the prize?"

"I think we are getting close. If I were you, I would get a spot over by that side of the tent. It will be the best seat in the house in a few minutes."

After another few minutes of hand-shaking and introductions. After a couple of more tiny bagels with lox on them. And after a final trip to the bathroom,

Patrick took up his position along with a few helpers along the north side of the tent.

Patrick noticed the crowd quiet as a few of younger in attendance who had not yet spent a lifetime damaging their ears by riding in powerful cars heard the slightest rumble. The shushing flew across the room. Patrick Patrick noticed that the doubt most attendees had been emoting had been replaced by hope. Because, as Patrick knew, they all wanted the last Blower to be found. They all wanted it to be real. Because, as true car aficionados, it was a better story for it to be real than to be a fake.

At Patrick's signal he and the few event helpers rolled up the north side of the tent. The crisp wind whisked any last cobwebs out of the crowd. The crowd pressed forward like a rush hour mob trying to get on the express train. The subtle thrum that only a few could hear before was replaced by a growing whine that could be heard by all in attendance. Howling like only the big blown four could SM 3912 went blasting by the open side of the tent. The wind it moved shaking the tent more than nature had.

Patrick had a stoic face as he watched huge smiles spread across everyone else's face in the room. Next, he heard a bloom of profanity in several languages all saying the same thing. They couldn't believe it was real. Patrick was stoked that he chose to introduce the Blower at speed. Instead of statically where the crowd would just pick and poke at it. Looking at serial numbers. Crawling around the car like an army of concours judges just looking for fault. But as the Blower sped by, it was a reminder to all that the car was a functional piece, not just a display piece. And that how a car drove, especially a Blower, was key to why it became famous in the first place.

The driver of the Blower had slowed the huge car, turned and made another pass. He was following Patrick's instructions to, 'do a pair of fly-bys. Like in *Top Gun*.' At the second pass, the crowd erupted into applause. Patrick had them. He knew it. And when the Blower finally pulled up and chuffed to a stop, the crowd didn't rush towards the icon. They stayed stuck to their spots. In awe of what they were seeing. Like a crowd at a rock concert is amazed when the singer jumps off stage and mixes it up with them. The item of fame and fascination becomes too real to believe.

With the hood up, no one in the crowd could recognize who was driving the car. And that little secret was just one more bit that would whip the crowd into a frenzy and have them writing glowing reviews in their head just like a baseball beat writer pens a story before the last out is recorded.

"Well, gentlemen," Patrick announced into a microphone that was handed to him, grabbing the attention away from the Blower for a second. "let me introduce to you. SM 3912, the missing Blower. And also let me introduce you to Blaine de Badenet."

With his introduction, Blaine emerged from the Blower with twinkle in his eye and wry smile. "Writers, most of you are writers, good luck finding the words to describe this motorcar in your papers. It is as fantastic a machine as I have ever had the pleasure of driving. Finer than all its contemporaries and more visceral than most anything on the road. Do come up and take a close look. And you will all get to drive it as well."

Patrick sat back while Blaine spoke for another twenty minutes about the Blower. Pointing out unique details. Calling attention to serial numbers and the like. And Blaine was, as far as he knew, telling the truth. Patrick and his team did not tell Blaine that the Blower was a re-creation. They flew him in yesterday to introduce the car and to act as litmus test as to the car's credibility. Blaine was skeptical yesterday but after spending hours with paperwork and the Blower, he was convinced enough to represent the car at its unveiling.

Listening to Blaine's Flemish tinged accent circumscribe a magical story around the Bentley and its history had Patrick smiling. There was no better choice in his mind to give this job to. The only other person Patrick thought could weave as wonderful a story and keep an audience of writer's as entertained, as Blaine was Faston. And that was never an option.

The more sensational of the writers were, of course, the ones who clambered to drive the Blower first. They all rushed to drive the legend. Then come back and blast Patrick with questions regarding the find. Patrick relished the questions, sticking to a simple story. Not varying from it. Not embellishing it. He and his team had one story about SM 3912 and that was the only one he would tell.

The hours passed and all the attendees but one were either leaving to catch flights or comparing the experience over a selection of wines and beers Patrick had provided including The Prisoner Shiraz, Alaska Kolsch and Pabst for the younger, hipper crowd Patrick knew liked old beers in cans. As Patrick walked over to the one man who had yet to drive or ride in the Blower he couldn't help but wink and nod in agreement at the snippets of conversations he was hearing. One man from the UK suggested he'd trade his Ferrari 250 for it. While another writer/restorer from California had a list of things he would give to own SM 3912, which included his wife, his house, his PV544 Panamericana racer, a timeshare he owned in Steamboat, a Basquiat lithograph, a Miele chronograph and his left nut.

There was always one in a crowd. The fish that swam upstream. And at the reveal, Patrick picked out

Peter Lennon as that person. Peter was a Bentley authority and had debunked his share of bunk stories regarding these cars.

"Peter, you don't seem as blown away, hah, pardon the pun, about my find."

Peter took a sip of his water then seemed to swipe his tongue over his teeth before answering. "I'm just a bit more reserved in my adulation. If you don't mind, would you mind walking me around the car yourself?"

"You don't want to ride along with Blaine? He knows all about the car."

The suggestion to ride with Blaine elicited a genuine laugh from Peter. "I took one ride with Blaine in the Mille Miglia in a short chassis Aston Martin and we skidded and ripped around the roads like our time mattered. Charming, and a handy wheelman, but I'll pass. I want to hear the story from the person who has spent the most time with the Blower since prying it out of Borland's mysterious manse."

"Man, that Borland was a lunatic-fringe sort." Patrick chuckled.

"So we all hear. How did he come by the Blower?" Peter pressed.

"Wouldn't say. Man, I asked him six ways from Sunday. Doing my best detective bit. But the man would not say. Only said he paid cash for it sometime in the fifties. That's it."

"That's it? To who? Boy or girl? In the UK or outside of it? Nothing?"

"Nothing. He even had us in and out of his estate in ten minutes. Just enough to agree to sell the car. Then he shooed us out like a couple of dogs." At least the part about being on Borland's estate was the truth, so Patrick could speak that nugget with confidence.

"See any other cars there? No. He had sheets over everything. Man, I am surprised he didn't wear a sheet and walk around his kooky castle like Casper."

"Alright. So you get the car. Arrange shipping. It comes here to Albany. And then what?"

Patrick paused, as it was impossible to make up new parts of the story as the questions got asked. So, he just tried to keep it as simple as possible. "When it got here, we freaked. I mean, I just looked at the thing for two days. Didn't even touch it. Just looked at it. I mean, it was like finding the Ark of the Covenant, I was afraid I would touch it and the rays of the old Bentley employees would beam out and melt me like in *Raider's of the Lost Ark.*"

"Seriously, Peter. We did nothing except dust her off. Lube everything. Change all the fluids. Repair a bit of wiring that was fiddly. Put some new tires on it. That was it. Man, you can tell, it runs great but leaks like a sieve. We could have resealed it, but why? Borland put the car up right. On blocks. Turned it over by hand regularly. Coated the whole thing in Cosmoline and junk. What a bear to clean off. But you can tell it looks fantastic."

"Can I call Borland?"

"You can. But don't think he would talk to you. But do give him a shout." Patrick was glad that Borland was such a hermit, he would just get more and more sick of people coming round his place about cars now and just retreat further and further into his decrepit, gothic cave.

Patrick watched as Peter flipped through a bunch of notes he had with him, then looked up and said, "Now, let's get on to the car. I have a lot of details I would like to cross-check regarding the car."

Patrick swallowed some spit that had collected at the sides of his mouth, then answered. "Sure man. I know some but not all the bookish stuff. But let's do it."

"First, there is the reinforced sump that SM 3912 was fitted with according to Michael Hay." And with that, Peter slunk down onto the ground and peered at the bottom of the Blower's oil-soaked undercarriage.

Patrick knelt down and craned his neck to get a peek at what Peter was doing. He was scraping a bit of the scum, dirt and oil that was painstakingly faux-finished on the bottom of the sump, away from certain areas.

"Reinforced or what?" Patrick asked projecting more confidence than he actually was feeling now. He had his man make a new sump once he found out that SM 3912 had one. It should pass muster.

"Hmm. It does look like the original sump is still here." Peter noted while rising to a stand. "Now, let's check something not quite so dirty."

Patrick ignored Peter's icy stare and just nodded agreement.

"What do you know about the steering?"

"Only that it is as heavy as John Goodman at low speeds but lightens up when you are on the go." Patrick tried to get Peter to laugh. He didn't.

"I was thinking more about the ratio." With that, Peter jumped in the car and cranked the wheel from lock to lock. He then did some scribbling in a pad. "That checks out as well. Just one more test."

"And what is that?" Patrick asked. Now, rather sure that the car would pass muster with all who inspected it.

"Wear in the accelerator linkage."

"Pfft. For what? I mean. Is there a standard?"

"No standard." Peter stated. "But there should be some existing wear. The mechanism was so complex that even Bentley recommended 'frequent lubrication' to the assembly."

Patrick felt his lunch of lox rise in his stomach. He had no idea if it was Minaz or his engine builder or who would be on the hook if this was not in spec to what Peter expected. Now, right now, Patrick was feeling the pressure to produce an exact replica of a famous car. A car so bloody famous that people would whip out feeler gauges and probe the linkages of the accelerator from pedal to carb. It took Peter ten minutes to check the whole system. All the while Patrick could feel the sweat dripping from armpit to waist. He was a mess.

Peter spent the next forty-five minutes checking, measuring, and comparing all parts of the Blower to notes and photos he had brought with him. Patrick couldn't believe how particular the man was in looking at the car. Patrick knew that he should not have allowed one of the few automotive journalists who don't just pass along the owner's or manufacturer's communication points to his unveiling. But, the reward and believability, and in turn the profits, would be that much greater if Peter blessed the blower as original.

Patrick always defaulted to over-the-top enthusiasm in times of doubt. And this was one of those times. "Hey man, stop getting all greasy and grab another bite to eat. Besides, this car is the real deal. No better barn find ever. Not even a cobra in a barn would be better than this."

"A cobra in a barn is pretty good. But you do have him beat. I have no choice but give my approval. Well found, Patrick."

"Thanks man." Patrick enthused while pumping Peter's hand furiously up and down. "Now, go and join some of the more the enthusiastic journalists in figuring out a way to have words capture how marvelous SM 3912 is."

"I'll pass." Was all Peter said and walked away while dialing his phone.

Patrick spent the next few hours talking with the reporters. Conjecturing about how much the Blower would bring at auction. Calling Minaz and his other conspirators to let them know it was a go. His most important call though was to the Pneu auction house. To let them know the sale was on.

A further nine hours later the Blower replica was being picked up by a classic car transport company and brought to JFK airport. The Blower replica would be put on cargo plane that would land in Paris tomorrow and from there, it would take a truck ride to get to Monaco. Patrick planned to accompany his creation the whole way in case any questions about duties or ownership or anything else popped up. This was the big one for Patrick. The one that would have him changing from servant to sir. And he wasn't going to leave anything to chance.

34
Newcastle, UK May 23, 2011

Faston thought that there was no other country so obsessed with their own history as England. The British, it seemed, had a stone marker, book, historian-in-residence or what have you for whatever insignificant and significant event that took place on English soil or was accomplished by a native of the United Kingdom. It was a country of documenters documenting classes, hierarchies, events and those involved. But what could make for a very boring historical tour of any village could also benefit the active archaeologist of any sort. Even those looking for missing cars and their missing drivers.

When Faston and Charles left Connecticut for Newcastle, they had no real plans as to what they would do when they arrived. Nothing. Just a hunch and some postmarks had pushed them towards this location to continue searching for the Blower. And unlike their last car-hunting trip to Italy and Austria for the 901 Porsche, they didn't even have time to arrange for decent lodgings. They had to join the flow of the itinerant hiker and tourist and put themselves in the hands of the local tourist board. A rather frightening thought for Faston. Heck, they hadn't even been able to fly into Newcastle on such short notice. Faston and Charles had arrived by train after flying into Heathrow.

Walking through the main Newcastle train station, Faston looked around for the tourist board office.

Charles, trailing a bit behind with his rag-tag bags, begged of Faston, "Where are we staying? A small local castle? Maybe a nice rental apartment you arranged?"

"I've no idea."

"Faston Hanks has no idea where he is staying?" Charles laughed.

"Keep laughing. Because if Faston Hanks has no idea where he is staying, that means Charles White has no idea where he is staying."

"Right. Need a hand looking through these?" Charles asked as they had stopped in front of a closed tourist office that had put out a rack of brochures for the local attractions, dining options and lodgings.

"Not likely," Faston retorted while reaching into his pocket. "I have this. The new Apple phone. I downloaded an app that uses geopositioning to recommend what in the past you would have had to paw through brochures to find. So, here we go." Shaking the phone up and down, Faston waited for the answer to his query.

"Ugh." Faston moaned.

"What?"

"It is recommending a Marriot."

"So."

"No so. We are not staying at a Marriott. No way. Let me just put in some different parameters and give it another shake."

"Yes, Faston. Another shake is always a good idea." Charles said as an aside which he wanted Faston to hear.

"Ugh. Another Marriott. Ridiculous." Faston was getting angry. And three more times shaking the phone and getting the same unsatisfactory answer, Faston turned off the phone, chucked it into his pocket and started combing through the pamphlets. Charles did the same.

"How about this one?" Charles asked, holding up a brochure that featured a small row house with small windows. The entire pamphlet was bordered with lace.

"No thanks. I'd rather stay at a cat-themed Bed and Breakfast."

"Then I think you would like the Catsenberg Arms." Charles smirked as he showed Faston the pamphlet for exactly that, a cat-themed B&B.

"Enough. Here. This is it." Faston stated while handing over a small packet of information to Charles. "It says it is the oldest guest house in Newcastle. And the oldest of anything is always worth visiting."

"Agreed."

Twenty minutes later, after calling to ensure the chosen lodgings had accommodations available for a couple of nights, Faston and Charles arrived at a pub called the Crown Posada. Small cross-hatched and stained glass windows reluctantly let some light from the inside reach the street. While its stone facade seemed to retreat away from the neighboring buildings. As if it was collapsing slowing away from the street. It looked, to Faston, like it wanted to just crumble and be swept away by time.

"Shall we, Charles?"

"After you."

"No, no. After you." Charles insisted while not budging an inch from his spot on the curb.

"Fine. Let's go. I'm exhausted. It's ten thirty at night. We might just be able to catch a pint and then to bed." Faston was speaking over his shoulder to Charles as he walked into the pub. So, not knowing where he was stepping, Faston tripped rather awkwardly, as if any trip was not awkward he thought to himself, and slammed into the only occupied table. In fact it was the only table in the pub. A rather snug snug. Glasses fell to the floor as in the tradition; the locals had not cleared the table during their long session. Several broke as they hit the dark oak floor. The cracking glass competing with Charles' laughter.

"A good slippering is in order for that sort of entrance, eh Botcher?" One of the table's occupants asked of his companion while looking down at Faston who was straining to get up from the floor without cutting himself.

"A slippering, Baskers? I would think that a proper codgering would be more the sort of thing."

Botcher and Basker, what odd names, Faston thought while gathering his bearings and trying to get in an apology as soon as the old pair stopped debating what to do to him. Not that Faston thought that either of the men could do much. Each looked to have crawled the earth and inhabited this pub for the better part of eighty years.

"I'd say a pummeling would do." Basker retorted.

"A pummeling would be far too pedestrian, Basker. Only a good old-fashioned brassing will make do when a table gets upturned." Botcher pondered while taking a sip of the remaining pint in his hand.

"A racking?" Basker asked.

"A bucketing?" Botcher quickly volleyed back.

"A tall cracking?"

"Or a short sacking?"

"Gentlemen," Faston finally interjected. "I don't really think there is reason to administer a slippering, pummeling, racking, bucketing or tall cracking."

"Don't forget the short sacking." The one Faston thought was Botcher responded.

"Yes, yes. The short sacking is admirably awful." Basker concurred.

"How about I buy you two a round of drinks?" Faston asked. "My friend and I could use one ourselves."

"That should do, the name is Basker."

"I do wish we could have laid into a heavy haying on this American chap, but a round of drinks makes that moot. I'm Botcher. I'll take a Gladiator."

"Another for me. I am feeling a touch combative. So a Gladiator is the bitter to imbibe." Basker agreed on the drink order.

"And me, as well." Charles winked as he grabbed a seat between Botcher and Basker.

Faston took a few steps over towards the bar. Luckily it was empty and he didn't have to play the English game of waiting for the bartender to nod to you so you knew it was your turn. Faston much preferred just to find a slot in a crowd and fight for his booze.

"You must be Faston?" The bartender asked as he extended a hand across the bar.

"Yes. We spoke on the phone then. Sorry about the entrance I made. Rather a mess. We won't treat your rooms like that. I guarantee it."

"Ah, no problem. I'm Thomas, and I see you've met Botcher and Basker. Good couple of blokes. I think."

"Yeah, I need to buy us all a round of Gladiator. I think it is the only thing that will keep Charles and I from getting a slippering."

Without looking up from his task of pouring four pints of ale, Thomas gave Faston a quick history of Botcher, Basker and the Crown Posada.

"Those two couldn't slipper a puppy. But that doesn't keep them from being quite animated about their ability to get into a scrap or three and have this pub live up to its nickname of the coffin. Both of them are ninety."

"I thought they looked eighty." Faston admitted.

"Only eighty?" Thomas said while placing one of the finished Gladiator Bitters on the bar. "They look older than that to me. Even older than the chap in the stained-glass window we are renowned for."

Glancing back over his shoulder, Faston took in the pre-Raphaelite stained glass depicting a sword-wielding man and liquid-pouring woman. It did look like a fine piece of bar decoration that rose above the brewer-provided promotional items.

Setting the last of the pints on the bar, Thomas continued. "Here are your ales. And hurry them back to those gents. Because back in the day they did some fighting. Both worked as youngsters for the local protective services before turning of age and joining the fight properly in the big one. I'm closing up the front door, but take your time. I'll show you to your rooms whenever you want."

Faston took a large sip of his Gladiator. "Nice bitter, this. Pretty sessionable. And thanks for the back story on the locals."

Making a triangle with his hands, Faston was able to pick up the four pints and make it the few steps back to the table where he found Basker, Botcher and Charles staring at each other. Silent. It seemed to Faston a rather tense situation.

Charles broke the silence. "Finally. Some ales. These two refused to speak about anything until some new drinks arrived."

Charles pushed across the ales to Botcher and Basker who simultaneously picked them up, nodded at each other and downed a third of the pint.

"Apology accepted." Botcher said.

"Welcome to the coffin." Basker warmly proffered.

Squeezing into the tiny snug next to Charles, Faston exhaled loudly and took another pull of his Gladiator, closed his eyes for a second and announced. "Now I feel human again."

"I'd say you'd have felt worse if it weren't for these beers." Botcher prodded.

"I'd say you were right." Faston agreed. "Thomas was telling me that you two did quite a bit of fighting a while back."

"We did. We did." Basker repeated between sips of his nearly emptied pint.

"And during the war that mattered most, WWII."

"It was. It was." Basker parroted as he finished his Gladiator.

Before answering, Faston looked at Botcher's pint and noticed it too was empty. So he went back to the bar and got Thomas to take a break from cleaning up the bar to pour four more pints. Even though he was not finished with his beer he wanted to catch up to the old guys. This time when Faston returned to the table he found Botcher and Basker talking Charles' ears off.

"Before we went overseas, Botcher and I did our bit in Newcastle. Lots of cleaning up."

"Lots of warnings, too. Worked for the local ARP. Put the lights out and all that. Helped the men who did the yelling." Basker added.

Almost choking on his Gladiator due to shock of hearing they worked for the ARP and the effort of trying to get his first pint down quickly, Faston held up his hand in a motion intended to get Botcher and Basker to hold their thought as he calmed his reflux. "You worked for the ARP?"

"I hardly believe it." Charles said looking dumbfounded, mouth agape like a child who just saw a fire truck pull up to his school.

Faston let Botcher and Basker in on why he was so shocked to hear they had been involved with the ARP. "Charles and I came here to do a bit of research on the local ARP chapter."

"We are living history." Botcher said while shrugging his shoulders.

"For the moment." Basker addended.

"Remember much from those times?" Faston coldly inquired.

Botcher glanced at Basker before answering. "What's my name? Where am I?"

"I like to eat pudding." Basker added with what seemed to Faston was a non sequitor.

Faston was quickly confused. "Sorry. I don't understand."

"Just because we're old," Botcher explained. "doesn't mean we've lost the plot."

"Great." Charles pronounced. "Let's test your memories. Remember a gentleman, an officer, by the name of Stephan Sidlow?"

"Sidlow. Not a name that sparks to me. How about you Basker?"

"Not me either." Basker said, then swirled some of his Gladiator around in his mouth as if he was trying to lubricate the entirety of his thought process through his palate.

"We didn't exactly tot around with the officers then. They yelled and we did as instructed." Botcher said as he played with his now empty pint glass. "Do you remember that one pfaft of man, Basker? The one who had us walk his dog?"

"Willows it was. Rather the Germans win than that man have become overlord of the British. Bombed to bits, him."

"Yes," Botcher noted while smiling. "The dog was even nicer after he bought the big one."

Faston felt sleep tugging at his senses and his eyelids. It was time for a good night's sleep. Botcher and Basker were wonderful guys, but Faston didn't feel that they would lead him to anything worthwhile tonight.

"Charles, let's get to bed. I'm done. D. O. N. E."
Faston said spelling out the word done slowly.

"Agreed. I'm not ninety, but not twenty either. I
could use some sleep too. Just one more question for our
new friends."

"Yes, Inquisitor?" Botcher winked.

"How can I help, sir?" Basker bowed.

"You might not remember a person. But most
boys love cars. Do you remember ever seeing a Blower
Bentley around when you were with the ARP?"

"A Birkin." Basker spat.

"A LeMans legend." Botcher said a bit wistfully.

Then in unison, Botcher and Basker answered.
"I do."

"We do."

"You do?" Charles asked with the sort of
trepidation of voice usually reserved for parts counters
when requiring a rare fastener in a very limited time.

"We do. Of course. Odd duck this Bentley
though." Botcher went on.

"Quite odd." Basker chimed in. "Didn't look
like one of the Birkin cars. Or one of the other racerish
cars."

"No. Not all." Botcher said while shaking his
head.

"So, what type of Blower was it?" Faston
propped.

"A rather large coupe." Basker said.

"Very large. Very, very large." Botcher added
with outstretched arms. "It looked like a doctor's Rolls
Royce. Or an esquire's car."

"Not the flash officer type Alvis or Bentley
often raced around during the war. Except the wheels
were red." Basker recalled with a rearward roll of his
eyes.

"No, not flashy at all. Saw it in town on several occasions. We'd always race to catch a glimpse of it." Botcher ended with.

"And this car was driven by an officer of the ARP?" Faston asked.

"I think so." The twins answered, again in unison.

"That's all you recall. That an officer drove around a Blower coupe. You don't know who? That's it?"

"All we know." Basker said, after which he looked to his brother for approval. And Faston noted some sort of unspoken communication going on between the two men. Then Basker continued. "But I am sure the ARP museum in town will know more than us."

"For sure. For sure." Botcher said as he nudged his brother as a signal for the two men to stumble towards their home.

Faston and Charles exchanged glances. Faston noted that Charles looked just as bamboozled as he felt. "Charles, how did we not know about the ARP museum here? How?"

"I've no idea, Faston. We did a thorough combing of the records we took from Tate."

"And I spent incalculable hours online searching for ARP records here. I just don't know how we missed it."

"It is rather smallish." Basker confided.

"Not even middish." Botcher added. "But, meet us here at nine tomorrow morning and we will walk you over."

"That sounds perfect. See you in the morning."

Leaving the close confines of the bar, Faston and Charles walked up to the even closer confines of their room. Two twin beds. A bath down the hall. A small corner sink. An armoire that was rickety, buckling under the weight of Faston's folded shirts. But, Faston thought, tonight it was perfect. Both Charles and Faston crept into bed and wound down from the day to the sounds of a centuries old building and the slight malty smell from downstairs. Faston was just moments away from getting some needed sleep when the phone rang.

Faston grabbed his phone off the floor, saw it was Peter, and answered. "Peter. How was the car?"

"Faston, I won't sugar-coat it. I just got back from Patrick's circus-like viewing of SM 3912. I feel it was the real deal. Maybe somehow restored a bit. Or messed with a little. Remarkable coachwork. It is an imposing beast. But I could not find anything on the car that I could stand behind and make a stink to the auctioneer about. Nothing to not have it cross the block."

Faston closed his eyes and took a few deep breaths, trying to push back the doubts rising up inside that the Blower he was chasing was a fantasy. That from the moment Aron got Faston's mind racing with obscure fuel records from WWII he was walking in the opposite direction of the Blower. With every day, taking a few steps farther away from any real progress. For heaven's sake, he was sleeping above a pub in Newcastle. Could all the decades of work by Tate's father have been futile? Could Stephan Sidlow just be another civil servant with nothing to do with the Bentley? Could Patrick really successfully negotiate with a known recluse and pry out of his hands one of his prized possessions?

"Peter, that is quite possibly the worst news I have received by phone. Ever."

"Sorry to bear the news, Faston. And let me just say don't read any classic car news for the next couple weeks. I am sure this will be the dominant story. All the other reporters at the viewing were thrilled and posting stories a la minute."

"Thanks for the quick update."

"So, are you flying back then?" Peter asked.

"I don't think so. I'll take a bit more time. There are six days to the auction. Follow some of the remaining paths and see where they go. We got, what I thought was, a promising lead just tonight that Charles and I will investigate tomorrow. You never know. Lots of museums have hung fakes of Old Master paintings thinking they were real until the real ones were found."

"True."

"I'm after the real SM 3912, Peter. So goodnight. I need to rest up. Not going until the end would be something I would always regret. So to the end."

"Goodnight, Faston."

"Charles." Faston called, but quickly noticed Charles had already slipped into a deep breathing sleep. His sheets rising and falling with his whimpering snore. Rolling onto his side, Faston looked out the small, unshaded window and repeated to himself 'The Blower is near. The Blower is near,' until he fell asleep.

35
Newcastle and Seaton Carew, November 10 1944

The attack that Stephan had signaled took ten days to put together. But the wait was worth it. His satisfaction at having played a big part in this latest assault made living amongst the enemy bearable again. The V rockets had trickled in over the past several days. No doubt to gauge effectiveness and sight-in the targeting. But today proved that the V attacks were real. And real damaging. So much so that Churchill spoke to Parliament, and in essence, all Allies, that London had indeed been under rocket attacks for several weeks.

This was a profound turn of events. Being among the British military leaders, Stephan had begun to tire of the more and more confident, smug and derisory attitude of them. The elite leaders of the Allies, believed the war was won in all but name. They believed that they had not only created a superior force, they doubted what the Germans could retaliate with.

The one-time socialist, now labor Mr. Herbert Morrison, Home Secretary, was so pompous that he claimed a few weeks back that Hitler had lost the battle of London. In the *Independent on Sunday* Stephan read that Morrison's Rocket Consequences Committee rejoiced as late as 5th September, 1944, saying "...the enemy is unlikely to be able to launch rockets or flying bombs against London on any appreciable scale so we have therefore directed that plans to meet the contingency of severe rocket attack should so far as possible be kept on a paper basis." What was happening now was exactly that, a severe rocket attack.

Well, the laugh was on Morrison now. Stephan got a special chuckle at Morrison's having to visit several V2 bomb sites which, until today, the public were told were 'gas main' or 'mystery explosions'. The bespectacled Morrison, caught agape over the massive carnage caused by the V2. Stephan saw the photos of the great man making a personal inspection. The public never did. Stephan knew the V2 was most powerful in its ability to cause panic. And the government of Britain knew this as well. Why else resort to such pathetic attempts to calm the public than to refer to the V2 carnage as 'mystery explosions'?

Stephan was sitting at home in Newcastle, listening to the news reports on his HMV deco-designed radio. The rich, book matched walnut case reminding him of the woodwork he'd seen on several officers' more formal Bentleys. He was fine-tuning the signal, hoping to get a clearer voice and confirmation of more and more carnage. And he did not have to listen much longer. The announcer who was talking about Churchill's announcement suddenly changed tack.

"There has been another, to what we now know to be rocket attacks from mainland Europe, in Aldgate." The announcer mournfully reported. "The first tally we have of damages has over a dozen dead and more than twice that wounded."

"Good. But you think with that much explosive on board, the dead would be more." Stephan spoke back to the announcer.

Stephan listened for a couple of more hours to the radio. There was another attack, in north London, but it hit an empty lot. Only one person was killed. Stephan didn't know how many Marks a V2 cost, but he was sure it was an expensive way to get the same effect as one bullet. But Stephan didn't let this fact get him down. He in fact, let it cheer him up. The rockets were coming at a rate that even he could not have hoped for.

Stephan noted that the sun was down far enough for him to head out to his appointment tonight. Sometimes he was given his instructions via the pigeons.

Other times there would be simple light flash communications from planes that flew off the coast. Tonight was one of the latter so Stephan pulled on his heavy, ARP-issued overcoat and walked out to where he kept the Blower garaged.

Looking over the Blower was always rewarding to Stephan. And after five years of ownership and near to 15,000 miles of hard travel, the big girl really looked OK. Some of the hastily applied midnight blue paint was chipping and crazing a bit. But that just gave the car an even more purposeful look. The red wheels still looked magnificent. They reminded Stephan of the wheels of a chariot.

Stephan walked around the Blower about once a month to give it a close inspection. Like a pilot before takeoff, ensuring his equipment was in fine fettle. All seemed to be in order. The folding top was looking a bit dirty, but Stephan was loath to clean it with the dirty places he had to travel to; it would just get filthy again. Bending over, Stephan looked under the Blower for any large leaks. The rear differential showed some weepage, as did the main sump but nothing out of the ordinary.

Lifting the bonnet, Stephan took in the large polished valve cover. Again, no major leaks. Tracing the cloth wrapped wires; he also noted no major problems. He then inspected his light-signaling mechanism. It still functioned well, although it had not been used as much recently as the pigeons were a safer and more reliable means of signaling. Stephan shut the bonnet and twice-checked that he secured the catches.

Over the half a decade of ownership the Blower had proven to be a reliable creature. Stephan never begrudged it the repairs it required. The only major one being a rebuilding of the gearbox occurring when a seal let go on a long run and all the oil leaked out, damaging the entire assembly. It was this that happened in the first few months of Stephan's ownership. A repair which got Stephan to start his inspections of the car to be more consistent. Other than the large rebuild of the gearbox, the Blower only required a new windscreen, a rebuilding of one wheel due to hitting a large bomb crater and minor fettling to switches and brakes.

Slipping inside the Bentley, Stephan relished the comfort and customization that five years of ownership had accomplished. The seats fit Stephan perfectly. The door arm rest was worn where Stephan liked to wedge his arm when driving the Bentley with one hand. The gear lever even showed some wear along the side that Stephan would sometimes methodically caress as he covered the stressful nighttime miles his jobs for the ARP and his mother country required.

The miles flew by and Stephan was soon near the bus station in Seaton Carew. This white, curved art deco design stood in great contrast to most of the more staid structures of this seaside village. The tall clock tower at one end of the bus station was where Stephan idled the Blower. He checked his watch, the car and the tower. All showed the time to be 9:35. Stephan had ten minutes to get to the location where he could see the airplane signal as it flew from north to south over the sea.

Stephan maneuvered the Blower along the coast and took up a spot not far from the eastern edge of the local golf course. It was a deserted locale and one that had a road leading on to the end of a small spit of land. It was here that Stephan parked the car, put down the top and waited. The cold, salty air did two jobs. One, keeping Stephan awake. The other, keeping the skies clear of clouds so that he could see the signals being sent to him.

The air to ground signals that Stephan was looking for were a very brief, bespoke sort of Morse code. Just a few quick flashes and longer pulses of light. There were only four options available for use. They were signals to leave the country, look for a more complex message in one week, send back location for rocket attacks or instructions to pick up another countryman.

The tedium of all this, thought Stephan. All so he could avoid having his own shortwave and in turn, being a suspect. No real way to explain what he was doing with a shortwave, so he did not want one. Ever. Stephan turned the collar up on his coat and tilted his eyes skyward. Concentrating on the smell of the leather and oil and the sounds of the beach and any potential approachers. In his ARP uniform, Stephan was confident he could talk his way out of any questioning by local staff.

Checking his watch and the Blower's clock, Stephan saw it was 9:45. And on cue, he saw the signals using his lovely new binoculars. No matter what state the war was in, the Germans were a timely bunch. And Stephan thanked them for that. He put the top back up on the Blower and began the drive back home. And when he arrived home, he would wait some more. Because his instructions were simply to go get his more complex orders by November 25th. *Maybe he should have risked the shortwave.* Beaurocracy seemed an equal foe to both sides in this war, thought Stephan.

36
Monaco, May 27, 2011

"We sold out of the catalog. And we were charging our highest price ever, two-hundred Euros." Vincent Fornel, head of Pneu Auctions said. He was seated in a blue velvet chair facing the window of the Designer Suite at the Hotel Metrople. Vincent had pushed back his masculine, brown leather chair and was looking out the top floor window after a light lunch that was brought to the room and that Patrick saw had cost six-hundred and twenty four Euros. For salad Nicoise, Pouilly-Fuise, fresh fruit and some Madelines it seemed rather high. And Patrick had loved the way the cost did not effect Vincent in the least. And if all went well in a few days, Patrick would too be able to pick up the tab of a six-hundred euro lunch and not blink. He too would soon be able to stay on the top floor of Hotel Metrople.

"Really? You sold out the catalog?" Claude Le Mevel asked, unbelieving. He had flown in yesterday. Patrick was glad to see the engine builder again. And more so when he saw that Claude had changed his hair color and wore some glasses in an effort to change his appearance slightly. "I may have angered one or two attendees, that is all." Claude had said as a reason for the change.

"And why would people buy the catalog?" Minaz questioned. The body man, or miracle worker as Patrick liked to think of him, had flown in a week ago with several members of his family. They were staying in a village an hour away from Monaco. Minaz, Patrick was learning, was a miser of considerable proportions.

"Because it is collectible. So people buy it." Vincent answered.

"How many did you print?" Minaz asked.

"As many as I could sell."

"And how is it collectible then?"

"Because it says 'collectible' right on the cover. See." Vincent said holding up the catalog which featured the word 'collectible' in a gold font down the entire length of the cover. "And I put it vertically so I could make it bigger."

"It almost has more space on the cover than the Blower." Patrick noted as he snacked on a Madeleine. The cover photograph of the Blower was a dramatic black and white cropping that highlighted the 'Villiers' blower itself and the unique coachwork of the bonnet. The whole catalog had been art-directed and laid out ahead of time. Just waiting for Patrick to assemble the car. The photo-shoot had been the day before the car was unveiled in Albany.

"It is almost as important, the word collectible. Let me be the artist of the sale. Minaz and Claude and others were the artists. The artisans of the car. True craftsmen. You, Patrick, were the patron. The Pope. The Medici. The Sun King. The man who had a need for something grand that only artists could provide. And provide they did. And in two days time, I will provide you with a remarkable performance. The podium is my milieu. The front of the room, my stage. And I have been teasing the audience for months now. The catalog is the first glimpse of the prize. I tease the car like the virgin girl who tried to sell her virginity online. I will have the most powerful men in the room fighting to conquer, to own, the Blower. The event." Vincent ended this in-room performance by snubbing out a cigarette that he had been holding, not smoking, and asked one final question. "Shall we go see the little whore?"

Minaz and Claude had silently agreed. So Patrick followed Vincent and the rest of his cabal out of the room, downstairs and out the revolving door of the hotel. Although the sun was shining, only rarely covered by the thinnest of clouds, the air was still cold. Patrick zipped up his tracksuit jacket and thrust his hands in his pockets.

"Shall we walk?" Vincent asked and began to stride down the bustling sidewalks without waiting for an answer.

Claude clapped his hands and followed suit, "The weather is wonderful, Quebec is still freezing now."

Minaz winced but shuffled to keep up.

Patrick, who was about to get into the hotel's courtesy Maserati, changed tack and joined the rest of the group.

Patrick let his eyes dance over the remarkable array of goods in the windows of the shops that the group passed en route to the auction location. There was watch store after watch store including Rolex and Chopard. A tobacconist who dealt in only custom blends. A perfumer who also only did custom blends. And then many clothiers offering custom-tailored suiting in fabrics Patrick had no idea their origins or quality. But Patrick Patrick did get the feeling that he would soon be the owner of a scent, a cigarette and a suit custom ordered to his specifications. Indeed, a world of his own devising and imagining would soon be opening up to him.

As the group met the water's edge after a fifteen-minute walk, they turned left and were finally able to see the event center that Vincent had secured for the event. The Espace Fontvieille. It was a stressed fabric tent, glowing white in the southern sun with four separate peaks that gave it a shape resembling a crown. There was a heli-pad hanging off the edge of the road over the water. Patrick thought of the high-bidders flying in to bid on the Blower, jumping out of their transport mere feet from the event.

As soon as the group was within 100 meters of the center, a guard who was dressed more like a tourist stopped them. He wore white pants; trim polo shirts, Persol sunglasses and white Pumas. They also wore earpieces, U-Boat watches and a hard-to-miss shoulder harnessed handgun.

Vincent held up his hands in mock submission. "Gentlemen. I thought there might be some people wanting to get too close to our prize car too soon. So I hired these gentlemen. You have heard of Blackwater? These men were sick of working in the Middle East, so I gave them less pay but better uniforms and a more attractive environment in which to ply their trade. There are fifteen of them around. So don't wander away."

As the group passed, Patrick could feel the eyes of the guards scan the group even though he could not see them through the dark brown Persols. Passing one more guard, who opened the door for them and waved a metal detector over them as they walked by, the foursome stopped when they scanned the room and didn't see the car. Patrick could tell that Minaz and Claude must have been waiting for the first glimpse of the Blower. Both let out a deep breath, and then turned their eyes toward Vincent.

Patrick looked around and was surprised not to see the Blower. Surprised would be a kind word. He was fully panicking. The Blower was supposed to be here. So, as calmly as he could muster he asked Vincent, "So, the Blower isn't here. I assume it is being held somewhere very secure?"

"Not to worry." Vincent said, pulling a remote from his pocket, aiming it at the stage and dramatically pushing a button on it.

Patrick could hear some clicks and whirs. Then, he and the rest of the group watched as a structure began rising from the elevated stage. It was a slow pace, and all the men stared, as the floor of the stage became the roof of a structure that revealed the Blower. Top up, unpolished, undetailed, mud from the test day still spattering its sides, it looked every bit the Prince of the automotive universe rising to take his rightful place. Patrick believed Minaz, Claude and Vincent to be its first supplicants. The bidders who would arrive in a few days would be its fervent worshippers.

Patrick stood by Vincent as Minaz and Claude rushed the stage like teenagers at a concert. Elbowing and nudging each other as they clambered up onto the stage and circled the Blower. Patrick reveled in the joy that each man showed. Sure, they were committing a crime. But it was a crime that wrung the best out of man. The challenge had let each of them accomplish more than any could have as individuals.

"If these two guys are this happy, what do you think the reaction of the bidders will be?" Patrick asked Vincent.

"Hysteria." Was Vincent's one word answer, delivered while still looking at the stage and smiling. Patrick could sense that Vincent was 100% sure now that they would hit it big. That both would pull off one of the biggest coups in classic car collecting history. Clasping Vincent on the back, Patrick walked with his co-conspirator towards the front of the Espace Fontvieille to join Minaz and Claude. The Blower still had a magnetic pull on Patrick that he could not ignore. It was like a Christmas wish granted that had to be played with right away. In the snow. In pajamas.

As they got close to the stage, Minaz and Claude could be heard ribbing each other about the quality of their handiwork.

"I think you might have been too rustic on your rolling of this fender edge, Minaz."

"Do you think so?" Minaz asked, his high-pitched voice rising higher with mockery.

"I do." Claude retorted. "And the louvering on the hood looks like it was done by a drunk wielding a wood chisel."

"Is that so?"

"It is." Claude stated while bending down to take a look at the undercarriage. "And here are more issues. The bottom of the unique step-plate seems to be too rounded off. And the frame rails themselves, are they from a repurposed fire engine?"

"Oh, my Claude. You have me worried." Minaz laughed. "Now let's look at your engine." He suggested while opening the bonnet.

"A beauty, eh? Faultless in every regard." Claude beamed.

"If the person doing the regarding is blind. I bet it doesn't even run."

"You have to hear it." Patrick said with the pride of a father watching the grandparents play with his newborn son. "Vincent, start it up for them. Claude, you've heard the motor of course, you built it. But, sitting in the chassis the resonance has changed a bit and it sounds so authentic."

"That is because everything about that motor is authentic." Claude said while staring at Minaz. "Unlike the bodywork."

Patrick watched as Vincent expertly ran through the complicated starting procedure with the result being the Blower bursting to life. Patrick didn't feel the need to say anything. And none of his cohorts felt the need either. They all just let the replica Blower's intoxicatingly real sounds and smells and sights do the talking.

37
South of London, December 7, 1944

'Shopping for Death'. That was what Stephan felt would
have been a good headline for the newspapers a fortnight
ago. His dark sense of humor had waned, but not been
extinguished by the challenging months and years
leading up to now. Stephan never played to a crowd with
his humor. Instead, he oftened joked distinctly for his
own amusement. And his bit of yellow-journalism
headline writing had made him chuckle.

The V2 attacks had been effective and
disheartening to the British populace. None more so than
the direct hit on the Woolworths on November 25th.
Those citizens might have been shopping for dresses,
socks or ties but they come home with death. Sweet,
dark, definitive death. But it would not be a 'death-
blow'. It was remarkable how the allies seemed to
bounce back from the biggest strikes that could be
thrown at them.

Today, December 7th, was a great example. The
Japanese had utterly surprised the Americans at Pearl
Harbor. Crippled the fleet. Got the upper hand. And
then…nothing. The Americans had pulled off a miracle
comeback. Stephan liked to think of December 7th
because it crystallized his desire to create his own
memorable day. To be the author of a plan that became a
touchstone of victory.

And that was the very reason why Stephan was
driving south again. Driving towards Penshurst and his
secret avian communication base. Stephan was aiming to
get to the grounds just after sunset and needed to press
the Blower in order to arrive in the first hour of
darkness. He had an urgent message to send to the
leaders back in Germany. While an even more urgent
message was to be awaiting him.

The sun seemed to be setting faster tonight than in previous days. Stephan knew this was not possible, but it didn't change the fact that it felt like it to him. So he pressed the Blower on. Dipping into the extra power whenever safe, and even when it didn't seem safe. He needed to make up some time. And there was only one way to do that. Drive like a demon, or his pre-war favorite driver, Rudolf Caracciola, fearless pilot of the Silver Arrows. *Now that is a car I would like to find after the war*, thought Stephan.

This daydreaming took a small percentage of Stephan's thinking off of his driving, and at the pace he was going, he needed to concentrate at 100 percent. So when he came over a small hillock at Paddock Woods he wasn't prepared for anything but open road. And that is not what confronted him. Without recognizing at first what he needed to avoid, he just tried to avoid it. Tried to avoid crumpling his car and most likely his neck. The blur of white that coursed across the road had no way through it.

The skid was uncontrollable. Having put almost his entire body weight into breaking so abruptly, and while the Blower was unweighted, had caused the big coupe to slew and slice across the road. The aggressive camber on the road didn't help as the Blower jumped from side to side trying to find traction in two directions at the same time.

Crashing the box from third to second helped use the engine compression to scrub more speed. The big four howled as it rammed past redline. Stephan peered through his panic and the dim light and wisps of tire smoke for a spot to aim the Blower. With stonewalls hemming him in, Stephan had one last desperate option left to avoid slamming into the moving roadblock. The emergency brake.

Knowing it would be impossible to turn the car quickly without hitting one of the stone walls on either his left or right side, Stephan cranked back the cable operated emergency brake. This had the effect of throwing the Blower into a quick, pivoting slide. The rear of the car swept past him on the right, the rear tires bumping on the slim grass border separating tarmac and stone.

The car was slowing. Stopping. Stephan had dipped the clutch and uncharacteristically, abruptly side-stepped the pedal. The Blower choked to a stop. Stephan closed his eyes for a moment to take stock of the situation. The acrid scent of overworked stoppers combined with spilt petrol and abraded tire gave the countryside the aura of a racetrack. Unfolding his hands from the wheel one finger at a time, Stephan completed taking stock of his situation by opening the door and getting a close look at the obstruction that almost caused him to crash.

Stephan had never seen so many white horses. There must have been twenty of them. Short, workmanlike horses filling the road and still finding their way onto it from a broken section of fence that topped the low stone wall. Scrambling up and over, the horses seemed to have no purpose other than to be where they should not be. In the dusk, under the stark thick branches of walnut and oak trees, it looked like a ghost herd.

Laughing out loud, Stephan walked over to get a closer look at one of the horses. To give one a pet to make sure that it was real and not a dream. One of the horses was bolder than the other and walked towards Stephan. Nuzzling at his pockets, no doubt looking for a treat, the horse was at ease. More so than Stephan, that was for sure as his pulse was still falling. Stroking the horse along its neck, Stephan got one more surprise. It was painted white.

Under the white paint was a regular chestnut-colored horse. Taking a quick peek at the rest of the horses milling around, he saw that they too were painted. Stephan had no idea why a farmer would paint his horses white, unless it was to make them more easily seen. And if that was the case, he was thankful. Because if the horses had been wearing their natural color he would not have seen the herd in time to avoid hitting them. The coat of cheap whitewash had saved his life, and that of a couple of the horses as well.

Getting back into the Blower, Stephan felt the elation that only came after narrowly avoiding serious injury. And, not that he would have ever requested the treatment, but it was exactly what he needed to carry on this evening with a positive, even lucky, demeanor.

The horses whinnied and circled tighter when Stephan fired the Blower up and revved the engine a few times to clear any of the extra petrol from the carbs that might have accumulated as a result of the hasty stop. It took a few points to get the Blower pointed in the right direction so he could get back on track to Penshurst. Slowly leaving the scene, the prow of the Blower parted the group of horses to reveal the deserted road that Stephan had counted on finding the whole way to his destination.

Chastened by the close call, Stephan kept out of the supercharger and made good speed, not great speed, the rest of the way. His assignment was too important to not complete because of an accident. Stephan hoped that what was going to be communicated to him was the massing of forces for an assault on English soil beyond the Channel Islands. The V2s had softened the resilience of the British some, and Stephan thought a bold attack would work. And an attack on England would be an exercise that his position would allow him to help in ways devastating to the defenses that Churchill relied upon. It would be the culmination of his decades of service to Germany.

Turning off the main road toward Penshurst, Stephan got on a secondary road the circled the property and finally onto the dirt path that lead to the coop he had used now for years without notice. Stephan turned the Blower around so it was pointing in the direction of the road; he always did this just in case he needed to leave quickly. Stepping out of the car, hearing the crunch of fallen leaves under his feet, Stephan walked towards the coop. He thought the birds were a bit noisier tonight than usual. They seemed to be not just cooing, but fluttering and jostling in the cramped airspace of the coop.

Stephan opened up the small door inset into the larger barn doors of the structure. "Settle down, my kids," Stephan said out loud, announcing his presence to his birds. He did not want to turn on his torch and startle the birds or potentially alert anyone nearby, so he let his eyes adjust to the darkness and got on with his task.

"I've travelled pretty far for you tonight." Stephan said, almost flirting with the birds. "And you wouldn't believe how close I came to getting into an accident." The birds usually calmed immediately when Stephan spoke to them. They would normally settle into a cooing pattern and preen and clean themselves on whatever perch they landed on. But tonight, the birds still jumped around and flitted back and forth, almost crashing into each other in the tiny confines of the coop.

"I am excited too, little friends." Stephan reasoned out loud with the birds. He always thought that animals had a sixth sense and knew when a situation was tense or serious. So, he tried to slow down, walk around, and pet his birds. And he wanted to locate his favorite bird to send his message to Germany with the best chance of arriving on time.

Stephan stumbled around looking for his favorite bird. It had a perfect set of grey circles on the left side of its head. And a chest that seemed a bit bigger than all the other birds. And besides being the bird that would carry his message to Germany, it should be bearing a message for him.

Stephan was not so familiar to name his birds, so he had no names to call out. He just peered around the rafters and the nooks in the ceilings looking for his private airman. Usually this bird stood proud among the rest. But tonight he could not see him in the dark of the coop.

"Damn." Stephan muttered and flicked on the torch. "Where are you?"

Turning around and sweeping the narrow beam over the walls, Stephan jumped back when he noticed movement to his left.

Dropping the torch on the filthy ground, Stephan unholstered his pistol and sighted down on what had made the noise.

Sharply lit by the torch which lay askew and flickering on the ground was a young boy of about twelve. The boy was clutching Stephan's favorite bird.

Glancing down, Stephan noticed that the bird's message packet was opened.

The boy was dressed in shoes too large for him. Threadbare pants and a sweater patched many times over what looked to be many years. The boy must have been from the surrounding village and not an employee or resident of Penshurst.

And he looked scared.

The gun which was extended an arm's length in front of Stephan was shaking slightly as his mind raced through the dozens of ways to handle this situation. None of which were pleasant.

He resorted to shocking profanity. "Who the fuck are you?"

The boy didn't answer. He just held Stephan's favorite bird tighter to his chest and pulled up knees.

"What the fuck are you doing here?" Stephan bellowed again over the cocked and shaking pistol.

The boy said something, but in so slight a voice that Stephan could not hear it, "What was that?" Stephan boomed.

"I'm sorry." The boy whimpered.

"Sorry for what?" Stephan grilled. "Sorry for trespassing. Sorry for scaring my birds. Sorry for being a nuisance."

"No," The boy contradicted Stephan in a quivering voice. "I'm sorry someone is going to try and kill the Prime Minister." The boy then held out the tiny paper message that had been attached to the pigeon he was clutching.

"What?" Stephan asked. "Give me that."

Reading the message, Stephan was the one now thrown off guard. The message was pretty clear. His superiors obviously wanted to make sure there was no chance the mission could be misinterpreted. The note simply said, 'Church on the hill to be targeted. Report back day and time.' And the frankness of the message hinted at the desperate state of affairs for the fatherland.

"Clever boy, figuring out that Church on the hill was the Prime Minister."

"Thank you, sir." The boy smiled slightly, Stephan thinking he had not heard too many compliments as of late.

"Now. I need to get that note into the hands of the proper authorities." Stephan said lowering his pistol to his side. "You can see I am a senior ARP officer. So, I need you to ensure your silence on this matter. It is of national security." Stephan then calmed his voice even more and spoke like a confidant of the boy. "I can trust you on this, can't I?"

"Yes sir." The boy proudly responded.

"Good. Now, does anyone know you were here?"

"No. No one, sir. I've just been spending time with my Aunt here and know no one in the village. I walk by myself."

"That is good to hear. Now go home." Stephan said.

"Yes, sir." The boy agreed and dusted himself off and walked past Stephan and towards the door that Stephan had walked through just minutes before.

The boy strode to the door without looking back. Stephan took this opportunity to raise his pistol, aim at the nape of the boy's neck, and pull the trigger.

The percussion scattered the pigeons into a blizzard of grey and white feathers. The boy fell instantly, a small hole in the back of his head and huge pool of blood streaming out of his face, or what was left of his face, onto the guano coated floor. Birds bounced off the walls and each other shedding feathers that hung in the air, drifted to the floor, and then stuck in the muck and blood.

Stephan slumped to the floor, dropping his body and the gun onto the muck, not caring one bit. That was it, thought Stephan. That was the last act I commit for my country. Stephan knew he would not be able to get anywhere near Winston Churchill for him to even attempt to harm the man. That was too much to ask, Stephan believed. If the war had come to that, the war would need to do without Stephan. If he needed to kill small boys...

It was time to clean up, Stephan decided. Taking his lighter out of his pocket, Stephan sparked it to life and burnt the tiny message in under a second. He then looked around the coop with his torch, finding the six birds that still had message tubes on their legs. Gathering up these birds, Stephan took off the tubes and slid them into his pocket. Opening all the windows and doors, he did his best to shoo the birds away into the still, black night. All but a few of the little messengers got the hint.

Continuing his methodical survey of the area, Stephan's eyes settled on the boy. Swallowing some bile, Stephan was overcome by the totality of what he had done today and in the previous decades of his service to Germany. He'd seen so many bodies in the past four years, several of the corpses his own doing. But this one hurt, it seemed to make him feel less and more human at the same time. This was the crossroads for Stephan. And he decided to take the road that lead to his disappearance.

Stephan searched the boy for any identifying items. He coolly groped his legs and arms feeling for anything that might contain his name. There was nothing except a very simple railroad watch. Unbuckling the watch, Stephan removed it and tucked it into his uniform's breast pocket. Then, grabbing the boy's feet, Stephan dragged the body back into the middle of the coop. He was so light, thought Stephan. So young. Stephan swept the ground with his foot looking for the hatch he knew was there and lead to a shallow storage compartment. Finding the hatch, Stephan pulled it open and pushed the body of the boy into the cramped space.

Shutting the hatch, Stephan was shocked to see that it stood open a few inches; the boy's slight torso too slight for his shabby sweater was just a bit too large to be hidden in the storage space. Stephan closed his eyes, took a deep breath and jumped up and then on to the hatch. It was still open. He jumped again. This time the hatch slammed to its stops with a snap of collar bone and ribs. Stephan immediately vomited, more from emotion than effort.

Staggering outside, Stephan was confronted with the largest bit of his equipment that needed to be disposed of because tonight was when he was going to change his skin and be gone. Be gone from England. Be gone from the war. And although he loved the Blower with the same affection many felt for their pets, Stephan knew he had to leave it behind. And not just parked up on the curb somewhere.

Stephan would leave the Blower here. But not just out in the woods. So, he climbed in and went through the elaborate starting procedure one last time. The Blower answering his call immediately. Finding reverse, Stephan backed down the lane about fifty yards and turned the Bentley to face the coop. Setting the brake, Stephan climbed out of the blower and began looking for a suitable branch. He quickly found a limb, snapped it off to the length he needed and jumped back into the Blower.

Dallying was never something Stephan did. So, he patted the Blower on the machined dash in a form of goodbye, engaged first and jumped towards the coop. Navigating the narrow lane at almost forty miles per hour was harrowing, but Stephan just focused on the door of the coop. Grabbing the branch off the passenger seat without taking his eyes off his target, Stephan then placed it between the seat and the throttle pedal. Sure the car would hit the door, Stephan tumbled out of the Blower, hearing his own ribs crack this time, as he hit the ground and rolled into a tree.

He caught his breath and looked up just as the Blower hit the door of the coop dead center. But the car was wider than the doors; it knocked out stones on both sides as it careened into the tight space. The few birds that remained finally flying out. The Blower slammed into the back of the stone coop. Engine still revving, as the stick kept the gas pumping, the coop began shedding stones to the ground. In just another few seconds, enough stones had fallen that the roof of the coop came crashing down on the Blower. The engine finally stopped. The whine of the Blower silenced.

Stephan stayed prone on the ground, looking up at the clear sky through the heavy canopy of trees. He listened to the odd crumble and groan of the totaled building. He ran through his mind the possibilities of where he would go now. The war was over. How had he been so foolish, so German, to think that the war would turn? Stephan felt the wave of emotion wash over him as he lay trying to think and block out the pain in his ribs. I deserve this pain, Stephan thought. The power of his feeling felt like the ocean. He could feel them sweep up from his feet and tumble over his head as they eased back into the woods.

For over an hour, Stephan didn't check the exact time, he let himself be something other than the weapon he had been for the past four years. He let himself be human. Nearly weeping at times for both his failures and his successes, Stephan gathered his energies and faculties. The silence was beautiful to Stephan. After nonstop years of bombs and yelling commanders and yes, even the thunderous bark of the Blower, Stephan needed the silence. Wherever he would go after here would have to be quiet.

The warm hum of a distant squadron of Spitfires pulled Stephan back to the noisy present. Even here in a deserted garden, acres from others, the noises of the war came round too soon. Pushing himself up on his elbow, and then to his knees, Stephan gasped for breath as his broken ribs caused each intake of air to feel like a fresh wound. Another few minutes of effort and concentration helped Stephan make it to his feet.

Gingerly stepping towards the coop, Stephan smiled at how effective his hiding of the Blower had been. He couldn't see any remnant of the car. It was as if there was no building there ever, just a roof of one set upon the ground. Only the smell of petrol and oil that would soon disperse gave any clue to the fact the Blower was buried under several tons of stone and wood and slate tiles. Walking around the circumference of the coop's foundation was equally rewarding, as the Blower was completely invisible from every angle. His last act as a soldier for the Reich had, like most of his others, been a success. Stephan said goodbye to the car he fondly thought of as J.H.

With the tasks at hand done, Stephan turned and walked down the access path towards the secondary road that intercepted the Penshurst grounds. Before brushing off the dirt that clung to his uniform, Stephan took a long pull from the cherry schnapps in his flask. He made himself once again into the dedicated ARP soldier that everyone on this island believed him to be. Taking short strides to reduce the pain in his side, Stephan put one foot in front of the other and walked towards his life after the war.

38
Newcastle, May 27, 2011

It was the fourth day now of Faston and Charles holing up in the small, disorganized and dusty Newcastle Museum of the ARP trying to find a link to the Blower. And this was on top of the several years' worth of time spent chasing the car. It seemed a long time ago that Faston was asked by Aron Stores after the 2008 Goodwood race to track down a few, veil-thin leads that might end with the Blower. So long, in fact, that Charles and he had both recently just been going through the motions of tracking down the Blower. But these last few days had given the quest purpose if not positivity.

Faston had never quite felt lower than this. He found it impossible to avoid information about the automotive find of the century in every classic car magazine, website and even some regular popular newspapers. There was even talk of the Blower having the potential to become the most expensive car ever sold at auction. Currently, that honor rested with the blue Bugatti Type 57 Atlantic acquired in a private sale by an anonymous buyer. Faston didn't really care whether the Blower sold for that type of money, what he cared about was whether or not the real Blower sold. Or, in a back up, that he could prove that the Blower Patrick was peddling was not real at all.

The reason Faston and Charles were still here, still slugging through box after unlabeled box, was that Alberto had phoned them yesterday with no more information. He was unable to find out more from the letters he used as a springboard to track down the vaporous trail of Stephan Sidlow. Alberto was not able to find out more about Stephan after he left university. From Thornley to Alberto to Faston himself a lot of people tried to track down Stephan yet none had. Faston was even beginning to have these slight feelings that maybe Stephan did not exist at all. At least with the Blower, Faston knew that it once was real. So, it was left to Charles and Faston to fight off the cobwebs and the allergies and plug away like good historians.

Newcastle's ARP museum was like many a small museum, one man's collection run amok and then turned over to the local community after said collector's passing. Faston guessed that the heirs must not have thought they could get much money at auction from the collection so they went with the tax angle by donating the lot to the city. And on that assumption, they were probably right, as historically significant documents were not always significantly valuable. Staffed by a codgering, dedicated group of volunteers, the museum was open only a couple of hours a day, three days a week. With more than half of its annual total of 300 visitors being children on school outings, it was not one of the UK's better historical holdings. But, for Faston and Charles's needs, it was hopefully enough.

Faston and Charles were doted over by the staff. Brought sandwiches, beer and boxes at a steady pace. And the staff was impossible to escape, as the whole museum compromised no more than five-hundred square feet. Over the past few days, there were two potential bright spots, or maybe flickering bits of hope spots.

Their first find was made only two hours into their search. After a cup of tea and introductions, Faston and Charles had set to work on the filing cabinet the docent had pointed to when asked where potential records of ARP personnel might be. After thumbing through a few files and attaches containing all sorts of beaurocratic paperwork from over seventy years ago, Faston found something interesting. It was a photograph of the front of an ARP spotting station. The sand-bagged location on the corner of the street overlooking a green was staffed by a woman and a man. The woman was peering into the large spotting scope. The man was writing down the horizontal and vertical angles and direction of flight, no doubt to be relayed to the home office in case the airplane was an enemy. Overall, the photo had a posed quality to it. It didn't seem to be reportage. But what caught Faston's eye was the car that was parked in the far back left part of the photo. Caught by accident it seems, as all you could make out was the bumper and a few inches of the bodywork. Faston wasn't totally positive, but pretty sure it was the, or at least a, Bentley bodied by Phillips. Unfortunately, no date or other writing appeared on the photograph. It was just a crumb that barely sustained the hungry historians and allowed them to make a few more steps back in time.

"Faston, I am going to make a photocopy of the picture we found the other day." Charles said. "It may be as close as we get to SM 3912. So, I do want a keepsake of it. It's either that or I bid on the thing that Patrick is selling."

Faston groaned to himself, then answered. "Make a copy for me, will you. I'll tack it up over my toolbox like a fisherman who had a glimpse of the big one that got away. And I didn't see a copier here."

"No, but one of the old guys said the chemist had one."

"The chemist? God, I love the UK. Take your time. It's what, about dinnertime? Pick up a snack while you're out too. There is that great little gastro-grocer down the street. Maybe get some premade stuff and we'll eat it here."

Faston could tell that Charles too was feeling the weight of coming up short. He recognized in him the expression of an athlete, though Charles was no athlete, who had tried hard but came up short in a fairly played contest. It was Charles though who had found the other bit of information regarding Stephan earlier today. It was a report from a rank and file ARP member about some questions he had regarding the Eastern Division manager, Stephan Sidlow.

The report was a two-page questioning of decisions Stephan had made that the writer felt were questionable and not in keeping with Stephan's charge of protecting the populace. The most vivid of the charges that the anonymous man made was that Stephan had relayed false coordinates about approaching bombers to home base. The man stated that he was present when he saw Stephan write down coordinates incorrectly and then call them in to the active airfields defending London with dire effects. Faston thought the complaint came across as panicky and picky. And all the complaints, like the wrongly reported coordinates could be attributed to simple human error. None the less, the complaint did make it all the way to Sir John Anderson's desk. Where it was summarily dismissed as ramblings and ravings. Sour grapes if you will. The actual hand written note on the case file read,

'Unsubstantiated information from an anonymous source. Unfortunately, not the first case of a war department employee acting like a slighted peacetime clerk.'

Ouch. But the report did add to the palette of facts that would not paint a romantic picture of Stephan Sidlow.

That was it. A sliver of a picture and an anonymous report were all that was found. Faston was still committed to finding out more though. The auction was not to commence for approximately 48 hours, so there was still time.

Faston's phone rang, causing a glare from the museum staff before he was able to answer it. A booming voice was on the opposite end. It was Aron.

"Tick tock, Faston."

"Tick tock indeed. Time is ending for our hunt. We are knee deep in it, Aron. Trying to get anything to cast a doubt on Patrick's Blower."

"So, the plan is now to just find some information to get the auction house to pull the car?" Aron asked.

"Exactly, I don't think we'll find the car now. But, like a sports team out of the playoffs, I enjoy playing the spoiler role."

"Well, spoil the bastard." Aron encouraged.

"We'll do our best. Sorry it's come to this. But we're going ten tenths till the end."

"That's all I can ask. Good luck." Aron offered, and then hung up.

Faston didn't dwell on Aron's call; he just kept digging into the documents as fast as he could while still ensuring he didn't pass over something valuable to the search. Faston worked until Charles finally returned from the food run.

"Hope you like the local oysters. Got a pie of them for you." Charles said, handing a still warm bag to Faston. Unlike the usual, Charles had perfect timing this go round. He was hungry and needed a break.

"That took a while." Faston commented, unwrapping the carrying bag to reveal a dense small pie topped with potatoes.

"And that is not potatoes, Faston. It's a horseradish and parsnip puree. Sounded uppity enough for you."

"Thanks, you didn't get the same?"

"No. Went with a cold roast sandwich. Proper man food."

"Proper indeed."

"Don't muck up the documents with that overpriced repast." Barked the last volunteer still in the building. The man who would lock up when Faston and Charles left. Neither Charles nor Faston responded, they just exchanged wry smiles and tucked into their dinners.

To get their minds off the search while they ate, Faston started up a favorite game he and Charles played. No board required. No facts to check. Pure subjectivity. And Faston was sure every car nut of every persuasion played it in some way shape or form. They called it, Dollar Garage. For a specified amount of money, the players had to state what three cars they would want to park in their dream garage. And most importantly, they had to give their collection a name. One of Faston's all-time favorite wins in this game was when, playing with a measly $30,000 budget, he came up with the Mr. T collection. Three remarkable T-top inclusive vehicles. Charles had laughed himself to defeat. Values were rounded off grossly to avoid any conflict over whether or not you could buy, say, a 1970 Chevrolet El Camino SS for $25,000 or $30,000. The winner was usually decided by the vanquished who most often said, 'you beat me, that's a better collection.'

"Alright Charles," Faston began, "$400,000 Garage. You first."

"Damn it." Charles cursed through a mouthful of food. "I had perfected a $100,000 and a six-million dollar garage just in case we would play. Thought I had the high and low covered. Damn the middle. Give me a minute."

Faston knew that Charles always came up with a theme first. A name. Then he would fill in the cars that fit that name. It was a technique that worked for Charles. Faston worked the opposite way. And it seemed that each was equally effective as both Charles and Faston seemed to admit defeat and, in turn, victory about equally.

"You are going down, Faston. The name of my collection, which I would print on a T-shirt and pass out to all lucky enough to view this collection, would be called...Are you ready?"

"Ready?" Faston obliged, and then took another bite of the creamy oyster pie.

"Aria. The aria collection. Because all of these cars would be ideal for making a trip to see an Opera."

"How cultured of you."

"Yes. First and grandest then. Because the cleverness does not come in here. 1930 Phantom II Barker Sedanca de Ville. Caned doors. Dual spares. In dark blue over cream coachwork. Blue disc wheels. Dark blue leather. Chauffer driven. It is well-proportioned. Well-bred. And well-done. Arrive in this and you will get more attention than Kiri Te Kanawa."

"Good one. What is that, $150,00 thousand?"

"One-fifty. Agreed. Two-fifty left. Minus $200,000 for a 1967 Mercedes 600 Pullman. The executive version, not the gross over-long limousine. In black over black leather. The leather replacing the factory velour, of course."

"Of course."

"6.3 liters. Air suspension. And a vertical grill that inspires awe and fear in all that see it. I might even add some flags of my own design to the fenders. In an African-dictator-goes-posh sort of way. Now finally."

"Finally. For fifty grand there are not that many cars I think would be appropriate for the opera, err, Aria Collection."

"Oh, I disagree. You are thinking of cars that one must be driven in. But, another rather nice way to arrive at the opera is to drive oneself."

"Really, have you ever been to the opera?"

"No. Doesn't matter. I know some people drive to the opera. And I also know wherever there are rich people driving there are valets. So, I figure, you still get to drive up to the front, even if you are stabbing the gas your self."

"Fine."

"Fine indeed. Alvis TD21 coupe. The vertical windscreen and square lines echoing the tuxedo and top hat I would wear. Spacious. Easy to drive. Rare as rare gets in the USA. I'd go for that nice Alvis blue-silver. Should look good under the lights. Wire wheels of course. No hood ornament on the Alivs TD21 which is a rather subdued thing. Subtle, something the world is missing these days, subtlety. Have you seen the size of watches recently? 50mm? Really. Anyway, there is something to be said for a car that costs but fifty grand and looks like three times that much. So, there it is the Aria Collection."

"Well done. My turn." Faston worked fast when playing this game. Especially when he went second, as he half paid attention to Charles, the other half of his mind worked on his collection.

"And what is your collections name?"

"Hyphen."

"Yawn." Charles mocked.

"1912 Gobron-Brillie. Wood-bodied skiff. Maybe the first 100 miles per hour capable car. Yawn at that. If you even know what I am talking about. $200,000. Next, that would have to be an Arnolt-Bristol. Only around 130 or so made. Rarer than rare. No replicas of it ruining the specialness. $100,000. That leaves me $100,000 to find the final car. Austin-Healey 100M. That should do nicely. All hyphenated. All remarkable and special and not yawn-inducing in the least."

"Although your cars are rather unique. The Healey."

"Austin hyphen Healey."

"The Healey, is a bit common. I rather prefer my collection."

"I do too." Faston had to admit to himself, his collection was even too esoteric for his own tastes. "You win. I would not want to own a Gobron-Brillie."

"Who would? Now, back to the stacks."

Faston and Charles returned to the search and worked silently. The hours passed not too slowly and not too fast. It was only when Faston noted that the sun was beginning to rise that he had realized just how late it was. It was almost six in the morning on the 28th. Faston was covered with records that he read and just set down on himself or near his position. He had beavered his way through a stack of papers that was over three feet in height. And his back and neck felt the worse for it. He needed a walk. Getting up from his seat, Faston walked towards the door and was just about to head out when Charles grumbled to him.

"You've got something stuck to your back."

Groping around his shoulders Faston tried to find what Charles was remarking on.

"No, a bit lower."

Changing his arm, Faston reached around his waist with his left arm and felt the scrap of paper clinging to his slim, cashmere v-neck sweater. Faston stood stock still and read and re-read the note. He felt nailed to the floor.

"Oye, get out of the way. I'm here to see if you all stole anything." Harrumphed the volunteer who was coming back to help them today.

"How far is Penshurst from here?" Faston demanded to know, grabbing the man roughly by the shoulder.

"The Palace?"

"I don't know." Faston fumbled. "I guess. Is there another Penshurst besides a Palace?"

"Easy. No other Penshurst I know. And...Phwooar. I'd say six hours."

"Charles, wrap up. We've got to get to Penshurst now."

"Why the hell would we go there? And where the hell is it?"

"It is down south." The volunteer answered. "But I've no idea why you'd go there. We've lots of castles and the like around town."

"We are going there because this little note." With that Faston handed the note to Charles. Imprinted on the yellowed, three-inch square or so scrap of paper was the initial S.S.

And in a tight, faded pencil script was the words; 'Penshurst. Unstaffed acreage. Suitable outbuildings. Accessible."

39
Monaco, May 27, 2011

Patrick Patrick thought it appropriate that he was having drinks in a casino with Wilkinson, Hertweck and Kiefer. They were, in essence, his whales. His bigger than big customers. They were three men from three different countries. Three different backgrounds. Three different business who wanted, even though they hadn't said it outright yet, the Blower to be theirs after the auction tomorrow evening.

Patrick had chosen the casino to meet these whales, as it was where one of his favorite movies, *Casino Royale*, was shot. To complete the feeling of being Bond for the day, Patrick had even gone ahead and ordered a Vesper. The very drink that Bond, played by Daniel Craig, had created on the spot in the film. Patrick loved the taste of the three parts gin, one part vodka and half a part Lillet, even though he had no idea what Lillet was.

Two Vespers into the evening, Patrick was feeling a delightful heaviness infuse his limbs. And an even more delightful sense of calm and confidence coursed through his mind. *This was the position he was meant to be in,* he thought. A man in control of the situation. So in charge and admired that men like Wilkinson, Hertweck and Kiefer would want to have drinks with him.

For three more hours, and two more Vespers, Patrick stayed and chatted with his whales. And with a dozen or so other Bentley enthusiasts who had needed to come talk to him. To congratulate him. And what he liked even more than the men who came and talked to him, were the ones who pointed him out to their wives or girlfriends. Often having to repeat the accusation that he was the one to find the car. The women seeming more disbelieving than the men. But with the belief that he was the star of the weekend along with the race winner, he could sense the women getting a flirtatious twinkle in their eyes.

Patrick almost wished that this feeling could last forever. That he could always be seen as the leader in his business. The he was the undisputed master of unearthing rare cars, not Faston. Because Patrick knew, in his heart, that Faston didn't run to rare cars. The rare cars ran to him. But after tomorrow, there would be a well-worn path to his soon to be much posher door.

Patrick was thinking about whether or not to order a final Vesper when he noticed a group of men approach him. Ugh, more non-bidders, Patrick guessed judging by how young the group of men looked. Were they wearing uniforms?

"Mr. Patrick Patrick?" The man in the lead asked in what Patrick Patrick thought to be an eastern European accent.

"Yes," Patrick answered. "What's up?"

"What is up, as you say, is we are from Interpol and have some questions for you regarding ownership, legitimacy and papers of the Bentley."

40
Penshurst Palace, May 28, 2011

Borrowing the morning docent's Ford Cortina for the drive to Penshurst had both good and bad side effects. Good, was the fact that the Cortina presented a stylish swash of small tail fins and tight dimensions. The bad, it was not a Lotus version and as such, ponderously lethargic. But by keeping the stock four pot on a boil it had not seen in years, Faston was able to keep up near the legal speed limit on most of the roads towards Penshurst.

Listening to the racket of the four and feeling the vibration through the seat of his pants for hours was maddening. Numbing. Frustrating. The miles didn't pass by as fast as he or Charles hoped. They crept by. They eeked by. But, methodically, they did go by. The miles uneagerly getting passed over by the thin tires of the Cortina only to be spat backwards, to be left behind.

Five and a half hours later, Faston and Charles arrived at the main gate of Penshurst. It was a dedicated tourist attraction. How in the hell could one of the world's most valuable cars be here for years without being found, thought Faston. It was then he remembered the note he had read and reread, it mentioned 'unstaffed acreage'. So, the acreage which would have been unstaffed eighty years ago is where he and Charles needed to start their search.

Having called ahead, Faston had already spoken to Piper Hartshorn, the curator of Penshurst. And it was no doubt Piper who was standing cross-armed and cross-legged as Charles and he pulled to a stop in the Cortina.

"Cute car." Piper noted with no other movement besides that of her thin lips into the open driver's side window of the Cortina.

"They are cute, aren't they?" Faston said while getting out of the Cortina much quicker than Charles. "You must be Piper."

"Yes. Pleasure to meet you." Piper said, untying one of her arms from the other and pivoting it at the elbow in front of her body for Faston to shake.

Shaking Piper's hand, Faston looked past her bored eyes and let them roam over the whole spread of Penshurst. Returning his gaze to Piper, Faston stopped shaking her hand and spoke to her, "Thanks for meeting us. Nice place to come to work every day."

"It has some charm. And I grew up here too. So, it is family home and place of employment. Trying to wring a bit of money out of this estate is harder than you would imagine."

Exchanging raised eyebrows with Charles, Faston let a small grin crease his face before speaking to Piper again. "Well then, I take it you played on these grounds quite a bit as child. Probably know every little hidden secret. Like, an old car sitting around somewhere that no one really thought much about?"

"Oh, we were allowed to roam some of the grounds. But Daddy has several hundred acres that he preferred we not walk through. So we didn't. And I don't know of any old cars around here. As I said on the phone earlier."

"But you do have several hundred acres of unexplored property?"

"I didn't say that. Now that Daddy has passed on my brother runs the estate and grounds and has opened them all with walking trails. And there is nothing out there. Lots of small buildings. But no cars spotted yet." Piper condescendingly noted.

"Be that as it may. We've driven a bit and could use a walk. So, just point us in the direction of what would have been considered 'unstaffed acreage' during the war and we will be on our way."

Spinning around without uncrossing her legs, Piper pointed towards a dense grove of old growth trees that encircled the castle on its north side. "That would be the area over there. Daddy and his Daddy didn't do too much on that property. It was a science experiment for them. The great age of experimentation that began in the 1880s. Leave the property alone and see what happens without man's hand mucking it up. Take a trail map and enjoy the walk."

"Oh, what if we do, crazy as it sounds, find this valuable car we are looking for?" Charles asked. "If you are tight for cash, Faston and I could help you monetize it."

"Monetize?" Faston repeated.

"Yes, we are quite the specialists in these matters."

"I know that." Piper said. "I looked you up while we spoke on the phone. Of course I would want you to sell it. Why else would I be willing to give you full access to the estate? Probably help pay the bills for a month or two."

"More like a decade or two." Faston jibbed.

"Noted." Charles said, tipping his fingers in a casual salute towards Piper. "Shall we walk, Faston?"

"Of course."

Faston and Charles walked in silence across the open grass near the castle, no doubt once kept clear to help strengthen its defenses, and into the woods. The late May weather felt more like late June weather and Faston was relieved when they got out of the full force of the sun and entered the cool, dark grove of trees. Within a few yards along the trail the woods swallowed them and hid the castle from view. Faston thought that a green

Bentley might have a good chance of remaining out of view even just a step or two off the main path.

"Nice backyard, huh?" Charles asked.

"Not bad. But think of the maintenance." Faston joked back.

"Right, I wouldn't want to take care of it either."

"So, it would take days to cover all this ground. Maybe weeks. So, how are we going to narrow down the search to something accomplishable in a few hours?"

Snapping a dead branch that hung over the path and using it as a walking stick, Charles took a while before answering Faston. "Didn't the scribble you find say something about outbuildings? And buildings are a more natural place for a Bentley than raw woodland."

"They did. Good plan. Let's hit the outbuildings." Faston said, then added. "If we find any."

Faston and Charles found their first outbuilding after about twenty minutes of walking. It was a colonnaded structure off the left of the path. There was no regular path towards it, so Faston and Charles tramped across the soft ground towards it.

"That looks big enough to hold a car or four." Charles said.

"It certainly does." Faston said while looking over the Greek influenced front. It seemed like a real temple. Not a structure that should be found in the woods.

"Well, here we are." Charles said, with a hand on the old, wooden double-height doors. "After you." Charles added while opening the door for Faston.

Stepping through the doors with rising expectations, Faston took a quick glance and all he saw was more woods. "A folly? That sums up this whole expedition of ours." The temple was just a façade, just one wall, built to amuse some long dead lord of the manor, thought Faston.

"You should build a folly on your property." Charles commented.

"Of what?"

"Maybe a giant B-squared for Blower Bentley. Or, concrete replica of Fenway Park."

"Funny." Lets get back on the trail.

"Why don't we get off the trail? Road less travelled and all that. We came through this door." Charles said, pointing back to the doors of the temple with his walking stick. "Why don't we keep walking that way, like the woods are the rooms of this temple. And I would rather walk through a temple of woods than just woods."

Faston nodded his head in agreement and followed Charles who was striding ahead looking like the logo of Johnnie Walker come to life. Minus the top hat.

"This is pretty pleasant walking through here. Caprice would love this stuff," Faston said to Charles. "But, do you ever ask why we trudge through the woods. Through greasy parts boxes. All that after cars."

"No." Charles said so quickly it was like a continuation of Faston's sentence. "You don't ask why you follow a passion. I ask all the time why I'm a teacher. But that is part job, part passion. And I constantly ask why I still clean my own house instead of hiring a lady."

"You don't clean your house."

"Besides the point. You know what I mean. Jobs and chores need rationalization. Passions don't. If you rationalize your passion you miss the point."

"But why cars?" Faston puzzled. "I think of them as really bits of history with more bits of history clinging to them. Like a doorway that a parent charts a child's growth on, owners leave marks on the cars they own. How they used them. How they cared, or didn't care for them."

"I think for me, with cars," Charles spoke sounding like he was thinking out loud, "It's that you bond with a good car like no other machine. Do you bond with a blender, dishwasher, or phone? You lose a phone and you miss the functionality but nothing else. A good car becomes a transcendent tool for living life a certain way. For getting you not just physically to a location, but mentally as well. Who hasn't sat in a car and immediately been transported somewhere else?"

"Like to the middle of a woods in England?"

"Exactly."

Over the next few hours, Faston and Charles walked without talking. They came across an old water mill, a large and listing wooden barn and three small stone houses. All empty. All reclaimed by the woods.

"Do you hear traffic?" Charles asked.

"I thought I did. I guess so." Faston answered looking around. Then finally catching glimpse of a passing car. "Yep, look there is a road."

Faston and Charles walked so far that they came to the edge of the property.

"Think it will be quicker to walk back along the road?" Charles asked in a defeated tone.

"Especially if we catch a bus or get picked up. It's been a while since I hitchhiked."

"After you." Faston invited Charles to go ahead of him.

"Thanks." Charles said and led the way. Then he paused and tapped a rough pile of wood.

"Look, another folly. Instead of just a façade. It is just a roof." Charles pointed to the pile of wood that made up a circular roof on the forest floor.

"Quite a unique folly at that."

"For sure." Charles agreed and gave the roof a final hearty stab with his walking stick. This time, breaking through the wood and coming to a halt with what Faston thought was an odd thud.

"Did that sound like metal to you?" Faston asked, daring to say it out loud.

"I believe it did." Charles answered through a huge grin.

41
Monaco May 28, 2011

Patrick was doing one more tap dance. And he knew it needed to be his finest performance. The agents at Interpol were going over the forged paperwork for the Blower more carefully than he could have imagined. They were also forcing him to give them Borland's phone number so that they could talk with the 'owner'. The agents were even phoning the registration department in England to try and check on the history of the Blower.

And to be tap dancing with a waning Vesper buzz was infuriating to Patrick.

"Mr. Patrick, would you mind sitting down? Pacing around the room is not helping this go faster." Said one of the agents.

"Really? It is helping me to feel better. You pulled me away from three of the largest potential buyers of my very real Blower Bentley. So, if you don't mind, I will continue my pacing."

"It is making you look nervous and maybe a little guilty." Another agent added.

"I didn't know you French cops followed so many clichés."

"We aren't all French. I am from Belgium." Said a third agent, shaking his head from side to side slowly.

'Oh, boy.' Patrick thought to himself.

"Now," began the Belgian agent. "Back to the paperwork. Or more precisely, lone piece of paper you have that ties the Bentley to Sir Borland."

"How much longer will this take? I need to text some people." Patrick harrumphed, the added. "Can I have my phone back so people don't think I'm dead?"

"In awhile." All three agents said in unison.

"And no one has called you, so I do not think that anyone is out beating the bushes for you yet," deadpanned the Belgian agent while unbuttoning the collar of his shirt and settling into his chair.

42
Penshurst May 28, 2011

It was ten in the evening and the small corner of woods that Faston and Charles had ended their walk at was turning into a nighttime construction zone. Generators hummed in the background as lights were sprouting up among the trees and beaming daytime-levels of lighting on the circular ruin. They had called in all the help they could get after Faston had pried up one of the softened boards of the roof and caught a glimpse of what could only be the recurved end of a Bentley bumper. The chrome pitted and dulled but still the shiniest item around.

Speaking above the din, Faston leaned into Charles. "Think the Interpol folks are bothering Patrick yet?"

"I'm sure of it. Inspired bit of counter punching that, calling your friends over at Interpol. Tax evasion is a big business with those boys."

"You two look like school boy pranksters." Piper said from behind Faston. She had been the first call he made after discovering what might be the Blower. She had proven more helpful than he would have thought. Rousing the local grounds keepers of the estate along with some nearby landscape contractors to provide the necessary machinery to excavate the site.

Once Piper had arrived at the scene to act as eyewitness and property representative, Faston had pried and broke away several more boards until he could see a bit more of the car. He had started at what was the front of the car as after three boards were removed he and Charles could make out the unmistakable casting of the Villiers blower assembly. This was the real SM 3912. Once the car was identified, Faston and Charles stopped and waited for the proper equipment to continue excavation.

Piper was at first put off that Faston wanted to haul the car out tonight. She couldn't understand why a photograph and her word weren't enough to stop the Pneu auction. So Faston had explained to her that photos could be forged much more easily than cars and that the powerful collectors and vendors in Monaco would get the auction going anyway. What Faston didn't say to Piper, but what drove him more than anything, was that he wanted to shut Patrick down for good. To end his career in a stunning fashion. To finally get this leach ostracized from the collector car community for good. And only an in-your-face, full tilt smashing of his lies would do that.

"We're ready." The head groundskeeper said to Piper, then added. "And sir. Step back."

The workmen had made quick progress, within three hours they had cleared a path to the ruin. Brought in their equipment. And made a sling out of lifting straps to remove the roof of what Piper had told Faston was an old pigeon coop not used by the estate since this area was put off limits by her family generations ago.

"Raise it up. Slowly, though."

With that command, the operator of the backhoe nudged the hydraulic controls of the Mahindra machine and saw tension gather on the straps. Moments later, creaks and groans rumbled up from the ruin. Struggling to lift the weight of the huge hand-carved timbers, the Mahindra shrieked until the roof finally swung free, less than an inch above the crumbled foundation.

Following the hand signals of the headman, the operator continued to lift the roof off the large stone base. One foot. Then two. Reaching three feet above the base, the operator nudged the backhoe to the left and guided the roof in one piece toward a clearing made just an hour earlier.

As everyone present swarmed to the edge of the circular ruin, snapping cell-phone pictures and high fiving each other, Faston and Charles walked slowly up to the edge of the site where a couple of workmen stepped aside to let the pair take a closer look. Faston and Charles' silence stood in stark contrast to the party atmosphere of the rest of those present. Even Piper was seen hugging the crew with a huge smile on her face.

But none of the others felt the exhausted elation of Faston and Charles. Faston felt like a marathoner completing his first 26.2 mile race. Glee mixed with joy and a healthy dose of discovering something everyone thought was lost for good. No matter the poor condition of the find.

If a rusted Bugatti from the bottom of a lake could draw a huge sum at auction, Faston knew this last of the missing Blowers would pull even more interest and money. But he had to admit; the Blower was in poor shape.

The first thing Faston noticed was that someone had changed the paint color. It was now a midnight blue. Though there was almost an equal amount of rust color present on the coachwork. Even the wire wheels had been treated to a color change, in their case to red.

The two-door coupe now rested surrounded by the broken boards of a shallow basement, looking like The Endurance surrounded by pack ice.

The Blower was not even in rolling condition. All four wheels were skewed in unnatural angles of castor and camber. The fabric of the top was non-existent. The leather was moist and tattered. The front crumbled and crushed from what looked like an impact with the wall of the coop. The cowl back suffered only vertical compression in areas where the beams had landed upon it. But, it was all there. And it was one of only 50 production Blowers ever produced.

Faston jumped into the pit next to the Blower to get a closer look. Tearing his pants on broken boards, he pressed forward until he was able to grasp the top of the driver's side door. Pushing back the top bows, Faston looked over the dash. Immediately, Faston could imagine the Blower in road-worthy condition again. The multiple gauges flicking with information and light. The metal dash polished to a gleam to offset the dark leather and carpet. Reaching over the door, Faston grabbed the gearlever and gave it a tug. Of course, it didn't budge but Faston hadn't really expected it to. Stepping back, Faston walked slowly around the car. Running his hand over the bodywork, wiping off decades of dirt and decay from the paintwork trying to complete his picture of SM 3912 at its ruddy, healthy best.

"Beautiful, isn't it?" Charles asked, interrupting Faston's romance with the Blower.

"Gorgeous. In every sense of the word." Faston replied. "Now, let's get this beauty packed up and on its way to Monaco. Piper, were you able to get a car carrier for us to drive?"

"No."

"What?" Faston asked, trying his best to remain calm.

"I did you one better." Piper revealed. "A car hauler is a bit rough and slow for a drive to Monaco. Let alone appearing in that town in such a rough machine. So, I called my friend at the local Porsche main dealer. He sent over their racecar hauler."

"And what is that?"

"It's over there." Piper pointed to the main road just seen through the trees. "It is a brand new Cayenne Turbo with some RUF parts here and there. Does any of this mean anything to you? Because it means nothing to me. Anyway, it is hooked up with a lightweight aero aluminum trailer. He said it would be comfortable at speeds up to ninety five. Able to do speeds of 120. And that that should be good enough."

"I would say so." Faston said while beaming over the deep blue Cayenne. "I have a secret weak spot for the Pepper, so I am not unhappy to drive one for eighteen hours or so."

"Glad to hear it." Piper smiled. "And I didn't want you to have to stop at a Little Chef or something worse, so I had cook pack a hamper for you."

"No one does hospitality in trying situations like the British." Faston replied with the slightest of head nods.

Faston returned his attention to the task of getting the Blower out of its tomb and onto the trailer. Loading up the remains of SM 3912 was made much easier by the open configuration of the trailer. A V-shaped front piece gave the trailer aerodynamics, but the open trailer part allowed easy loading and unloading. Especially when the car you were loading was not even in rolling condition. The backhoe had to carry the remains to the trailer and gingerly place them on the trailer. A process that Faston was surprised didn't damage the car further. A piece or two of the body work did fall off, but the workmen gathered them up and strapped them to the trailer. A tarp was snugged down over the entire load to the point that the covered hulk could be mistaken for a pile of wood.

With the Blower secured, Faston and Charles prepared to head off to Monaco. Saying their goodbyes quickly and thanking each of the workmen personally, it was a few ticks before midnight when Faston clicked the gearshift into drive and headed off the grounds of Penshurst.

Punching the destination in to the navigation system, Faston thought of a few things for Charles to do. "Charles, give Aron a call. Let him know that we have the Blower. Then, ring up the Sergeant we spoke to earlier from Interpol. Explain our situation, I'm sure he'll be happy to help us put away Patrick after having met him."

"It's after midnight, should I call Aron now?"

"I think this is one time that Aron wouldn't mind be awakened. I know I wouldn't."

43

Monaco, May 29 2011 5:14 PM

With the only stops made enroute determined by the Cayenne's prodigious thirst for petrol, Faston and Charles made it to Monaco in around 15 hours when usually the trip would take closer to 18. Espressos and Red Bulls did their best to keep Faston and Charles awake now, even though both had managed to grab a fitful hour or two of sleep on the drive. The best aid to awareness that Faston had found was the warm, herb-scented air of southern France that poured in the open windows of the Cayenne.

Interpol demanded to meet Faston and Charles when they crossed into Monaco to determine if the rusting hulk they hauled in was the real SM 3912. They wanted to ensure they would not look like fools. Pulling into the hotel car park that was the prearranged meeting place, Charles and Faston saw a rather large group of officers, almost two dozen in total.

Stepping out of the Cayenne, Faston stretched down to touch his toes, then walked over toward the group of men.

"You must be Faston. I am Sergeant Demont. We have spoken together several times now."

"Thanks for your help, Sergeant. Quite a group you have here. What do you need from me? The auction starts in under an hour."

The Sergeant shrugged as if he had all the time in the world. "I just need for you to step back and for these gentlemen from the Bentley Driver's Club to look at the car. They too, do not want to look like fools and stand behind a forgery. So, I fear they will be quite thorough."

While Faston was speaking with Demont, the three representatives of the BDC had already uncovered the Blower and were swarming over it with flashlights and cameras like crime-scene investigators. Or a panel of concours judges. One of the men was even underneath a portion of the car, his head just millimeters from the rusting, shifting mass.

"Please, sit down while they verify the find." Demont offered.

"No thanks, I'll stand." Faston answered after exhaling a large breath.

Fifteen hours of driving coupled with his nerves weren't allowing Faston to sit down and rest. Pacing around the parking garage Faston tried to act calm and collected, not a strong suit of his. Checking his Ward Ascari watch so often that he decided to unclasp it and shove it in his pocket to not watch the time crawl minute by minute closer to the auction time.

Charles on the other hand, lain down against a concrete support and was sleeping away this stoppage.

After dozens of phone calls, double that amount of fact checking in books and numerous huddles, the men of the BDC had a quick chat with the men of Interpol. Hoping that this was the end of the inquisition into a find that was without a doubt the real SM 3912, Faston walked over to Demont.

Strapping his Ward back on his wrist, Faston asked the Interpol Sergeant what the result was. "So?"

"It is real, for sure. Everyone is quite embarrassed at having been put under the spell of a fake, an excellent fake. None better, all agree. Probably worth a half-million dollars as a forgery. But, you have the real one. So, lets go stop the sale of Mr. Patrick and Pneu's copy."

With the answer he wanted to hear, Faston finally allowed himself a glance at his watch. "It's five after six. The auction has begun."

"No worries, Monaco is a small place, and we will escort you."

Five minutes later, after a chaotic, thrilling drive through the winding streets of Monaco, Faston and what he came to think of as his Interpol entourage arrived at Espace Fontvieille.

The Interpol officers quickly dismounted from their Opels and surrounded the white, tented structure while Faston parked the trailered Bentley in front of the main entrance. Flashing his credentials to the guard at one of the side entrances, Demont quietly led Faston and Charles into the auction. All of Patrick's guards were now replaced with Interpol officers.

Staying out of the line of sight of the stage, Faston, Charles and Demont gathered themselves and looked around. The crowded tent was filled to capacity. Faston guessing that there must be at least 2,500 people with seats. Another dozen was standing along the curved back wall. The dress code was casual rich. Faston noticed the expensive watches and exclusive small run wardrobes of the smiling potential bidders. Among the crowd Faston noticed a few well-known celebrity car collectors here to watch or maybe even bid. No matter, Faston was impressed by the turnout for a one-car auction.

Turning his attention from the crowd to the stage, Faston looked over the whole reason that he and Charles had pressed to find the real story behind SM 3912. But, the recreation that Patrick had created was, Faston had to admit, beautiful. And under the stage lights it commanded the room. Faston next noted that the Blower re-creation was idling. The burble of the big four a bass track for the ramblings coming from the person speaking podium.

"Who the hell is that?" Faston asked Demont.

"I think it is Sir Borland himself." Demont answered, pointing to a projection on the wall that showed the estate where this replica was supposedly found.

"Does he sound drunk to you?" Faston asked.

"A bit." Demont underplayed.

Faston thought he heard Sir Borland talking about duck hunting, not the car in front of him when, smiling, Vincent Fornel hurried to the podium.

"Thank you very much, Sir Borland." Vincent said, while escorting Borland to a nearby chair off to the side of the podium. Fumbling to get Borland to sit upright brought a couple of condescending snickers from the audience.

Returning to the podium, Vincent straightened his tie, and then began. "I'd like to thank Sir Borland for his, uh, remarkable memories of the Blower and the excellent but secret care he lavished upon it over the past decades. But to the present. The months of waiting are over, shall we start our bidding at one million Euros."

"Subtle he isn't." Charles noted as over a dozen paddles shot in the air to participate in the bidding. "Not even a how are you. A bit prostitute like."

"An apt comparison." Demont whispered.

"Three million Euros, in the back." Vincent excitedly cheered into the microphone. Ten bidders were still active. "Do I have five million Euros? I do. Thank you."

While the bidding slowed but inexorably climbed, Faston glanced around the room and this time spotted Patrick. "Hey, Charles. There's Patrick. In the third row."

Charles turned and zeroed in on Patrick. "Who's he chatting up?"

Faston took a moment to search his memory to recall if he knew the Indian-looking man on Patrick's

left or the thin, elderly man on his right. "No idea."
Feeling frustrated with watching this charade continue,
Faston wanted to push Demont into action.
"Demont, I can't watch this anymore. Bidding at
seven and a half million Euros. Not fair to the bidders.
Let's get moving."

With a calm, emotionless voice Demont twisted
his head and spoke a few words into the microphone
mounted on his vest's epaulet. Searching the room,
Faston caught sight of the Interpol agents break through
each of the eight entrances. Striding down the aisles
towards the podium and the elevated, burbling Bentley,
Faston saw no escape possible for Patrick.

Nudging Charles with his elbow, Faston
reported to Charles. "Vincent just saw them."

"And so did the bidders." Charles noted as all
the heads in the crowd swung to the nearest pair of
Interpol agents focused on reaching the stage.

Vincent's cheerleading for money stopped. He
paused. But Faston wasn't surprised when the skilled
conman tried to spin the situation. "Gentlemen, thank
you for coming." Vincent graciously said while
sweeping the room with his hand. "The winning bidder
will no doubt welcome some protection from Europe's
finest. Was the figure eight million Euros?"

This time, the call for more money didn't elicit a
single hand from the crowd. All were savvy enough to
want to see the scene in front of them play out before
bidding higher.

When all the Interpol agents positioned
themselves in front of the stage and to the left and right
of Patrick and his two friends Demont patted Faston on
the back and winked as he walked toward the stage.
"Shall we handle this as was discussed?"

"Of course." Faston answered and then walked
out with Charles to where the Cayenne and Blower were

parked. Reacquainting themselves with the representatives of the BDC, the group uncovered the remains of SM 3912.

Less than a minute later, Faston and Charles beamed when they heard a huge gasp of disbelief rip through the crowd. Excited voices in dozens of languages rose to be heard over one another. Then the sound of chairs being moved and pushed gave way to the sound of footsteps, soft loafers and loud stilettos, click-clacking at double-time pace toward he and Charles.

44
Litchfield, CT September 4, 2011

Finishing a relaxing dinner outside in the newest part of the garden that Caprice had finished installing over the summer, Faston, Charles and Caprice were catching up on the small business of the day and the large turns of events from the past few months. A small table, in a sunken square garden guarded on one side a by a twenty-foot long water feature which cooled the air and made a perfect place to escape the late summer heat now served as footrest for Faston. He contemplated that this would be the last peaceful moment before his favorite event, The Rolex Vintage Fall Festival.

Scraping the bowl of the last bit of fig and honey ice cream, Faston set the bowl on the ground for the dogs to lick clean.

"He looks as frothy as Vincent and Patrick when Interpol showed them the real SM 3912." Charles noted.

"Yes, he does." Faston agreed, reaching down and wiping Cooper's face with his napkin.

"So," Caprice drew out, "are you two having to go back to Europe for their trial."

"I hope so." Charles said. "Would like nothing better than to point from the stand at those two and say 'guilty'."

Faston rolled his eyes, and then disagreed. "No, we won't. We just had to write some depositions about the real car. We are done. But that group. Wow. They went through an incredible amount of effort. It was leaps and bounds above the last big fake on the market, that Ferrari P4. I mean, Patrick sourced a new body from India. A replica engine from Montreal. You know Charles, the replica just sold for one point two million dollars."

"I did. And I would have to say after seeing it, it was probably worth that. The fact that it was at the center of the biggest collector car scandal no doubt helped the value climb."

"It did. I bet that all that money will go to legal fees." Caprice said.

"The one time I wouldn't mind the lawyers getting a huge chunk." Charles piped in. "No need for those guys to profit from their scandal."

"One point two million for a replica." Caprice said in disbelief. "What will the real one sell for?"

"Don't know if it will go up for sale now. Piper took a moment and figured a great way for the Blower to bring people to Penshurst. She's partnered with a restorer to rebuild the Blower on the grounds of Penshurst. Sort of a living museum. And the project will take a decade at least. They will also have a memorial to the boy whose skeleton they found in the coop, underneath where the Blower was. Must have been Stephan's last victim, they still haven't identified him."

"Can't think of a better result for either car or boy. Better than the car going to some collector who would just stow it away like most of the other Blowers." Charles said. "But Piper did say she would loan the car to me and Alberto to support our Imperial War Museum show at the beginning of 2012."

"Yeah, a book deal and a museum show." Faston said, punching Charles softly in the arm. "Well done."

"Thanks. The upside of all this chasing around. We didn't just find a car. We found the only effective spy that was operating in England during WWII. Stephan Sidlow is a remarkable character. He walked such a fine line of spy and soldier. We plan on calling the show 'SS. England's Protector. England's Enemy.' The more we dug into it, Stephan did a lot of good things to help the people of England; had to, or he would have never risen to his rank. But then, the deaths caused by the few raids we can prove were a result of his actions led to over 2,400 dead civilians and countless more wounded. And that is a lot of bad. Like a serial-killer doctor. You've got to save enough lives to have the opportunity to take them."

"The summer break is up and researching this man has taken up all your time." Caprice detailed. "So, have you any idea what happened to him after the war? Where did he go? Back to Germany? To South America? Inquiring minds want to know, Charles."

Raising his eyebrows at Faston, Charles swallowed the last bit of his Leopold Brother's Apple Whiskey, crunched his cube of ice and answered Caprice. "We've no idea."

AUTHOR'S NOTES AND THANKS

According to Michael Hay in *Bentley 4 ¼-Litre Supercharged*, SM 3912 was delivered new to Lord Brougham and Vaux and has not been heard of since 1939. Of the fifty chassis covered in this book it is the only one whose fate is not known. Alan Bodfish of the Bentley Driver's Club was a great help in getting me photographs and further information on SM 3912 including the name of the last known owner, D.H. Sessions.

Further tactile details of the Blower Bentley were thanks to the Cussler Museum in Arvada, Colorado, whose caretaker was kind enough to allow me access off-hours to crawl all over and under a real Blower Bentley. This gave me insights into the starting procedure, feel of leather, grip of cord and just solidified the huge presence of these mythic cars.

To create an accurate picture of England during WWII, I relied on two books more than any others. For specifications of Home Front service uniforms and functional details I looked often at Martin Brayley's *The British Home Front 1939-1945* with its evocative illustrations by Malcolm MacGregor. While Felicity Goodall's *Voices From the Home Front* provided a glimpse into the lives of English citizens and gave me primary source material for describing the efforts and complications of life in a country struggling to win a war. Every letter and journal highlighted in *Voices* has enough drama and passion to inspire a novel of its own.

It is important to note that the efforts of Patrick Patrick to build a highly accurate forgery of the chassis SM 3912 is not without precedence. There is a growing trade in replica exotic cars. Some of the more high-profile cases include a P4 Ferrari crafted in Thailand.

Two faked Type 35B Bugattis sold in Germany. The Auto-Union withdrawn by Christie's at the last moment when it was revealed it was a rebuilt car on a different, non-championship chassis. A buyer in England receiving an £84,000 settlement over a misrepresented Bentley built up of new and old parts. Finally, and most dramatic, the 'Red Passion' raid by Italian police on a criminal ring that built fake Ferrari 360 Modenas. They seized 14 complete and 8 under-construction cars.

So, if you are in the market for a classic car – buyer beware.

And a final thanks to Frank Barrett and Nicole French whose help makes my prose more polished than it really is.

Also from Kevin Gosselin

Hunt for 901 is the debut novel by gourmet chef and automotive writer Kevin Gosselin. It's protagonist, Faston Hanks, is a Connecticut innkeeper, car historian, and automotive archeologist known for his ability to find lost automotive treasures: an automotive Indiana Jones. He is also a gourmand who won't let an adventure stand in the way of a good meal.

When Austrian musician, Heidi Ruff, arrives at his inn, begging Faston to help her find her father, his answer is simple, "I don't find people."

"You might this time," replies the Austrian. "In 1963, Porsche's 901 prototype went missing after its debut at a German auto show. My father was the one who lost it."

Thus begins Faston's hunt for the Holy Grail of Porsches, searching all over Europe for clues that will lead them to the missing 901 prototype. As Faston and his geriatric sidekick, Charles Ivory, close in on the long-lost Porsche and Heidi's mysterious father, they discover they are not alone in trying to find this most famous of Porsches. Who will be the first to find it?

Also from MX Publishing

The story concerns Mike Brookes and his Pegasus Car Company as they attempt to build and enter a two car team for the 1957 Targa Florio road race in Sicily. Pegasus build road-going sports cars but Brookes wants to take them onto an international stage to compete with the likes of Ferrari, Maserati, and Mercedes. He selects the Targa Florio as it is the toughest road race in the world, combining a car breaking mountain section with a long flat-out 180mph straight.

Available from all good bookstores and Amazon Kindle, Kobo Books, iBooks for the iPad and several other formats.

Also from MX Publishing

Close To Holmes

A Look at the Connections Between Historical London, Sherlock Holmes and Sir Arthur Conan Doyle.

Eliminate The Impossible

An Examination of the World of

Sherlock Holmes on Page and Screen.

The Norwood Author

Arthur Conan Doyle and the Norwood Years (1891 - 1894)

www.mxpublishing.com

Also From MX Publishing

In Search of Dr Watson

Wonderful biography of Dr.Watson from expert Molly Carr.

Arthur Conan Doyle, Sherlock Holmes and Devon

A Complete Tour Guide and Companion.

The Lost Stories of Sherlock Holmes

Eight more stories from the pen of John H Watson – compiled by Tony Reynolds.

www.mxpublishing.com

Also From MX Publishing

Watsons Afghan Adventure

Fascinating biography of Watson's time in Afghanistan from US Army veteran Kieran McMullen.

Shadowfall

Sherlock Holmes, ancient relics and demons and mystic characters. A supernatural Holmes pastiche.

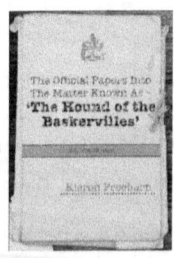

Official Papers of The Hound of The Baskervilles

Very unusual collection of the original police papers from The Hound case.

www.mxpublishing.com

Also From MX Publishing

The Sign of Fear

The first adventure of the 'female Sherlock Holmes'. A delightful fun adventure with your favourite supporting Holmes characters.

A Study in Crimson

The second adventure of the 'female Sherlock Holmes' with a host of sub- plots and new characters joining Watson and Fanshaw

The Chronology of Arthur Conan Doyle

The definitive chronology used by historians and libraries worldwide.

www.mxpublishing.com

Also From MX Publishing

Aside Arthur Conan Doyle

A collection of twenty stories from ACD's close friend Bertram Fletcher Robinson.

Bertram Fletcher Robinson

The comprehensive biography of the assistant plot producer of The Hound of The Baskervilles

Wheels of Anarchy

Reprint and introduction to Max Pemberton's thriller from 100 years ago. One of the first spy thrillers of its kind.

www.mxpublishing.com

Also From MX Publishing

Bobbles and Plum

Four playlets from PG Wodehouse 'lost' for over 100 years – found and reprinted with an excellent commentary

Tras Las He huellas de Arthur Conan Doyle (in Spanish)

Un viaje ilustrado por Devon.

The Case of The Grave Accusation

The creator of Sherlock Holmes has been accused of murder. Only Holmes and Watson can stop the destruction of the Holmes legacy.

www.mxpublishing.com

Also From MX Publishing

The Outstanding Mysteries of
Sherlock Holmes

With thirteen Homes stories and
illustrations Kelly re-creates the
gas-lit, fog-enshrouded world of
Victorian London

Rendezvous at The Populaire

Sherlock Holmes has retired,
injured from an encounter with
Moriarty. He's tempted out of
retirement for an epic battle with
the Phantom of the opera.

Baker Street Beat

An eclectic collection of articles,
essays, radio plays and 'general
scribblings' about Sherlock
Holmes from Dr.Dan Andriacco.